Adrenaline is a better pickup than coffee . . .

Maggie just wanted to go to a Marriott and soak in a Jacuzzi. Instead, she began the drive back to her condo.

Fifteen minutes later, she pulled into her driveway and remembered that she needed batteries for her garage door opener; it had been working sporadically for weeks now. She said a small prayer, promising abstinence—not a big sacrifice—if God would allow her garage door opener to work one more time. But of course the opener didn't open.

She let out a deep sigh. She could either spend the night in her car or trek to her front door via the three feet of snow on her sidewalk. The temperature in the car was descending its way to match the chill outside, so Maggie left the comfort of her Corolla and tunneled to her front door.

When she got to the front door, she was cold, wet, and miserable. She unlocked the front door and flipped on the living room light.

Her mind couldn't make sense of the destruction she saw.

The door slammed behind her. "Ho! Ho! Ho!"

Maggie turned and saw Psycho Phil standing behind her in a Santa Claus costume, minus the white wig and beard.

TO GIVE OR DECEIVE

Don't miss the first mystery featuring Maggie Connors

A TAX DEDUCTIBLE DEATH

"*A Tax Deductible Death* is an amusing investigative tale with several twists and turns that will surprise the reader. . . . Fun [and] wonderful."
—*Midwest Book Review*

Berkley Prime Crime books by Malinda Terreri

A TAX DEDUCTIBLE DEATH
TO GIVE OR DECEIVE

TO GIVE OR DECEIVE

MALINDA TERRERI

BERKLEY PRIME CRIME, NEW YORK

TO GIVE OR DECEIVE

A Berkley Prime Crime Book / published by arrangement with the author

PRINTING HISTORY
Berkley Prime Crime mass-market edition / October 2002

Copyright © 2002 by Malinda Terreri.
Cover art and design by Tony Greco and Associates.

Visit our website at
www.penguinputnam.com

ISBN: 0-425-18691-1

Berkley Prime Crime Books are published
by The Berkley Publishing Group,
a division of Penguin Putnam Inc.,
375 Hudson Street, New York, New York 10014.
The name BERKLEY PRIME CRIME and the
BERKLEY PRIME CRIME design
are trademarks belonging to Penguin Putnam Inc.

PRINTED IN THE UNITED STATES OF AMERICA

10 9 8 7 6 5 4 3 2 1

For my parents,
Ann and Dave Ferry

Acknowledgments

Special thanks to Dave King for his editorial help, to Vicki Merrill for suggesting the title, and to Bill Ferry and Scott Harper for providing background information.

Chapter 1

Tuesday, December 21

I slid the paper clip between my incisor and front tooth, but the piece of lodged spinach would not budge. I had excused myself to the bathroom to perform this delicate surgery as soon as my tongue detected the tooth barnacle and before my client noticed. The only tool I could find for the job in my suitcase-sized purse was the paper clip from my lost bank deposit.

I tried my vegetable extraction again.

This time the paper clip made a noise I usually hear just before my dental hygienist says, "Oops," and the spinach came free. I smiled in the mirror. I was back to looking my professional best, exuding confidence and ready for the most critical meeting of my career. I left the rest room with less tooth enamel than when I entered, and returned to the dining room. I was a few feet from my table when the high heel of my new pumps caught on the restaurant's carpet.

There was a moment of vertigo, then the CEO of Saint Louis General Hospital and I toppled onto the floor in a clamorous lump of body parts, mashed food, and breaking dishes. I landed with my face jammed in his crotch and my feet tangled in the tablecloth above my head. Thankfully, my pleated suit skirt flipped down to hide my face, which was now as crimson as my hair. On the other hand, this meant my ass and underwear were sticking out for all to see, which might have been all right if I was wearing a sexy pair of thong underwear to complement my Prada suit. But this wasn't date night, it was an afternoon business lunch, so I had on practical, big, white, Tuesday-afternoon underwear that was worn to a comfort level that didn't sanction public viewings. I didn't reach my hand around to check, but I think it was the pair that had a few holes above what was left of the elastic leg band in the back.

For a moment everyone in the restaurant was silent.

Then Charles rolled away, howling in pain from the impact of my chin on his nuts, and that snapped everyone out of their shock.

"Ohmygod! Ohmygod! I'm so sorry."

I stood and pulled my suit skirt down so my fellow diners could divert their attention from my ass to the man I had tackled out of his chair.

Charles got to his feet but scrunched over, using the table for support. "What the hell happened?"

I bent over and retrieved his glasses, which were hiding under an overturned salad plate. I couldn't decide whether to give him the short answer or the long one. The truth was, my new shoes were $330 Ferragamo pumps that had been on sale, then marked down further for pre-Christmas clearance on a day when my $89 store credit was going to expire, making my effective cost for these shoes only nine dollars. And the nine-dollar price tag easily justified the fact that they were about a size too big. But if I told him about the bargain buy of slightly big Ferragamo pumps, I had to explain why I bought them even though I had almost $7 million in my portfolio and could easily afford to buy the right size shoes at full price. How do you explain to a client you want to impress that a shoe sale is a shoe sale?

Better to go with the short answer.

I wiped salad dressing off his glasses. "My heel caught on the carpet, and I tripped."

"Oh," he said, through still-clenched teeth.

By now, waiters swarmed in, offering help, as they should in a restaurant this overpriced. Ten minutes later, the food and broken dishes were gone from around our feet. The musician at the grand piano resumed his soft melodies, and the atmosphere in the restaurant returned to one of posh dignity.

We were seated again, enjoying our replacement entrées. Charles had ordered a broiled piece of fish with a side of cottage cheese and bottled water. This explained how he managed to be in his midsixties with the physique of a man in his forties. He was a wiry man, and under his custom-tailored suit you could tell he spent time at a gym or, more likely, had a personal trainer visit him at his estate.

Before me was a deep-fried piece of chicken smothered in cheese, a side of double stuffed cheese mashed potatoes, and the dental-trauma-causing spinach salad with two bites missing. Although it was lunchtime, I was already on my sixth or seventh Pepsi of the day. My workout regimen consisted of an occasional body-shaking sneeze—which I counted as an abdominal crunch—and a constant stream of caffeine to boost my metabolism into overdrive and keep the extra pounds off my five-foot-two frame. So far, it seemed to be working, but now that I had turned thirty, it was probably time to consider more drastic options such as eating a fresh vegetable once a week and trading in the escalators for the stairs.

Charles moved the bouquet of fresh flowers off to the side and out of our line of sight.

"I know you wanted to talk with me," he said, "but I've got something I need to tell you first. I'm going to cut right to the chase and say it."

"By all means."

"You've been handling my account for about eight years, and the deferred comp retirement plans for our seven hospitals for about a year. Both I and the executives at our other hospitals have been very happy with everything you've done. But I'm afraid we have decided to make some changes."

My fork dropped to my plate. "What changes?" Suddenly, months of planning dangled above the toilet.

"Frankly, I'm a little disappointed with Hamilton Securities. I can't understand why a firm as large and as respected as Hamilton isn't more advanced in their retirement account support. We need a firm who can offer us more options."

My breathing returned to normal. I wouldn't have to flush my plans.

"The fact that you want to change brokerage houses is good news," I said, "and the reason I wanted to get together."

He stopped chewing. "It is?"

I stabbed a piece of chicken with my fork and took a deep breath. "Charles, let me ask you a hypothetical question since my financial consultant employment contract with Hamilton Securities prevents me from asking anything more direct."

He nodded.

I glanced around the restaurant to make sure none of my coworkers had come in. "If your financial consultant—who I might add, has faithfully and profitably served your account and the retirement accounts of the seventy-two executives in your hospital network—if that purely hypothetical financial consultant decided to leave her current brokerage house and become independent, would you be comfortable with that?"

He pondered a moment. "It depends on what exactly 'independent' means. How would this hypothetical consultant execute trades and handle administration for an account our size? We've probably got about thirty-five million dollars in assets with you."

"That's a good question. Hypothetically, the financial consultant could sign an agreement with, say, a firm called First Alliance. They provide independent financial consultants with complete back-office support, a means to clear trades, all the office licensing and registration, and some additional services that Hamilton doesn't offer you."

"Such as . . ."

"Well, for one thing, you and the other executives could have on-line access to your accounts with real-time account information."

"That's what we're looking for."

"And this hypothetical financial consultant would be able to offer a wider platform of investment vehicles. Instead of only having the Westgate Family of mutual funds for your employee retirement accounts, you would have over seven thousand funds to choose from."

"That would certainly be a plus. But how risky is this, for you and for me?"

"There isn't any risk for you. All monies are cleared through First Alliance. It's not as though I'd keep cash in a piggy bank in my office. And you would still have access to some of the top analysts and fund managers in the industry. My risk, quite frankly, is in how many clients feel comfortable making this change. For me, the benefits easily outweigh the risk. I'll be able to give my clients a wider range of services while simultaneously relieving myself of the constant pressure to push Hamilton's proprietary products."

I didn't mention that my payout would also increase

from Hamilton's 50 percent commission on my earnings to 85 percent with First Alliance.

"When would a change like this happen? Hypothetically."

"Our hypothetical financial consultant gets one hundred percent vested in Hamilton stock options a week
from today, on December 28th, so she would hypothetically give notice the day after that. Next Wednesday."

He chewed on his fish and considered the situation.

"The financial consultant already has office space
leased and furnished, telephone lines installed, and
everything else in place, so it should be a smooth tran-
sition." I handed him my new business card. "And her
hypothetical assistant Stacy is joining her, too."

"How many clients are you talking to and what's
their response been so far?"

I leaned forward and smiled. "I'm meeting with a
handful of my bigger accounts, and you're the first."

"I guess you wait until after the move to invite your
other accounts to join you?"

"Ethically, I can't really work counterproductive to
my employment contract with Hamilton, so yes, that is
my plan. And it sounds as though my employment
change is perfect timing for the hospital, too."

"There is a small fly in the ointment," he said.

He paused, and I waited to see what was going to
happen to my world.

"I'm not in a position to rubber-stamp my approval
and tell you to go ahead and transfer everything. We've
already started the review process with two other
firms."

I took a sip of Pepsi and tried to act calm. "Who
else are you talking to?"

He mentioned two other brokers. One I didn't know,
and the other I knew to be extremely aggressive.

"To keep things fair, the best I can do is to include
you in the review . . . if you're interested."

"I am. What do you need from me?"

"A copy of your résumé. Testimonials from three clients. A statement as to why you want the hospital's retirement account. And a profile of any support people who would be involved in our account. I'll need a dozen copies of all this, along with any other materials you think would be beneficial."

No mouth swab for DNA analysis? "When do you need this by?"

"We have a committee meeting on Friday, December 31st. I need your materials the day before."

"All of this by the thirtieth?"

"I'm sorry Maggie. We should have talked sooner, but I had no idea what you were planning. I thought this would be bad news."

I nodded, mentally reviewing the avalanche of paperwork I needed to create.

"Do you think you can pull all of that together?" he said.

"Charles, it won't be a problem. Being able to give my accounts a better level of support is why I'm pursuing my own shop." It sounded good. Too bad it wasn't true.

"That's just great, Maggie. You don't know how relieved I feel. This whole thing has been putting a real damper on my holiday spirit, and it turns out I was concerned for nothing. It's going to make my vacation much more enjoyable."

"You're going away for the holidays?"

"I'm taking the family to Saint Johns for a Christmas getaway. I'll be out of town until next Thursday."

"Why Saint Johns?"

He drank a sip of water before answering. "It's a great place to avoid the Christmas commercialism, kick back, and appreciate the important things in life. How about you? What are your plans?"

Preparing the boatload of bullshit you just requested. "I'll be spending the holidays close to home so I can finalize arrangements for my new office."

"You work too hard, Maggie, which is probably why you're such a great financial consultant. But take it from a heart attack survivor: You should enjoy life while you can."

I nodded absently, but my mind was reviewing which three clients to ask for testimonials.

We talked a little longer about Saint Johns, then I caught the waiter's attention and motioned for the check. He brought the bill over and laid it beside my plate. I picked up my purse that had been hanging on the back of my chair and rummaged for my wallet.

I didn't see it.

The waiter stood beside me, shifting his weight from foot to foot, waiting for me to find some way to pay for the eighty-five-dollar lunch we had consumed.

I dug more thoroughly and then searched the floor to see if it had fallen out earlier. I didn't see any sign of it. Then I remembered. It hadn't been there when I'd searched for the paper clip in the bathroom. I had it last in my blue purse, and I had grabbed my black purse this morning before leaving home.

"Charles, I hate to tell you this, but it looks like I don't have my wallet."

"I'll come back," the waiter said.

"This has been some lunch. You broadside me, head-butt my gonads, solicit my account away from your current employer—"

"Hypothetically."

"—and then you want me to pick up the tab?"

"I think that pretty well sums it up."

"Is this the same level of service I can expect in the future?"

I grinned. "Probably."

He fished for his wallet and tossed his gold card on the bill. "It's a good thing your recommendation of Palimo Tech has made me the money it has, or you would be washing dishes."

"Thanks. I owe you. Are you still going to make the Palimo party tomorrow?"

"Wouldn't miss hearing Tiger Woods speak. Ruth and I have it marked on our social calendar."

"I'll have a nice bottle of champagne and some caviar waiting for you in your hotel room to make up for this lunch."

"I'd say that would be a fair trade, but I hate caviar. Could you do cashews instead?"

"Consider it done," I said.

We said our good-byes, I drove home to retrieve my wallet, and at one o'clock, I pulled into the Hamilton Securities parking garage.

This was my ninth year with Hamilton. Last year I had almost ended up in the unemployment line after my production had dropped dramatically, thanks to the unfortunate demise of a number of my wealthiest but most ancient clients. Then I got tangled up in an IRS investigation of one of my clients. For doing my civic duty above and beyond the call of duty, I netted a few attempts on my life and an unusually large thirteen-million-dollar reward payment from the fine folks at the IRS. Not that the IRS had much of a choice. If they didn't give me the money, it would have been confiscated by the Caymanian government, and by paying me, they got about six million dollars back in taxes I had to then pay. But even after paying taxes, it was still better than my previous financial situation in which my checking account was overdrawn and I had eighteen grand in credit card debt.

I was raised in a typical middle-class suburb of Saint Louis, and it still didn't feel right having so many zeros on my balance sheet. Not that I was complaining. But I ended up like one of those sappy million-dollar lottery winners who still go to work the next morning. The only difference was that I used my small fortune to attract the riches of others. The hospital's deferred comp plan was one of the biggest accounts I nabbed, comprising almost a third of my assets under management. That account also helped me increase my client base to 280 households, so my total assets under management were around $110 million. Commissions and bonuses put my income around $550,000 a year. By going out on my own, I hoped to increase that by almost $400,000.

Not that it was all a matter of money attracting money. I had done well for my clients as well as doing well by them. For instance, I'd discovered Palimo Technologies six months or so ago. Palimo was a large biotech that was one of hundreds working to develop an AIDS vaccine. With 15,000 people worldwide becoming HIV infected every day, the demand for a vaccine was overwhelming. Palimo caught my attention when they hired Dr. Richard Craig away from the world's leading biotech firm in Liverpool. Dr. Craig had a powerful, worldwide reputation in the scientific community, and I knew that if Palimo had the resources to support him, the stock was worth a closer look. I started buying Palimo stock at 17¾. And so did all my clients.

Since then, the company had put out a string of releases on successful trials. The holiday party was to celebrate the opening of their new headquarters and their plans to submit an effective vaccine to the FDA for approval early in the new year. Their stock was currently trading at 72⅜.

I was on a roll. It was the perfect time to strike out on my own.

One of the side effects of being a workaholic is that it left me little time to spend my bonanza. I still drove a beige Toyota Corolla. I still lived in the same condo. And I still felt guilty for not calling my parents often enough.

I walked into the foyer of Hamilton Securities feeling a little like Benedict Arnold. Thankfully, rather than being greeted by a firing squad, I was welcomed by the familiar combination of brass accents, an ever-green marble floor, and a mammoth mahogany reception desk. Because Christmas was just a few days away, everything was decked out with poinsettias and evergreens. The three receptionists sitting behind the desk wore wireless headsets and were busy transferring calls as I walked by. They each acknowledged my return with a nod of their head.

A ten-foot-high glass wall with the Hamilton logo in the middle and fountain water shimmering down either side separated the reception area from the Hamilton bullpen: an area comprised of rookie stockbrokers surgically attached to their phones. Surrounding the bullpen were the private offices of brokers earning $250,000 plus.

My private office was the sixth from the reception area. Although it was called an office, like the other Hamilton offices, the walls only went halfway up to the ceiling and there wasn't a door. This made my attempts at collusion even more difficult. I'd like to say that to camouflage information dealing with my departure—rent agreements for the new office, letter-head proofs, clearing house agreements, etc.—I purposely created a paper disaster in my office. But the truth was that when it came to paperwork, I was a little messy. The two chairs normally reserved for visiting clients were filled with stacks of unread annual reports and copies of articles I needed to forward to clients concerning their holdings. The credenza behind my desk was equally cluttered.

I motioned for Stacy to follow me into my office, and then I gave her a quick, whispered summary of my meeting with Charles Witmer.

She let out a long sigh. "Mag, I told you about the bigger apartment I found. I'm supposed to sign a lease for it tomorrow. If I don't, they have another person waiting to rent it. But I can't afford it if I'm not making what you offered at the new office."

"Go ahead and lease the apartment. Everything is going to be fine. It just won't be official for a little bit longer."

She nodded her head, and I felt the weight of the commitment transfer to my shoulders before she returned to her desk.

I cleared a spot on my desk and reviewed some trade confirmations from orders placed before I left for lunch. I was halfway through the stack when Stacy yelled that Diane Brown was on line one. I glanced around to see if the mention of my PR woman's name immediately caused everyone to conclude that I was leaving Hamilton. No one seemed to notice or care. I picked up the phone.

"Hi, Diane, this is Maggie."

"Is this a good time to talk?"

"Not really, but I can't think of a better time. What have you got for me?"

"I should have the press release finished on Thursday regarding the opening of your new office. Where would you like my assistant to send the proof?"

I lowered my voice. "There's going to be a small delay. I don't want to announce my new office opening until after I get confirmation that a certain account is transferring with me, and they're scheduled to make a decision next Friday."

"Not a problem, I'll move the dates back on the press release. It won't be sent to the papers until you approve."

As soon as I hung up the phone, my intercom beeped. "Maggie, this is Mike. Could you come see me?"

My heart skipped a beat. "On my way."

Mike Ambrose supervised about fifty brokers in this branch of Hamilton Securities. To manage so many personality types, his job required the patience of a preschool teacher, the negotiating skills of a lobbyist, and the multitasking abilities of an air traffic controller.

He was a great manager, but his patience and flexibility probably didn't extend to brokers about to jump ship.

I left my office and walked to his, trying to convince myself with each step that there was no way he could know what I was planning. His secretary wasn't at her desk and his door was slightly ajar, so I knocked and then poked my head in. "You wanted to see me?"

He was on the phone and motioned for me to come in and have a seat in the conference area of his office.

His office was maybe three times the size of mine and a reflection of the reception area: elegant and organized. His glass desktop held three pieces of paper, a picture of his beautiful blond family, and his telephone. In the conference area there were two burgundy leather wingback chairs that faced a matching leather love seat. On the glass coffee table was a copy of today's *Wall Street Journal* and a vase of fresh flowers.

I took a seat in one of the wingbacks and was about to pick up the *Wall Street* when he hung up the phone and joined me, sitting in the love seat across from me.

"So how are plans coming for the Palimo party?" he said.

Probably not a prelude to getting fired. "I think I've got it all pulled together. Two buses will leave here at eleven-thirty tomorrow morning. I'll have about twenty clients on each bus. Clayton Catering is serving lunch, and when that's over, there will be a movie. By the time the movie finishes, we should be in Jeff City."

"Any idea what the outing is going to set you back?"

"With hotel accommodations for everyone, the buses, and food and drinks during the trip, I'm guessing about $15,000."

He let out a low whistle.

"Palimo is going to reimburse me for half of it," I said.

"How much of a position are you carrying with Palimo right now?"

"I have about sixty-five clients in Palimo with a total

of 72,000 shares. Plus, I've got about 25,000 shares myself." I looked at the ground when I said this. I knew holding that many shares of one stock would worry Mike.

"That's a lot of shares." He rubbed his chin and then leaned forward, resting his elbows on his knees and folding his hands together. His dark blue suit high-lighted his blue eyes, which exposed a genuine look of concern. "I know you like this stock a lot, Maggie; I'm just a little worried about how heavily weighted you are. You're familiar with the adage that says eighty percent of your business comes from twenty percent of your accounts?"

I nodded.

"Are the sixty-five accounts you have in Palimo your larger accounts?"

I nodded again. I knew where he was going with this.

"Maggie, if you burn these accounts, you burn your business. You know as well as I do that the rest of your client base is in CDs and mutual funds, and they don't generate the commission dollars you depend on. That's an awfully big risk to take, especially when you have so many shares yourself." He paused again. "What's it trading at these days?"

"It's around seventy-two dollars a share. My average purchase price is about twenty-four dollars."

"Your clients must be very happy."

"I think they'll be even happier once Palimo gets FDA approval."

"I know you're a smart broker and can make your own decisions. I'm just a little uncomfortable with you having such a large position. There isn't any such thing as a sure thing when it comes to the stock market, and you never know what could happen to a company—even a well-respected, billion-dollar company like Pal-imo."

"I talk with Palimo's president at least once a week,

and I can assure you that everything is fine, and they aren't expecting any research surprises."

"But my point is, you don't know what could bring a company down. What if some stupid E-mail virus gets in and wipes out critical research information? What if some homophobic skinheads blow up their laboratory? Things like that you can never expect but should always be prepared for. Besides, it's not as if your clients won't make money. You've done your job. Take your profits."

"I'm just looking for a twenty percent bounce once the research results are announced, and then I plan on selling half of my position and my clients' positions."

"That's certainly a good plan. I'd feel better if you would think about unloading some sooner rather than later."

I nodded halfheartedly, and he could tell my mind was already made up.

"Well, the goodwill you're creating with the Palimo party should really benefit your production in January."

"I'm counting on it," I said, feeling a fresh wave of guilt since this time next week, I would have to sit in this same chair and tell this guy I was leaving his firm.

"But you better keep an eye on the stock price and make sure you don't get too close to managing five percent of the stock, or you'll have the SEC on your back."

I nodded again and hoped he was winding our meeting to an end.

"Any plans for the holidays?" he said.

Other than pilfering client files to help me illegally solicit them for my new office? "I'm thinking about heading down to the Ozarks with a few friends," I lied.

"Well, have a good time tomorrow at Palimo, and let me know how things turn out."

When I got back to my office, the CEO of Palimo was ringing in on line one. I grabbed the phone. "Hi David, how are you doing?"

"It depends. Any idea what the sticker price is going to be for you and your clients?"

"I'll know more by tomorrow, but it looks like it will be close to sixteen grand," I said, adding a little cushion.

"Well, just forward the receipts to Jennifer, and she'll make sure you get our donation."

"How are the plans coming for the party?"

"Great, really great. This is going to be one heck of a party. Did I tell you we booked Steve Martin *and* Tiger Woods?"

He had, several times. "This is going to be a lot of fun."

"Hey, I meant to ask you your date's name."

"I'm not bringing one."

"You have to. The seating arrangements are already set, and you'll be the odd duck out at our table."

"Well it won't be the first time. The guy I invited couldn't get the afternoon off." My second lie in ten minutes. I was getting good at this.

"What's he do that's so important he can't take some time off for a little holiday fun?"

"He . . . works for the government," I said.

"Hell, they'll never miss him. What part of the government does he work for?"

"You're beginning to sound like my mother."

"So be a good girl and spill. What's his name and what's he do?"

"You know, we spend entirely too much time on the phone together."

"You're stalling."

"It's Tim Gallen. He's a . . . special agent."

"FBI?"

"The Criminal Investigation Division of the Internal Revenue Service." I sighed. It was like saying my boyfriend happened to be a leper. "You probably don't even want his type at your party, so I'll come solo."

"No way. Tell this Tim character he's welcome to come as long as he doesn't audit me."

"I can't make any promises. But like I said, he's got to work, so he can't make it."

"Nonsense, I've got an offer you can't refuse. I'll send my jet to pick him up so he doesn't have to waste three hours driving over here."

"Don't send your jet. You're spending enough to get me and my clients there as it is."

"Believe me, sending my jet over will be the cheapest expense of the party. Besides, Maggie, when's the last time you've been to a really great party?"

"It's been too long."

"Fine, tell this Tim character to be in the chartered plane area of Lambert Airport tomorrow around four-thirty, and my plane will pick him up and have him here by five-thirty. The Learjet is blue and green with a big Palimo logo. He can't miss it. I'm anxious to meet the guy that can keep up with you."

So was I.

I thanked him and hung up.

I flipped through my business card file and found Tim's. I picked up the phone to call him and then let the phone fall back into the cradle. I was stressed out enough trying to finish last-minute details for this bus trip and finalize preparations for my new office. The last thing my nerves needed was to get slam-dunked by Tim Gallen.

I walked out to Stacy's desk and leaned against a file cabinet. "Hey Stacy, any suggestions on a man I can commandeer for the Palimo party? David is insisting I bring a date."

"My grandfather just got released from hip surgery. He might be up for a good time."

"I was hoping for someone who still has his own teeth."

"Well if you're going to be picky, you'll have a

tough time finding someone you haven't pissed off already."

I stopped leaning and stood with my hands on my hips. "I'm not in the habit of pissing off men."

"What happened to that good-looking IRS agent that used to come around?"

"That's a bad example."

"Uh-huh. What happened to him?"

"I was supposed to have dinner with him one night, and a meeting I had with a client ran late. When I tried to call him from the car, my cell phone died. He thought I stood him up."

"But you guys were really hitting it off for a while."

"Well there was some other stuff, too. I don't think he would be interested. But enough about him. Any other suggestions?"

"You're in sales, for God's sake, give Mr. IRS a call and promise him sexual favors if he goes."

I wandered back into my office, trying to figure out why Mr. IRS made me so nervous. Maybe it was because my preferred way of doing my taxes was to start with the refund box and work my way back. Maybe it was because he had penetrating eyes and rugged good looks with the added bonus that he carried a government-issued gun. But I think the real reason was that Tim Gallen was someone I couldn't push around, and I always enjoyed the challenge of a little male mental manipulation.

But I needed a date.

I punched in his number and got his voice mail.

"Hi Tim, it's Maggie. It's been a while so I thought I'd give you a call and see what you're up to. I've got this function tomorrow, and I thought I'd see if you wanted to go with me. Steve Martin and Tiger Woods will be there. Anyway, you've got my number. Call me if you're interested."

Time for a reassuring Pepsi. I was halfway to the cafeteria when I heard the receptionist page me for a phone call. I turned the corner to my office and Stacy was motioning wildly toward the phone. "He's on line one."

"Who?"

"Mr. IRS."

"God, that was quick. I thought he'd let me twist in the wind awhile before calling to tell me why he can't go."

"Nice positive mental attitude."

"The foundation of a great sales career."

I went into my office and picked up the phone. "Hi Tim, I didn't expect to hear from you so soon. How've you been?"

"I'm doing pretty good. But you sounded a little desperate on my voice mail."

"Sorry, I didn't mean to. I've got a lot of things going on."

"So . . . Steve Martin and Tiger Woods?"

"They'll be eating at our table if you want to go. It's a black-tie Christmas party at Palimo Tech tomorrow."

"It could be fun to watch them eat, I suppose. What time is this bash?"

"Palimo's headquarters is in Jefferson City. I'm taking clients over by bus at eleven-thirty. There are tours of the new Palimo headquarters from four to five, followed by a cocktail reception. Dinner is at six-thirty, and the entertainment starts after that. David, who is the CEO of Palimo, said his jet could pick you up around four-thirty, and he could have you at Palimo by five-thirty."

"Just in time to swallow a free beer and grab some dinner. Yeah, I think I could make that, but on one condition. Do you have plans for New Year's Eve?"

I twirled the phone cord around my finger and smiled. "I might be available."

"I'll make you a deal. I'll be your poster boy date

tomorrow if you'll baby-sit my sister's kids on New Year's Eve."

I dropped the phone cord I had been playing with.

"I'm not spending New Year's with a bunch of rug rats."

"I was going to, but I've got a date. And they're not rug rats. Nick is seven, Alexandra is five, and Baby Kate just turned two. You'll love them."

I should have known. I felt like I had just asked out my second-grade teacher. "Thanks for the offer, but I'm not sure I'm qualified to spend New Year's changing diapers."

"Okay, give my best to your Palimo buddies. My guess is, with the money they throw around, it'll be a great party."

"Yeah, you're going to miss a good time."

There was a long pause.

"Any chance one of your coworkers needs some free champagne and a private jet ride?" I'd never been afraid to ask for a referral, and asking now helped lessen the humiliation of the baby-sitting offer.

"If I run into anyone, I'll pass your name on."

I wanted to hang up, but instead I said, "Come on Tim. Can't you cut me some slack? I told you before I was sorry about missing our dinner. I tried to get a hold of you, but my cell phone died, what else could I do?"

"It's not just that, and you know it. Your work always seems to takes priority over your personal life."

"Isn't that like the pot calling the kettle black?"

"I catch criminals. I'm doing a service for my fellow citizens."

"And managing investors' funds so they can have a comfortable retirement isn't helping people?"

"You make a tidy profit off of it."

"You say that like it's a sin."

"Greed warps people. I know. I see a lot of it."

"I drive a ten-year-old Toyota. How greedy can I be?"

"But that's what I mean about being warped. You're so wrapped up in making money that you don't have time to enjoy it, and what's the point of that?"

I started to reply, then stopped. I knew what he said wasn't true, but I couldn't put my finger on just why at the moment. Instead, I lowered my voice so I couldn't be overheard. "I'm making some changes that I think you would approve of. One of them involves my job, but I can't talk about it right now."

"Now that's something I'd like to hear more about," he said. "Where do you want me to be for this party and when?"

"Thanks." I gave him David's instructions.

"I'll bring pictures of my sister's kids."

I rolled my eyes and told him I would see him tomorrow.

As I hung up the phone, Stacy walked into my office. "You're broker of the day, and there's a woman in the lobby who wants to open an account."

"I was going to run a few errands before my meeting with Vandenberg. I'm not sure I have time unless she's carrying bags of cash."

"She's not, but I think you should meet with her anyway. I'm bringing her back."

I cleared off one of my client chairs and tried to do some quick straightening. Stacy returned with my new client. She had scraggly brown hair, and she stared at the floor as she walked. I guessed she was in her late thirties, and she looked like those had been hard years.

I extended my hand and introduced myself. She glanced up for only a moment and then returned her gaze to the floor.

"Ms. Connors—"

"Please, call me Maggie." I motioned for her to have a seat, and then I sat down at my desk.

"Maggie, I heard on the news last night that this kid

at Truman University took a thousand dollars and
turned it into a hundred thousand dollars by investing
in something called options." She picked at her finger-
nail, then she looked up and stared me in the eyes.
"I've only got five hundred dollars. Can you turn it
into $50,000 for me?"

"I'm sorry, I didn't get your name."

"Donna, Donna Trundle."

I scribbled her name down on my pad of paper while
I thought of where to begin.

"Ms. Trundle, option investing is a risky business.
You can lose money just as quickly as you make it. In
fact, you can even lose more money than when you
started and end up owing money. For that reason, investors need to have a certain investment portfolio and
experience before I can recommend options trading. I
saw the story you mentioned, and I'm afraid that's the
exception rather than the rule."

She had gone back to staring at the floor, and her
head seemed to hang a little lower as I spoke.

"Additionally," I said, feeling like I was whipping a
puppy, "it's important when you start investing that
you get a solid base of investments with minimal risk,
like certificates of deposit, and then add investments
with a little more risk, such as mutual funds, as your
portfolio expands. Hamilton has a nice book for beginning investors. I'd be happy to give you a free copy
to look over. But the truth is, I only work with accounts
with a minimum of $500,000 in assets—"

"Ms. Connors," she said without looking up, "I have
a daughter who is four years old. She has bone cancer.
If you ever saw what cancer can do to a child, it would
break your heart in ways you didn't know were possible. I'm not a rich woman. In fact, at the end of the
month I'm going to get evicted from my apartment
'cause I've spent my rent money doing what I could
for Elizabeth. I don't have insurance, and I got no other
alternatives. I sold my car this morning for $500, and

I was hoping you could do something to help me."

"Isn't there a hospice or something that could help you?"

"I've been everywhere and applied for everything." Her voice was flat as though she had already cried out all of her tears. "This godforsaken cancer is unbearable when a child is on painkillers. And my Elizabeth, she's got nothing. She's going to die on the streets of Saint Louis."

"Can't the government—"

Stacy stuck her head in my office. "Maggie, I'm sorry for interrupting, but Phil Scranton is on the phone."

"Tell him I'm in a meeting."

"I did. He's insistent."

"Please tell him I'll call him back in a few minutes."

"I did, but he's very upset about Palimo and said he has to talk to you."

"Donna, I'm terribly sorry. Would you mind if I took this call quickly?"

"I've gotta go the bathroom," she said.

Phil Scranton, aka Psycho Phil. He was one of those blue-collar types who had gotten into the market but belonged in a passbook savings account. A handyman at a local nursing home, he had been a walk-in client more than a year ago, had barely made the $5,000 minimum deposit, and since then was convinced he was J. Pierpont Stanley. If he wasn't calling me for weekly updates or asking what I thought of this or that penny stock, he was ranting and raving because one of his stocks took a dip.

I sighed and picked up the phone. "Connors."

"What's this shit I hear about a Palimo party?"

"I don't know. What have you heard about a Palimo party?"

"I hear you're throwing a party for all your clients who have stock in Palimo. I've got sixty-eight shares, so why wasn't I invited? Aren't I good enough?"

"No, it's not that at all." Actually, it was. "The party isn't for everyone on my client list who owns Palimo. You need to own a certain number of shares—"

"How many?"

I did some quick math, based on what I knew of his account. "One hundred."

"Fine. Buy me some more."

I punched up his account. Evidently, some of his stocks were doing better than I remembered. If he sold his other holdings, he did have enough to buy the additional shares, even after my commissions. Not that it improved his chances of getting a Palimo invite.

"You realize that would mean putting everything you've got into Palimo? I can't, in good conscience, recommend—"

"What's the matter, it's a good stock, right? You recommended I buy it six months ago. And you've been telling me it's about to jump when they announce this . . . whatever."

"Well, yes. But good stock or not, no one should put everything they've got in a single financial vehicle. It's not responsible."

"I don't care. Do it. And send a limo to pick me up."

"No, I'm not sending a limo for you. This is a black-tie party for clients with portfolios over $500,000."

"Yeah, I got a black tie. I'll be there."

He hung up.

I rolled my eyes. I dialed his number and got a busy signal. There was no way this idiot was going to the Palimo party. I needed to make that perfectly clear to him. If I wasn't leaving the firm next week, I would have transferred his account to Client Services—a no-man's-land of orphaned, pain-in-the-ass clients serviced by a salaried Hamilton broker.

I waited a minute and then tried his line again. This time the phone rang, but no one answered. As I listened to the phone ring, I realized Donna Trundle hadn't returned. I hung up and walked to the bathroom to check on her. The stalls were empty, so I returned to my office.

"Stacy, did you see what happened to Donna Trundle?"

"The broker-of-the-day client? I showed her where the bathroom was and left her there."

I did a quick loop around the office to see if she had wandered into another financial consultant's office but didn't find her. I checked the bathroom again and the cafeteria, but there was no sign of her. I walked to the front door to see if she was outside the building at the bus stop but still didn't see her. I did notice that the snow the weathermen had been predicting for the last week had finally started falling.

Damn. I'd been ready to write her a check from my own account, and she probably thought I took Phil's call just to get rid of her.

I returned to my office and ripped the page from my notepad with Donna's name on it. "Stacy, please see if you can track down a phone number and an address for this woman." I handed her the page. "It's starting to snow, so I'm going to take off and run a few errands before for my meeting with Stanley Vandenberg. Do you have copies of his portfolio updates?"

She handed me a folder. "But not so fast," she said. "You have one more walk-in account."

"Who is it?"

"A little old lady. And this one does have a bag of cash."

"You're kidding me."

"That's what the receptionist said."

"Fine, I'll go get her, but after this, I'm done for the day."

When I began my career as a broker, being broker of the day was the highlight of the month. It was a chance to take a break from cold-calling often hostile prospects and deal with people who actually had money they wanted to invest. But at this point in my career, walk-ins rarely had a couple hundred thousand they wanted to give to a stranger to invest, and so broker of the day became more of a nuisance.

I walked to the reception area and saw an elderly lady with enormous snow boots sitting with a brown grocery bag.

"I'm Maggie Connors, and you are?"

"In need of some advice." She stood and shook my hand. "And don't tell me not to open my mouth when I'm in manure up to my neck."

"I'm going to go out on a limb and say that particular piece of advice would never have occurred to me."

"Then we're off to a good start. My name's Eleanor Cosgrove, and I need some investment counseling."

"I'd be happy to help you. Why don't we go back to my office and discuss this?"

She pointed her finger at her ear. "What was that?"

"I said, let's go back to my office so we can discuss this."

She nodded, and I led the way. Back at my office, I took a seat, and she placed the brown bag on my desk before sitting down.

"What's this?" I said.

"Come again?" She cupped her hand to her ear. "You're going to have to speak up, dearie, because I couldn't hear a pin drop if it was a bowling pin dropped off a cliff onto a tin-roof barn."

I chuckled. These were not the analogies of my typical client. "What's in the bag?" I said, louder.

"Go ahead and have a peek."

I looked inside and it was, indeed, filled with cash. One-dollar bills.

"Do you mind if I ask why you have all this cash?"

"It all started when the government sent me a check for $103 from some old savings and loan account my husband had. Evidently that S and L went belly-up a long time ago. I tried to deposit the money at my bank, but they done pissed me off."

"The government or your bank?" I said.

"The bank! Getting decent service from them is like trying to turn a pair of boots back into a cow. They wanted to charge me fifty cents for making a deposit, can you believe it? Charging me money for giving them money. Then they told me my monthly fee was going up, and I said enough was enough. Why the hell should they charge me fees so they can take my money and then loan it out to other people? I think they're a little screwy in the head."

"So you got your balance paid out in singles?"

"They wanted to give me a check, but I said no siree bob." She looked over the top of her glasses. "I wanted to be as big a pain in the ass to them as they were to me. Anyhow, I got your card from a fellow giving a seminar at Autumn Oaks, and here I am. I'd like to open an account and make a deposit. I've got $1,782."

She opened up her purse and got out her wallet, stood up and handed me her driver's license, and then returned to her seat.

I picked up the card and looked at it. The photo was grainy, and they say if you look like your driver's license, you're too sick to drive. But still . . .

"Ms. Cosgrove?" I said. "This isn't you in the picture."

"What?" She grabbed the license and stared at it. "That damn Department of Motor Vehicles. A department of imbeciles if you ask me. They sent me that license yesterday with a note saying they were backlogged and were sorry about the delay. Damn fools. My old one hadn't even expired yet."

She pulled out another license and handed it to me. This one had her picture and was good for another six months.

"Could I ask a favor? I'm afraid to throw out this bad license because it'll be too hard to cut up—scissors

and my arthritis don't mix. But I don't want the trash-
men to get it. Maybe you could cut it up for me?"

"Would you like me to have it shredded with our
confidential documents?"

"That would be mighty nice of you," she said.

I dropped it into a box beside my desk that was
labeled Shred.

"Now, back to your new account. I'm afraid our accounts aren't free, either. Hamilton charges a thirty-
five-dollar monthly fee to maintain your account, and
we require a five-thousand-dollar minimum deposit."

"I realize the cheapest oats are the ones that have
already been through the horse, but I can't afford that
kind of money. At least not now." She shook her head
in disgust. "I'm afraid I've done wasted your time.
Should have known better than to trust that fool Vandenberg."

"Vandenberg? Stanley Vandenberg of Vandenberg
Funeral Home?"

"That's right. That's who I got your card from. He
holds regular seminars over at Autumn Oaks, drumming up business. Ghoulish, if you ask me."

Not for Stanley Vandenberg. He was one of my most
peculiar clients. Normally, I liked a person who loved
his or her work, but when that person was an under-
taker . . .

Eleanor stood up, and I did the same.

"I'm sorry I wasn't able to help you," I said. "I saw
an ad on TV the other day that Federal Union Bank
was offering free checking accounts. You might have
better luck there."

"That's mighty nice of you." She dug into her blue
vinyl purse and produced a bag of sprinkle-covered
Christmas cookies, which she set on my desk. "I baked
these yesterday, and you look like you could use a few
pounds, so why don't you take 'em and enjoy 'em."

Before I could refuse, she said good-bye and left.

What a waste of twenty minutes. After she turned

the corner to the reception area, I dropped the bag of cookies into the trash. I wasn't going to take a chance that the main ingredients included possum or hound hair.

"As of right now, I'm not here," I said to Stacy. "By the way, in case Psycho Phil calls back, he thinks he's going to the Palimo Party, but he's not. If anyone else calls concerning the Palimo party, have them buzz me on my cell. Also, would you please call the Hilton and make sure that there's a bottle of Dom and a ton of fresh cashews in the Witmers' room tomorrow night?"

"I'm on it," she said and turned her attention to the phone.

And now it was time for my date with death's merchandiser.

Chapter 2

The snow was falling fast and furious when I stepped outside. I pulled my winter coat closer and tried to step my way across the street to the parking garage using the footprints left by others. I wasn't that successful and ended up packing snow into my slightly big, now-a-little-less-fabulous pumps.

When I got to the parking garage, I stomped the extra snow off my shoes, which pushed some wet stuff further down to my toes. I walked with slushy feet over to the elevators, punched the elevator button, and rode to the bottom level.

I spotted my Corolla without any problem. It was a grime and road-salt-covered mess next to my boss's gleaming, hand-polished Mercedes and the expensive imports of my coworkers. Maybe Tim had a point about my spending habits, but the Corolla was paid for, ran reliably, and got me where I needed to go, so what was the problem?

Ten minutes later, I turned my car off Highway 270

and onto Manchester Road, one of the most commercially developed and sought-after stretches of roads in West County. A block away from the highway, I turned into a snow-covered parking lot. Funeral homes evidently aren't as quickly cleared as, say, fast-food places. The front parking lot was empty of cars, so I continued around to the back. There I saw my client's parked car, if *car* was the right word.

Stanley Vandenberg's everyday driving vehicle was a 1940s hearse. It seemed as long as a football field, from the chrome swan on the coffin-shaped hood to the back bumper with Packard embossed in the middle. Valets tried to close when they saw him coming, and it was quite a sight when Stanley stopped for a Whopper at the Burger King drive-through.

A large Ace Rents truck was parked in a No Parking zone, and the rest of the lot was empty except for six more modern hearses parked off to the side. I tucked my Corolla into the shadow of the Packard, a tugboat next to a battleship, and hoofed through the snow one more time in my now far-from-fabulous Ferragamo pumps. Four Victorian pillars accented the entrance, with lion statues flanking either side. I stomped my feet on the greeting mat before entering.

When I turned the brass door handle, the smell of flowers rushed out like spring at the Botanical Gardens. Nondescript music softly bounced off the rose-colored marble floors before dissolving into the ornate, sixteen-foot-high ceiling. There wasn't anyone to greet me, so I continued down a hallway toward the muffled mixture of men's voices and construction noises.

The sounds led to a room marked Visitation Room Number Four. Inside, three men in Ace Rents uniforms were putting up several television monitors at the head of the room. They seemed uneasy as they clanged and banged their way around. Video cables snaked between arrangements of pink, yellow, and orange gladiolus, along with carnations, peace lilies, and white rose arrangements that littered the aisles. I wondered what kind of bizarre funeral the honorable Vandenberg Funeral Home had committed itself to.

"Can you tell me where I can find Stanley Vandenberg?" I asked the group.

"He's in his office," one of the uniformed men said.

"Thanks."

I walked a little farther and found my favorite area of the funeral home: a bright, glass-enclosed atrium that flooded the surrounding visitation rooms with light and created a peaceful atmosphere. Sliding glass doors from all four sides invited mourners to stroll into the meticulously landscaped gardens. There were several teak benches beckoning visitors to relax and enjoy the sounds of the bubbling waterfall. The setting looked particularly beautiful now when the rest of the Saint Louis landscape was so barren.

I stood there relishing the tranquillity when I became aware of an off-key rendition of "When the Saints Come Marching In." My client probably never noticed how his singing improved as his hearing deteriorated.

I walked into his office. "Mr. Vandenberg?"

Stanley Vandenberg kept singing to himself and dusting the framed obituaries that lined the walls of the small office. On his shoulder was Socrates, an obnoxious Amazon parrot with equally bad singing abilities. The two made quite a pair. My client had white hair shaved very short with lots of pink scalp showing through on the top, which is why he usually wore a derby. His head jutted forward from his slightly stooped body, and when he walked, his mouth was always open, which made him look a tad confused. His head looked slightly big for his body, which seemed to have shrunk during his seventy plus years of living. With his pants pulled up a little too high at the top and a little too short at the bottom, he looked like he belonged on a shopping mall bench shouting comments at the passersby, not running one of the most popular funeral homes in Saint Louis.

And running the Vandenberg Funeral Home had been profitable, until recently. Several years ago, Mr. Vandenberg had almost five million in investments with me. Since then, the polite funeral home days of high gross sales to bereaved widows had apparently passed on and been replaced with cutthroat competition and preneed sales. Unfortunately, my client never let a little thing like profitability stand in the way of throwing outlandish and often quirky ceremonies for which the Vandenberg Funeral Home was famous. Mr. Vandenberg had liquidated most of his portfolio to keep financing his funeral home, which did a monthly dance in and out of the red. In fact, about the only asset I'd managed to persuade him to retain was Palimo.

Although he was no longer one of my wealthier accounts, Stanley Vandenberg was a connector for me. Over the years, he had referred numerous widows who were faced with the daunting task of investing for the first time in their lives. Unlike Eleanor Cosgrove, most of the referrals turned out to be very lucrative accounts for me.

"Mr. Vandenberg?" I yelled louder.

He turned, and Socrates flew to his perch in the corner. "Ah, Maggie, come in. Let me take your coat."

Stanley relieved me of my coat, and we sat down in the lounge area of his office.

"So what's going on in Visitation Room Number Four?" I said.

"Oh, you'll never believe it," answered an elderly lady making her way into the office. She carried a tray of coffee.

"Maggie," said Stanley, "you remember Grace, my right-hand man."

"Actually, I used to function more as his right brain, and that got tiresome, so I just took over the whole gray matter." She handed me a cup of coffee. "But

Stanley will have to tell you about Visitation Room Number Four."

"La, la, la, la, la, la, laaaaaaa," Socrates said, singing the scales.

"It's nothing special," Stanley said and then sipped his coffee. "We have a seven-thirty ceremony scheduled for Emily Dickinson."

"Correct me if I'm wrong," I said, "but I thought Emily Dickinson died a long time ago. And what's with the TVs?"

"Well, it's true that someone named Emily Dickinson did die many years ago," Stanley said, grinning over his coffee, "but our guest of honor believed she was the original Emily."

"Is this going to be another one of your ceremonies that ends up on *Entertainment Tonight*?"

"You never know," Stanley said. "As the story goes, our Miss Dickinson had been calling all of her relatives to her mansion every six months or so for the last three years, so they could witness her last words. She'd be all dressed in black, lying in a huge four-poster bed with seventy pounds of covers on top of her and the cameras rolling."

"Miss Dickinson wanted the historic moment documented," Grace said.

Stanley nodded. "So, with the cameras rolling and all her relatives surrounding her, she would fold her arms over her chest, close her eyes and say, 'The fog is rising.' But the damn thing of it was, she wouldn't die. Over and over again she'd tell people that the fog was rising and her weather forecast was clear as a bell."

"Too bad her mind wasn't," Grace said.

"To be or not to be," Socrates said, and then let out several loud squawks.

"So what happened?" I said.

Stanley slapped his hands together and grinned. "That's the good part."

"It is not the good part," Grace said.

"Well, tell me, and I'll decide if it's the good part," I said. Would we ever get around to our portfolio review?

"Finally, one night, with everyone gathered around to see Emily say her famous last words, this frail old lady who probably couldn't have weighed more than ninety pounds—"

"Including the fake eyelashes," Grace added.

"—well, this little old Emily Dickinson impersonator, well she . . . I don't know how else to say it . . . she passed some gas that actually did make it seem like the fog was rising."

"More like a napalm cloud, I understand," Grace said, laughing.

The parrot flew over to sit on Stanley's shoulder. "Hush, Socrates, hush," the bird said to himself.

"Poor girl was on some kind of fiber diet, apparently," Stanley said. "Anyway, little Emily's eyes grew wide with horror as she realized that fourteen relatives and a cameraman standing there to witness her last words were about to suffocate. So, finally she says, 'Pardon me, I seem to have fluffed.' And then the old woman drops deader than a flattened cat on an expressway!"

"You're not serious."

"Swear to God. View the tape if you don't believe us."

I thought of the TVs. "The relatives aren't playing the tape while she's laid out, are they?"

"Got to," Stanley said, nodding his head for emphasis. "Says so in her will. If the relatives don't play it, all of the woman's money goes to her canary. And this old lady had a ton of money, not a lot of common sense, but a ton of money."

"What's for dinner?" the bird said.

I reached for my file folder on Stanley's portfolio. "Speaking of money—"

"Uncle, who is this delicious morsel?"

A cultured, British accent. I turned to find a man in the doorway, wearing a black suit and black shirt. He crossed the room like a panther about to lunch on a gazelle and slid into the spot next to me on the love seat. His left arm automatically wrapped around the back of my seat and his other hand picked up my right hand.

"Maggie Connors," Stanley said, "allow me to introduce my nephew, Malcolm Vandenberg."

"Guilty as charged," Malcolm said and flashed a wickedly mischievous smile before bending down and kissing my hand.

Uncle and nephew couldn't have looked more different. Malcolm had a ravenlike face with a long, pointed nose, dark eyes, and a black goatee. His hair was cut above his shirt collar, but the top was long, and one lock hung down his forehead somewhat defiantly. It was hard to tell how old he was, maybe somewhere in his midthirties.

I leaned back to regain some personal space, but he seemed to close the distance again without moving.

"Maggie is the Hamilton broker I was telling you about," Stanley said.

"It's a pleasure to meet you," I said. It was hard not to stammer.

"I regret not meeting before," he said.

His voice was a seductive blend of confidence, nonchalance, and honey-coated contemptuousness.

I tried to move the conversation back to a safe area. "Do you work here with your uncle?"

"No, no. Dead people are not to my taste." He flicked his hand a few times in the air, dismissing the business his uncle and prior Vandenberg generations had worked so hard to build. "That embalming smell gets into your veins and starts to creep into your soul."

"You're a dead man. You're a dead man," the bird cackled.

"Don't believe a word of what he says," Stanley said with a hint of disgust. "Malcolm has been the extra pair of hands I've needed lately."

"Where does the English accent come from?"

Malcolm cocked his head to the side. "I grew up in Liverpool."

"My brother stayed in England after he got out of the service," Stanley said. "Malcolm put himself through law school by working as a mortician. Maggie, I bet you didn't realize the Vandenberg Funeral Home business was international."

I shook my head. "So, Malcolm, what brings you to the States?"

"I got bored practicing law there and decided last year I needed a change of venue."

"Malcolm is a junior associate for George, Bransford and Jacobs."

"What type of law do you practice?"

"I'm a tax attorney, or was. Now I spend most of my time doing grunt work for the senile, senior partner, John George. It's part of the cost of starting over in a new country."

"But when he's not helping his clients screw the government out of money, he gives me a helping hand around here."

"Mostly with the finances," Malcolm quickly added.

"Speaking of finances, that reminds me," I said to Mr. Vandenberg, "I wanted to thank you for referring Eleanor Cosgrove."

He frowned. "Eleanor opened an account with you?"

"No, our fees were too high for her. But, I appreciate you thinking of me."

"She's quite a hoot, isn't she?" He grinned and then sipped his coffee.

"I guess 'hoot' is one way to describe her. Talking with Eleanor, I felt like I was stuck in an old *Hee Haw* episode. She actually came in with two driver's licenses and a grocery bag filled with one-dollar bills."

"Nothing Eleanor does would surprise me."

One of the Ace Rents guys appeared in the doorway and asked Stanley to come approve the setup. The parrot left with Stanley. Grace excused herself as well to check on something, and suddenly I found myself alone with Malcolm. I slid out of my seat and walked to the wall to examine the framed obituaries of celebrities who had been serviced by the Vandenberg Funeral Home.

He crossed the room and stood behind me. "So, Miss Connors, how do you plan on dying?"

"A brain aneurysm during multiple orgasm wouldn't be a bad way to go," I said, and then regretted my remark as soon as I turned to look at him. His cold elegance seemed a little creepy now that it was just the two of us.

"Maybe I could help you with that. But first I'd have to know if you made preneed arrangements with my uncle."

He moved closer. I turned my attention back to reading obituaries to avoid further eye contact with him. "Stanley talks to me about it all the time," I said, "but the truth is, I'm hoping for immortality."

"As a tax attorney, I can tell you there is no such thing as an unclaimed death, only unclaimed assets. I find most people need a slap-in-the-ass wake-up call to realize that death claims everyone." His voice was deep, soft, and mesmerizing. "Have you had your wake-up call?" he whispered.

He then lifted my suit skirt and gave me a painful slap on the ass, his hand lingering a few seconds before he pulled it away.

I was so utterly shocked that I didn't react. By the time I realized I needed to knee him in his brains, Stanley walked into the office.

"You two look like you've been up to something," Stanley said with a frown. "What did I miss?"

Malcolm returned to the love seat and stretched out

as if nothing had happened. "Miss Connors and I were discussing the importance of preneed arrangements."

"She's planning on immortality, I've heard it before." Stanley hung his head for a moment in mock defeat, and then brightened up. "But you know what, Maggie? We got some new coffins in last week. Real beauties. You'll go nuts when you see them. And if you buy today, then you lock in at today's prices. I don't have to tell you what inflation can do to the cost of money."

I stood there still turning several colors of burgundy from Malcolm's advance. It wasn't *my* death I was thinking about.

"Excuse me, Stanley," Grace said from the doorway, "we've got a situation on our hands. Tim Easton was killed in a private plane accident about an hour ago."

"The sports anchor from *Channel 10 News*?" Stanley said.

"That's him, or was him," Grace said. "We're going to have to combine all the visitation rooms for the viewing, which I'm guessing will be Thursday evening. It's going to be a busy night, and we'd better clear our schedules for tomorrow, too."

Several phone lines started ringing.

Stanley turned to me. "I'm sorry, but I'll have to reschedule our portfolio review."

Malcolm sat upright on the love seat and raised his hands in a cautionary stance. "Uncle, I know this is going to be a big funeral, but we're going to have to stay strictly in the family's budget—no Vandenberg contributions. I'm still trying to reconcile your books, and I don't think it is going to be a favorable mistake that I find. We need some fiscal responsibility right now."

"Oh, screw fiscal responsibility," Stanley said, noticeably irritated by Malcolm's patronizing tone. "I'll get Sunshine Flowers to work on the arrangements right away."

"Stanley," Grace said, "Sunshine isn't going to bill us, so we have to pay up front for what we order."

"That's just absurd, but I'll take care of it." Stanley looked like a general about to go into battle. "Did the Aegean Elite come in?"

Grace nodded.

"Hotdiggitydog!" Stanley slapped his hands together. "Perfect timing! Didn't I tell you we needed to stock a high-end casket for the holidays? We'll have to completely rearrange the Selection Room."

"Uncle, Tim Easton isn't going to get the Aegean unless his family contracts for it."

"We'll consider it a loss leader. Do you know how many people will be through here on Thursday? Think of the advertising impact of seeing one of Saint Louis's favorite sports anchors in the Aegean Elite." Then the expression on Stanley's face changed. "The Palimo shindig is tomorrow."

"What Palimo shindig?" Grace said.

Stanley rubbed his head. "You know, the bus trip to Palimo headquarters. We leave from Hamilton at eleven-thirty and return Thursday morning."

Grace's hands were on her hips. "You never told me about it."

"Uncle, you should still go. Grace and I can get things organized here."

Grace and Malcolm shared a look, and I guessed they wanted Stanley away from the funeral home to keep him from pushing the place into Chapter Eleven.

I'd finally calmed down to the point that I could put vowels and consonants together. "Mr. Vandenberg, we should be back late Thursday morning, so you won't miss Mr. Easton's service."

Stanley stared at me but was lost in thought. "I really want to go," he said. "You two promise to call me with updates? Don't forget we'll need to make arrangements with the police for traffic control."

Grace and Malcolm both nodded and seemed surprised at his decision.

"Uncle, I can even give you a ride over to Hamilton tomorrow if you'd like. I'd like to open a new brokerage account with Miss Connors, and this way you won't have to leave your Packard in the parking garage overnight. I know how you hate paying for two parking spaces."

Malcolm's account was one I could do without. "I'm sorry, Malcolm. Because of my client commitments, I only accept accounts with $500,000 or more in assets." I tried to keep my tone businesslike, although I was still pissed beyond words.

"Not a problem. In fact, John George dumped two estates on me that I need to liquidate. I think they're worth about $800,000. I'll stop by in the morning, and we can work out the details."

"Tomorrow's not good for me. I have a lot of last-minute arrangements before the Palimo party."

"Oh, please Maggie," Stanley said. "I would feel so much better if you met with Malcolm. Then at least this visit wouldn't have been a total waste of your time."

Socrates was squawking again, and the constant noise and commotion were getting tiresome.

"What do you say, Miss Connors? Are you up to it?"

Malcolm's words hung in the air, mocking me, while Stanley benignly waited for my answer.

I smiled sweetly. "Malcolm, I would love to handle your account. Is ten o'clock good for you?"

He nodded. "Even if it's bad, it will still be good."

"That sounds like it will work out for everyone," Stanley said.

I accepted my coat from Stanley and bolted from the office to avoid being alone with Malcolm again. Outside, I tromped through the snow to my car, but when I went to unlock my car, I realized I forgot my purse.

I kicked an innocent tire, sending frozen shock waves up my leg and wedging more of the cold, wet stuff into my shoe. Back to the funeral home.

I returned to Stanley's office, but everyone had disappeared, along with my purse. I walked back into the hallway and found Grace coming out of a visitation room.

"Excuse me Grace, I left my purse in Stanley's office, but it's not there."

"Check with Stanley. He's upstairs with Kirby, rearranging the Selection Room. Go down this hallway to the elevator and take it to the second floor."

I thanked her and walked to the elevators. When the doors opened on the second floor, I found myself in a hallway with large windows overlooking the top of the atrium.

"This is all wrong!" It was Stanley's voice coming from the room to my right. "Kirby, when you lay out the caskets, you need to remember some very important merchandising points."

I walked closer and listened outside the door, curious to know how caskets were peddled.

"We separate the caskets into four price points," Stanley said, "but they need to be interspersed so it's not obvious. That way I can start people at the second-tier pricing, move them to the top to shell-shock them, down to the fourth tier for shabby product comparison, and then bounce them back to where I want them at the second tier."

There was a long pause.

"Am I making any sense to you, boy?"

"Not really," the young man said.

"How 'bout this. Let's move the expensive caskets over here to the right, and I want wide aisles leading up to them. Make the aisles narrow and uninviting to get to the cheap ones over there. Do you know why we put the more expensive ones to the right?"

"Not a clue," the young man said.

"Are you right-handed or left-handed?" Stanley asked.

"Left-handed."

"Figures, but eighty-five percent of the population is right-handed. Studies show that when right-handed people get lost in the woods, they tend to walk in a big circle to the right. We want them to do the same thing here. Simple enough? Now help me slide this one over."

I walked into the room.

"Hey Maggie, look at these caskets: velvet, inner-spring support system. Aren't they great?"

I nodded. *No sound system?*

"Bet you're looking for your purse. I gave it to Malcolm."

I sighed. "And he would be?"

"Downstairs someplace."

I turned and went back to the elevator. When the doors opened, Malcolm was standing there.

"Your chariot, madam," he said, "and your purse."

I stepped onto the elevator. My mace was in my purse, but my knee was ready now.

"For a woman who manages so many millions of dollars, I'm surprised you couldn't manage to remember your purse. I hope it wasn't because I upset you. I was only being playful. Please forgive me."

Damn, for the second time he completely caught me off guard, this time with unexpected sincerity. I assured him I was fine, just running late for a dinner meeting.

We reached the first floor, and he said good-bye. He wanted to go back upstairs to check on his uncle.

I made my way to my car with purse in hand. My former grime-covered Corolla was now a big snowy marshmallow with at least five inches of snow on every horizontal surface. I glanced back to make sure I didn't have an audience and began using my arm as a make-shift snow scraper. They had been predicting snow for days. Who knew I would actually need a scraper to-day?

I didn't bother clearing the windshield, figuring the wipers could do that, and concentrated on getting enough snow off the back and side windows for minimum visibility. I would be okay as long as I didn't have to change lanes or merge into or out of traffic. I'm sure neither of those talents would be needed in my ride back to Clayton. I climbed inside my Corolla and shut the door, but not before accidentally knocking inside a few inches of snow from the car roof.

Even with 85,000 miles and a ton of snow all over it, my Corolla started without hesitation. I flipped the heat on high, something I should have done when I began my snow reallocation, and turned on the windshield wipers.

Nothing happened. They were frozen to my windshield.

Back out into the cold.

The snow was the deepest on my windshield, and with each sweep of my arm I managed to push more snow inside my coat sleeve. I finally cleared most of the snow from my windshield and located the wiper blades. I snapped them against the windshield a couple of times to shake off the ice and then jumped back into my car.

I turned on the wipers again. I heard a motor hum, but no movement. Evidently, windshield wipers should not be used as snow scrapers.

At least the heat was working. I flipped off my now-never-again-to-be-fabulous snow-covered pumps and jammed my feet as high as they could go into the heating vents to return feeling to my frozen extremities. While I enjoyed a few minutes of luxurious thawing, I flipped on the radio to get the details on Tim Easton's death. The plane had been caught in the snowstorm and gone down over the Ozarks. I was mildly saddened. I had never been a sports fan, but he wasn't a bad guy.

One more meeting, and this nightmare day would be over. One more week and I would have my own brokerage business, assuming the hospital didn't make a bad decision.

The drive to Clayton, which usually takes about twenty minutes, took an hour. The snow was falling too heavily and too fast for the road crews and my broken windshield wipers. Every few miles I had to pull over and clear my windshield, but finding a spot to pull over to wasn't easy. Luckily, I was headed into town, and most traffic was exiting the city, or my commute would have been even worse. It was ten after seven when I arrived at the restaurant and found my client impatiently drumming his fingers at our table.

I apologized for my tardiness and blamed the snow. The same waiter from my lunch meeting waited on us, and he didn't seem particularly happy to see me again. While we waited for our meals to arrive, I gave my client my hypothetical spiel about leaving Hamilton. It turned out that both the client and his five million dollars were fine with me going independent. We had just finished dessert and I was beginning to think that maybe this day wasn't a total disaster when the waiter appeared with the check.

I retrieved my purse from the back of my chair and began fishing for my wallet. Inside my purse I found everything that had been there from lunch, including my paper clip/dental tool, but no wallet.

I reviewed the day's events. I was sure I'd retrieved my wallet after lunch, but I didn't remember seeing it at the Vandenbergs. Had it fallen out?

My client wasn't upset about picking up the check, but the waiter looked at me as if I made a habit of chiseling my clients out of meals. Of course, as far as he knew, I did. I chose not to make an issue of it with the dish jockey and instead apologized profusely to my client and headed for the door.

Chapter 3

I planned on getting to the office early but had stayed up too late last night doing paperwork, which translated into multiple beatings of my alarm clock's slumber bar. Eventually, I yanked the clock's plug from the wall and drifted back into a deep sleep without the nagging beep, beep, beep serenade every ten minutes. When I regained full consciousness at eight-thirty, I shouldn't have been surprised that I overslept, but I was.

It was after nine-thirty when my wiperless Corolla and I made it into the Hamilton parking garage. I needed a new car and a tropical vacation. Stacy was in my office tidying up when I arrived.

"I thought it might be good to give your clients the impression that you're organized," she said. My stacks and piles had all been transferred, not too meticulously, into a single oversized cardboard box. "I'll have someone from the mail room relocate this box for the day."

"You're a genius." I glanced at the front of the day's *Wall Street Journal*. "Hey, did you find an address for that woman from yesterday?"

"Donna Trundle? No, I checked the phone book and called information but didn't find anything. As soon as we get through this Palimo trip, I'll do some more investigating."

I nodded. "I'm going to the cafeteria for a Pepsi. Can I get you anything?"

"If they got in any emotionally well-balanced, financially independent bodybuilders, pick me up one."

"Make it two," said another secretary walking by.

"I don't think I have enough quarters, but I'll look."

Word of the Palimo party had made the gossip grapevine, and several brokers in the cafeteria wanted my firsthand account of the expensive outing. It was almost ten o'clock before I returned from the cafeteria with Pepsi and Oreos in hand. I opened my Pepsi and popped an Oreo in my mouth.

"Ms. Connors, you're even more ravishing this morning than you were last night."

I looked up and saw Stanley and Malcolm Vandenberg staring down at me. My teeth were probably as black as Malcolm's custom-tailored suit. I swallowed a gulp of soda and hoped it washed some of the cookie residue from my teeth.

"I'm sorry, I forgot—"

"It's ten on the nose. Are we interrupting your breakfast? Would you prefer we wait in the lobby?" Malcolm cocked his head to the side and smiled devilishly. Then, without waiting for my reply, he made himself comfortable in one of my chairs. Stanley took the seat next to my desk and draped his trench coat over a clear spot on my credenza.

I swallowed another gulp of Pepsi and tried to covertly swish it around before swallowing.

"I'm sorry, gentlemen. I've got a lot of stuff going

on this morning, and I'm usually more organized. I'll
get a new account form from my assistant and be right
back."

Stacy wasn't at her desk, which gave me an opportunity to search for a form and use a tissue to rid my
front teeth of the Oreo leftovers. I took my time looking for the form so I could finish my impromptu dental
hygiene.

"Maggie?" Stanley said, standing behind me. He
was holding his coat again. "I know you and Malcolm
have some business to discuss, and I need to meet
someone before we leave for Palimo, so I'm going to
catch up with you later."

I nodded and opened another drawer in Stacy's desk.

When I returned with the form, Malcolm stood and
blocked my way to my desk. "You look like you're
missing something," he said and tilted my chin up with
his hand.

I stepped back to regain control of my chin and give
myself room to swing. "What exactly do you mean?"

"This was sticking out from under the edge of your
desk." He handed me my wallet.

I'd forgotten it was gone, which probably explained
why I misplaced it so often. I flipped it open and found
all my credit cards and cash were right where they
were supposed to be.

"You really didn't give me enough time to swipe
anything," he said.

I blushed slightly. "I can't tell you what a relief it
is to have this back."

He sat down. "Happy enough to give me a discount
on my stock trades?"

"Not that happy." I walked around to my desk and
tucked my wallet back into my purse, which was lying
on the floor. "Actually, perhaps you might be better
served at one of the discount houses or using an on-
line broker."

"No, I don't like my chances of finding another broker with legs as good as yours. Let me check something." He walked around to where I was sitting, pulled me up, and then bent down and sniffed my neck. "I thought so. You smell good, too."

I pushed him away. "Malcolm, I think I might have given you a wrong first impression."

"My first impression was that you didn't like me."

"Your impression was right," I said, still standing. "Here's the deal. If you need someone to do estate evaluations and liquidations, I'd be happy to help. But anything beyond that isn't going to fly."

"There's something about a stiff, uptight woman that's a real turn-on for me." His voice was a velvety purr. "Must be the environmental hazard of being raised in a funeral home."

I cringed. "Take it or leave it, and I think you should leave it."

He dismissed my ultimatum with a flick of his wrist. "I'll take it, and I'll get right to the point, because I have another meeting shortly." Now his tone was all business.

I grabbed a notepad.

"I have two estates that I'm currently settling. The Stenner estate should be worth about $280,000 and the Lanz estate should be worth about $525,000. Would you please give me an evaluation for the Stenner estate as of May 18th of this year, and the Lanz estate as of June 9th of this year."

I looked up from my notes. "Those are the dates of death?"

"Yes, and then I'll need current evaluations. I'd like you to go ahead and liquidate the stocks today, using market orders. Here is an inventory list and the stock certificates for both estates."

I flipped through the ornate pages. Most of the certificates had been issued in the sixties. He had quite a few blue-chip stocks, and it would take some deciphering to figure out their current value because of the

number of stock splits companies had gone through in
the last forty or so years. He was probably undervaluing the estates by about 30 percent.

I took down the new account information for his law
firm and opened up an account for each of the estates.
Selling about a million dollars in stocks would earn me
almost fifteen thousand in commissions, and for that I
would put up with a few passes. I finished the paperwork and thanked him for opening the accounts. I
hoped to get him out of my office as soon as possible
so I could check on some last-minute Palimo details
before clients started arriving.

"I also need to open up a margin account for my
uncle."

I frowned. "Your uncle doesn't believe in borrowing
on margin."

"He needs the money to finance some business expenditures."

"I'll give him the paperwork on the bus ride to Palimo."

"That won't be necessary. He gave me power of
attorney for his account, so perhaps we can get the
paperwork taken care of right now."

I remembered the battles over the sports anchor's
funeral. "He gave you power of attorney?"

"Here's your copy," he said and handed the paper
over that documented his claim. "As long as he keeps
creative control of the funerals, he doesn't care if I run
everything else. And that place needs some fiscal responsibility if it is going to survive."

I nodded. "You realize that when you establish a
margin account and borrow against it, if the value of
the stocks decline, you're at risk for putting up more
money?"

"Thank you for your concern, Maggie, but I understand how margin accounts work."

I retrieved the margin account forms from my bottom drawer. Something didn't feel right about this.

Malcolm signed in several places as Stanley's power of attorney, promising that he understood the terms of the account and the risks involved.

"How soon could I get an advance against the account?" he said.

"I can get a check today, if you'd like. How much do you need?"

"Why don't we start off with a hundred thousand."

I filled out the paperwork requesting the check. "You said you had an appointment soon. Is it nearby?"

He nodded.

"I can have this check ready for you before I leave for Palimo if you'd like to stop back."

"My, beautiful and efficient. Are you sure you don't want to have dinner with me tomorrow night? It would be an experience you'd never forget."

His self-confidence had a darkness that was both intriguing and disconcerting.

"Sorry, I don't date clients."

"Hmmmm. We'll have to work on that." He bent down as if he was going to kiss me. "Enjoy your trip."

He walked out of my office, leaving me still expecting the kiss.

I watched him pass the reception area. It was odd how people gave him the right of way when he approached. Probably a reaction to his height and black-on-black fashion statement. He did make for an eyeful.

Stacy walked into my office. "The buses are here."

"Let's go take a look."

We grabbed our winter coats and strolled to the front door. Parked in front of Hamilton Securities in a no-parking zone were two custom buses from Carlson Travels. They were each about forty-five-feet long. We walked to the closest bus, and I knocked on the door.

It opened with a hiss. "Are you Maggie Connors?" the driver said.

"Yeah, can we take a look around?"

"Come on in."

Stacy and I climbed up and were stunned by the opulence.

"This isn't your ordinary Partridge Family bus," Stacy said.

The front third of the bus had rows of creamy leather captain's chairs, the kind you always pass on a plane as you make your way back to coach. Mounted from the ceiling every few rows were nine-inch television screens for your viewing pleasure.

"This coach has an in-motion satellite system, so your clients can watch a new-release movie while we travel," the driver said. "And back here is the galley."

We followed him to the middle of the bus, which had a good-sized kitchen and wet bar. All the countertops were Corian and the fixtures brass.

"It's amazing what all you can pack into a bus," I said.

"This leads to the bathroom." The driver opened a door to the left of the galley to give us a view of the spacious rest room.

"Look back here," Stacy said.

In the back of the bus was a lounge area with a horseshoe-shaped leather couch and a Corian conference table in the middle. For those in the back of the bus, there was a thirty-two-inch television to enjoy.

"This is going to be a very comfortable trip," I said. "Is the other bus laid out the same?"

"Carbon copy," the driver said.

There was a knock from the front of the bus.

"That's probably the caterer," Stacy said. "They wanted to get set up before clients start arriving. I'll get them settled."

"Thanks. I need to get back. And would you put some Palimo annual reports on the bus conference tables?"

"I've got them boxed up and ready to go."

Back in my office, I checked the price of Palimo. It

was down 5 percent. I punched up the latest news. One of Palimo's leading scientists had been killed in a car accident, and the stock was dropping in response.

I immediately called Richard Craig. He was the head of research for Palimo's Saint Louis facility and also my client.

"Richard Craig," said a haggard voice.

"Hi, Richard, it's Maggie at Hamilton."

"Maggie, this isn't a good time."

"I'm so sorry. I just saw the news on Edward."

"They told us he was on his way to work this morning and pulled onto the highway in front of a tractor trailer." There was a long pause, and I waited while Richard found the words to go on. "Edward was killed instantly."

"I'm sorry, Richard. Is there anything I can do for you? I know you two were really close."

"Yeah, dump all my stocks and bonds."

I paused, not sure if he was serious.

"Are you there, Maggie?"

"Yes. I'm not sure what to say. Why do you want to get out of the market?"

"I don't know. I've been getting tired of the whole research grind for quite a while now, and I guess Edward's death pushed me over the edge. I want to get out of the business and enjoy life for a while. Maybe return to England. I don't know."

My heart skipped a beat. "Is there something you're not telling me? I don't mean to be crass, but is Edward's death going to affect the outcome of the study? Is that your concern?"

"No, no. Everything will be fine. All of our research methodologies are in place, and I'll see the project through to the end. I promise."

I called up his account on my computer. "We liquidated most of your stock holdings last month and put the proceeds in the money market. Looks like you've still got about $50,000 in bonds and a few shares of

Palimo. To sell your Palimo, I'll need a copy of your 144. Can you fax it to me?"

"I didn't file one yet. Why don't you slide this order through. I think it's only for a hundred shares; I doubt anyone notices."

Certain executive positions, such as head of research, were privy to insider information that would affect a stock's price, and the SEC kept these executives on a tight leash. Whenever a company executive bought or sold their own company's shares, they had to file a form stating the date and the number of shares. This helped the SEC track executives' trades and acted as a deterrent to those dumping stocks before low earnings were announced to the public, or perhaps buying up shares before announcing a new breakthrough. It was because of these restrictions that Richard, ironically, owned less Palimo stock than any of my major clients. He liked liquidity.

"There's no such thing as sliding through an insider trade," I said. "This stuff is all computerized, so the question is not if you will get caught but when. I'm not ready to lose my securities license, so when you get your 144 filed, send me a copy, and we'll sell the shares then."

"All right, all right, just dump the bonds and send me a check for the proceeds," he said and then hung up on me.

Richard never dealt with pressure well. I got the impression that he preferred to experience life from behind a microscope.

I filled out sell orders for his bond portfolio. Despite a recent market correction, Richard would still net about $185,000.

My next call was to the Palimo CEO in Jefferson City, who again assured me that everything was fine. He had thought about postponing the Christmas party, but there were too many people on their way that couldn't be reached.

The next hour was a flurry of phone calls. I decided the dip in Palimo's price was a buying opportunity and started calling clients to give them the news. I also needed to update those clients going to the Palimo party. By the time the buses were ready to roll out of town, I had bought an additional 5,000 shares for clients and another 1,000 for myself. The downside was that I was frantically filling out buy orders instead of calmly greeting clients as they arrived. I scrambled to get on my bus before it left and didn't even get a chance to say hello to my clients on the other bus.

As my bus pulled beside the other one and we passed to take the lead, I saw Psycho Phil's ugly mug smiling at me from a window seat. I silently cursed at a mutant detail I had forgotten to take care of.

It started snowing halfway to Jefferson City, which slowed our travel to a crawl. We arrived at our hotel about an hour late. I herded the clients from my bus into the hotel, and Stacy worked on getting the clients from the other bus checked in.

When I reached my hotel room, I quickly changed out of my business suit and into a form-fitting black gown. The front had a high, conservative neckline and long sleeves made out of black chiffon. The back was a different story—it plunged to my waist. The black dress with my auburn hair made quite a statement, and as I stared at myself in the mirror, I wondered if it was too much. But I hadn't packed an alternative, so there wasn't anything I could do about it. And, what the heck, it was the holidays and time to loosen up.

I walked to the elevator and had to admit, it felt good to spend an evening playing dress-up instead of being in sweats, curled up on a couch, and reading financial reports. Outside the hotel I found the two buses had been retired for the evening and standing in were five stretch limousines. The drive to Palimo took less than five minutes. The limos would spend the evening shuttling people back and forth, so clients could come and go when they wanted.

At five o'clock, I joined four other clients for a limo ride to the new Palimo headquarters. The snow was still falling, but it didn't seem to bother the limo driver. He said he'd already made one trip over and so had the other limos.

The limo driver slowed the car as we approached the Palimo headquarters, and someone in the car gave an audible gasp. The building was comprised of two stainless steel and glass drums that rose up seven stories and were joined in the middle by an expansive atrium topped off by a glass barrel vault. Spotlights illuminated the exterior and highlighted the falling snow, which made the building look magical.

We entered through the center atrium and stopped. The extravagant seven-story entrance made the luxury-yacht buses we'd ridden in this afternoon look shabby. Above the artificial lake in the center—fountain was too mild a description—the upper levels rose like an inverted cascade to maximize the view from any level in the building. A magnificent spiral staircase wound around the atrium's perimeter and formed the building's liquid spine. For those wanting a quicker way to the top, glass elevators in the four corners of the main area offered a breathtaking view of the center court before disappearing down to the two underground floors that housed the company's secretive laboratories. Above us was a steel and glass floor that seemed suspended in air over the lake and served as the reception area for tonight's festivities.

The building's design created a free flow of space that was unlike any other commercial building I had seen. The Palimo building oozed of high-tech accomplishments and environmental responsibility, characteristics that suited the company well.

A representative from Palimo was waiting to greet us. Many of my clients had already arrived. The Palimo rep divided us into groups of eight to ten and gave us tours of the new digs. I kept my eyes open to make sure I was nowhere near Psycho Phil, but I soon spotted him at the bar wearing a powder-blue polyester suit that must have come from a Sears clearance rack. At least from some of our previous phone conversations, I knew he was a fairly mellow drunk, so I quit worrying. Maybe he would quietly get drunk and then pass out without actually talking to anyone.

My other, more civilized clients were very impressed with the building's design, although I did hear a few rumblings about how the expense was going to affect the bottom line. The laboratories were off limits to visitors, so in the reception area they had a multimedia presentation explaining the medical progress Palimo had made and their plans for the future. It was overwhelming and exciting.

When we made it back to the reception area, I spied David Chambers, the Palimo CEO, talking with a woman I didn't recognize and Paul and Horace Goldberg. Paul and Horace were twin brothers in their eighties. Goldberg Homes had built about 30 percent of all the homes in Saint Louis's West County. They had been millionaires by the time they reached their forties.

"Hey, Maggie, you're just in time," David said. "Let me introduce you to Stephanie Wolf. She's in the process of trying to shake some change out of these old codgers to keep her hospice afloat."

"It's nice to meet you," she said, extending her hand.

"You're not trying to weasel money out of these guys that I could be investing for them, are you?" I said.

"Guilty as charged." She smiled, somewhat embarrassed. "I'm afraid I don't have much of a choice. I run a hospice for children and their families, and most of the families we serve live below the poverty line. Because of some government cutbacks, I have to close our doors at the end of the month if I don't find a white knight who can give us some funding."

"She is trying to convince these tightwads to each buy a thousand shares."

"Shares of what?" I said.

"Shares of Hope," Stephanie said. "They are honorary certificates we issue as part of our fund-raising effort to forge partnerships with the community."

"How much is a share?" I said.

"A wiz," Paul said.

Ten bucks a share? $10,000? I smiled. "You guys probably have that much between your sofa cushions."

"I don't keep that much change lying around," Horace said.

"I have eleven families that we are currently assisting," Stephanie said, "all with children under the age of ten with life expectancies of less than two months. Their families have no money, no insurance. And we have a waiting list that stretches forever." She started digging in her purse. "There is no excuse for this level of suffering in a country as prosperous as the United States."

I thought about Donna Trundle—the woman from yesterday—seeking money for her daughter with bone cancer. I'd meant to give her a check and still would if I could find her.

Stephanie handed me a picture of a baby with enormous blue eyes. The eyes had a wisdom that contrasted harshly with the small, pale face that seemed haunted and full of pain. The little girl couldn't have been more than six months old.

"This is a picture of Sarah. She's dying from leukemia. If I don't raise enough money tonight, this poor child will spend her final days living with her family in a beat-up station wagon. They won't be able to ease her pain because they have no money for food or medication. And her mother refuses to go to a shelter because her oldest child was once attacked there."

"Good God," I said, "but a hospital can't refuse medical aid to someone because they can't pay."

"That's true," Stephanie said, "but you've got to understand, this isn't like a gunshot wound. These are impoverished families dealing with long-term illnesses, and often the parent has a distrust of the system, which keeps them from seeking help."

"Why don't you kick out a donation, Maggie?" Paul said. "It's the end of the year. I'm sure your tax return could use a charitable write-off."

I rubbed my chin. "A thousand shares, huh?"

"I'll make you a deal, Maggie. Whatever you donate, Horace and I will each match."

"What do you mean, 'Horace and I will match'?" Horace said.

"Oh come on, you old fool, it's Christmas."

Stephanie noticeably sucked in her breath and waited for my answer.

"You're on, guys. But if you're going to match my donation, then why don't we each do three thousand shares?"

Paul choked slightly on his champagne. "Good God, Maggie. That's a lot of cash."

"You're sure you got that kind of money?" Horace said.

"I think I can shake it loose. You guys won't even miss it."

"Fine, but here's the condition. Ms. Wolf, as soon as you receive Maggie's donation, fax me a copy of the check, and then we'll forward our donations. But, Maggie, if you change your mind for any reason, try to lower the donation, or weasel out, the whole deal is off."

"Boy, you guys are making such a big fuss over this. I should think a donation like this would be pocket change for you."

"I guess you're a better financial manager than we realized," Paul said.

Stephanie charged me and flung her arms around me. "Oh my God, you're an angel. I haven' slept for days worrying over this. And when I called L'avid, he suggested I network at this meeting tonight . . . but I had no idea."

Nonprofits are always touchy-feely, but I was surprised she was getting this excited over three donations of $30,000. Maybe $90,000 goes a lot farther in a hospice than I imagined.

We each gave her a business card with information on how she could reach us.

"And one more thing, Maggie," Horace said. "You need to give your check to Ms. Wolf by next week, because if we're going to do a donation this size, we need to declare it this year."

I spied Tim entering the reception area.

"Not a problem. I'll get my check to Stephanie by the beginning of next week. And if you'll all excuse me for a moment, a friend of mine just arrived that I need to greet."

By the time I made it across the reception area to Tim, a waiter had already given him a glass of champagne.

"You're a sight for sore eyes," he said.

He put his drink down on an adjacent table and then turned to hug me. When his hands felt the smoothness of my back, he said, "Did you get the dress on sale since it's only half there?"

I turned and modeled my gown for him.

"My, you do scrub up rather nice, Miss Connors."

A month of traipsing in and out of dressing rooms and pulling dresses on and off in search of the perfect dress had just paid off. "You look pretty good yourself."

Tim looked perfectly at ease in his black tuxedo, white shirt with small black buttons, and a black bow tie. He was Harrison Ford—but younger.

"Thanks for inviting me," he said.

We were both facing the windowed back wall. Outdoor spotlights aimed in the air lit up the snow that was falling wildly. It was like standing in a shaken snow globe with a handsome, gun-toting man at my side. It didn't get better than this.

"Enjoy your trip?" I said.

"I gotta admit the plane ride over here was a pretty cool way to travel."

"The snow didn't give you any problems?"

"Not at all. Got here right on time."

Richard Craig was walking back from the bar and bumped Tim.

"Oh, Tim, I'd like you to meet one of the busiest brains behind Palimo. This is Richard Craig. He's Palimo's vice president of research and development and one of my clients. He heads up Palimo's field research center in Saint Louis."

Richard stopped and shook Tim's hand. "It's a pleasure to meet you."

Although it was early in the evening, Richard was already slurring his words.

"I'm sorry again about Edward," I said, and then turned to Tim. "Richard lost a colleague this afternoon."

"My condolences," Tim said.

Richard nodded and took another drink.

"One of our best scientists was killed today," he told Tim. "I can't believe that over the weekend we're partying on my yacht, and Edward dies in a car accident this morning. To make things worse, they went ahead with this damn dog and pony show and required mandatory attendance. This goddamn place sucks every bit of life out of you that they can. I can't wait to get out of it."

"Where would you be on a yacht in this kind of weather?" Tim said, obviously trying to change the subject to something lighter.

"In the Mediterranean. We were—"

"You have a yacht in the Mediterranean?" Tim said.

I watched it happen, right in front of my eyes. Tim switched into his IRS mode.

"You'd be surprised at the perks you get when you toe the company line," Richard said. "What business are you in?"

"I'm a special agent with the Criminal Investigation Division of the Internal Revenue Service."

Richard's face turned ashen. "Bet that's a lot to get on one little business card. Well, I'm dry," he said, tilting his empty glass at us. "I'm heading back to the bar, and then I need to take a piss. Nice meeting you."

We watched him wobble back to the bar.

"You really know how to add life to a party," I said.

"Maggie, any idea what a Palimo scientist earns?"

"Yes, but we're not here on IRS time, and I can't discuss my client's financial situation without a warrant. I think we've been down this road before."

"Well, perhaps another conversation with Richard—"

"Tim, turn off the IRS antennae for just one night, and let's have a good time. I didn't buy this dress to help you investigate another one of my clients."

He smiled sweetly and slid his hand down my back and rested it on my hip. "That is some dress, and I notice by the slit at the bottom that you actually shaved those legs of yours."

"It's the holidays. I decided to make an extra effort."

"So what kind of employment changes are you making?" Tim said.

The lights flashed, and then a waiter announced they were ready to begin dinner.

"Let's talk about it later," I said. "Right now I could use a plateful of food."

Tim and I took our seats with David Chambers and his wife, Tiger Woods and his date, Steve Martin and his wife, and two couples I hadn't met yet. A few minutes after we were seated, Tiger Woods excused himself to deliver the predinner speech. It was an inspiring talk discussing the challenges of life with AIDS.

When the speech was over, waiters and waitresses appeared to serve the meal. First came a shrimp cocktail, followed by a spring salad. Then it was onto the main course, which was a choice of filet mignon, lobster, or chicken alfredo.

"So tell me about this employment change you're making," Tim whispered after we were served.

"I've decided to go out on my own," I said softly so our fellow diners wouldn't hear—not that any of them were paying attention as they sucked down the free wine.

"Because . . ."

"Lots of reasons. I'm tired of the office politics, of having to push Hamilton proprietary products. And I want to make more money and work less. I know you think that's greedy—"

"Not at all, especially the work less part. It's not having money I object to, it's letting it control you. So how exactly do you go about setting up your own shop?"

"I signed an agreement with a firm that will provide all the back office support I need and execute my trades. They take a percentage of my commission, which is a heck of a lot less than what Hamilton takes."

"Are you going to work from home?"

"I thought about it, but I think I need to go to an office every morning, so I rented some space in Clayton."

"When does this all go into effect?"

I motioned the waiter to bring more wine. "I'm planning on giving notice on Tuesday. I have about $300,000 in stock options I get vested in on Monday. But enough about me and Hamilton Securities, what's going on with you these days?"

He leaned back in his chair. "I've just finished a big

trafficking case. This guy was using a network of private planes to smuggle drugs in from Mexico."

"I saw that on the news. Why were you involved? I thought we had ATF agents for that."

"We follow the money. The Service tends to get into anything where large sums of cash change hands."

The waiter arrived with the wine.

"So, are you harassing Richard Craig because your caseload is lightening up?

He smiled. "I can neither confirm nor deny that Richard Craig is under investigation."

I leaned closer to Tim. "You don't think Craig is involved in drugs, do you?"

"No, I don't."

"Aren't drugs the usual source of unreported income in your tax investigations?"

"Yes, but unreported income can come from all sorts of places. We've had restaurant owners skim cash from the business or doctors not declare all of their income. There are lots of ways to make money disappear."

"But Richard Craig is on a straight salary. I don't think they get commissions in the research lab."

"Yeah, you're right. And maybe the guy has a trust fund. You never know. I just had a hunch. Why don't we talk about something other than Richard Craig?"

Tim started telling fascinating stories about his recent cases, and before I knew it, our dinners were done and the waiters were serving a simple yet decadent chocolate soufflé.

"So," I said, after swallowing a mouthful of soufflé, "all we've talked about is the Service tonight. What's going on with your love life these days?"

"Not much. I've been pretty wrapped up with work lately."

"Well, you must have poked your nose out of your IRS manuals for a few minutes. What about the woman you have a date with on New Year's?"

"Oh, yeah. I forgot."

"Well?" I said.

"Well, what?"

"Who is she?"

"Just an old girlfriend I've been wanting to get to know again."

I tried to play the disinterested third person, but it wasn't easy. "What does she do?"

"Let's not talk about her right now. Are you dating anyone these days?"

"Not really."

He reached into his pocket for his wallet. He flipped the wallet open, and I noticed his IRS identification badge and his photo ID. He looked good even in that picture. In the pocket where he kept his money, he produced a photo and handed it to me. It was a picture of three brown-headed kids: two girls and a boy.

"Don't tell me. . . ." I said.

"You don't think I forgot about our agreement for New Year's?"

"Don't make me start the new year by baby-sitting some screaming urchins."

"A deal's a deal." He leaned forward and pointed to the boy. "That's Nick. The baby is Kate, and the one in the middle is Alexandra."

"They look very angelic. It probably took a whole team of kid wranglers to get them to look like this."

"No, they're great kids. You'll love them. It will be fun, you'll see."

Yeah, right. I handed the picture back.

Steve Martin concluded the dinner with a speech that made people laugh, cry, and want to donate more money for AIDS research. After dinner the bar stations were opened in the reception area and Earth, Wind and Fire began playing.

During the course of the evening, I managed to spend some time with most of my clients. Those I talked with seemed overly impressed with Palimo and excited about the stock's future. Many wanted to increase their already heavy positions. I also succeeded in avoiding Phil, who was eventually carried insensate out to the limos. I guess he had his fun. There was only one client I hadn't seen.

I spotted Stacy on her way to one of the bars and caught up with her.

"Have you seen Stanley Vandenberg tonight?" I said.

"Yeah, he was here. He left early because he wasn't feeling well."

"That's too bad, I—"

The crowd cleared from the bar, and we gave the bartender our requests. Stacy ordered a gin and tonic, and I ordered red wine. Once we had our drinks, we returned to the main section of the reception area.

"Tim was asking me questions about Palimo," Stacy said. "And I don't think it was because he's interested in the stock."

"What kind of questions?"

"He wanted to know about the scientists. How many of them there were and how much money they made."

"What did you tell him?"

"The truth. I didn't have any idea."

"You're a good woman. I'm afraid Tim has his IRS hat on tonight, and he's gunning for Richard Craig, so do what you can to divert Tim. Richard has enough stress with Edward dying."

"Did someone mention my name?" Tim said, walking up behind me.

"Stacy tells me you're still poking around with questions about Richard Craig."

"If you two will excuse me, I think I'll find somewhere else to be," Stacy said and then left.

"Can't take your IRS hat off for a minute, hmmm?" I put my hand on my hip. "And you say I'm obsessed."

"The difference is that I'm trying to do good for our fellow taxpayers. I'd like to discuss this more, but I've got to get going to catch my plane to Saint Louis."

I angled my leg to give Tim the full advantage of the dress's revealing slit. "You really can't stay the night?" Then I remembered he had a date for New Year's and tucked my leg back inside the dress.

He stood in front of me and tipped my chin up, then bent down and kissed me. On my forehead.

"No, I've got to get going. But how about meeting for dinner tomorrow night? There's something I'd like to talk to you about."

The disappointment of a forehead kiss was quickly erased by the dinner invitation. "That would be nice."

"Good. Do you want to meet at MiaMia at around six?"

I nodded.

He smiled and then disappeared.

Earth, Wind and Fire stopped playing around midnight, and the party wound down soon after. I thanked David again for his hospitality and congratulated him on a successful evening. By the time I was ready to leave, all of my clients had been shuttled back to the hotel. I took the last limo back by myself, enjoying the short, peaceful ride without having to make small talk with anyone.

I took the elevator to the top floor and began the labyrinth walk back to my room. It was a two-room hotel suite. The main room was a kitchen/living room combination, and then there was a separate bedroom with a bathroom. I kicked off my shoes and then grabbed a Pepsi out of the refrigerator. Now that the Palimo party was over, my life would calm down considerably.

Safe and secure, I climbed into bed to enjoy what would be my last peaceful night's sleep in a while.

Chapter 4

Thursday, December 23

After my clients had breakfast in the hotel restaurant and then checked out of their rooms, I went down to settle the bill. I wore an emerald green silk suit, which was festive while still businesslike. I stood at the front desk examining my manicure while the desk clerk printed my bill. It literally took ten minutes for the computer to spit out the pages detailing the expenses of my clients' stay. $8,890.34. I handed over my VISA. Thank God Malcolm had found my wallet.

By nine-thirty, everyone was loaded on the buses, and we began the trip back to Saint Louis. The caterer served coffee and danishes, although everyone had just eaten. With more caffeine and carbohydrates in hand, we settled in for the movie and the three-hour ride.

The return trip didn't take as long as the trip over. We parked in front of Hamilton right after noon. I thanked everyone for coming, and they each scurried through the snow to their waiting cars in the parking garage.

I tipped the bus drivers and settled up with the caterer, getting receipts from both. I desperately wanted to go home and relax, but I needed to check on any fires that had erupted during our absence.

On my way to my office, my manager Mike caught up with me.

"I hear your party was a hit," he said, patting me on the back.

"News travels fast, or did you have a mole?"

"Bernice Johnson called me from the hotel this morning to say what a fabulous broker you are and suggested I give you a big Christmas bonus."

"Did you tell her Hamilton doesn't do bonuses?"

"No, but I agreed you deserved something for all the work you've done. I had a guy call me yesterday who needs a retirement plan set up for his business. He has a half dozen car dealerships here in Saint Louis. Think you would be interested?"

He was offering me a freebie big account, and I was supposed to look him in the eye in a few days and tell him I was leaving? With the hope that most of my clients were coming with me? I couldn't have felt more guilty if he'd given me his kidney.

"My plate is kind of full right now," I said.

He knocked on my forehead. "Hello, has an alien life-form taken over your body? Are you out of your mind turning this account down?"

"It's just been a long couple of days. Of course I'd love the account."

"I'll have my secretary give you the account details."

I thanked him and made my way to my office. Back at my desk, I got out the various bills from the Palimo trip. The sooner I faxed them to David's secretary at Palimo for reimbursement, the sooner I would get paid.

The bill from the caterer included lunch and refreshments for forty-two on the trip to Jefferson City, and breakfast for forty on the way back. I searched the hotel invoice and added up the number of single and double occupancies I was charged for: forty-one. It was possible that not everyone wanted breakfast on the return trip—Psycho Phil, for one, was probably too hungover—but why would fewer people have stayed overnight? I was examining the itemized portion of the bill when my phone rang.

"Maggie, it's Richard Craig."

"Hi, Richard. How are you doing?"

"I'd be doing a lot better if your asshole boyfriend wasn't pestering me with questions on how much money I make and how I spend it. Can you call off the dogs?" He sounded frantic.

"I'm sorry Richard. When it comes to taxes, I've got no influence with Tim. But he's reasonable. All you have—"

"He wants me to go to his office today after lunch and have what he calls a 'little chat.' I've got no time for that. Edward's funeral is this afternoon."

"I'm sure Tim would understand if you need to re-schedule."

"Thanks. You've been no help at all," he said and hung up.

I was still trying to figure out what that was all about when my second phone line lit up.

"Hi Maggie, it's Diane Brown. I just called to let you know the press release is ready for your review. Where would you like my assistant to send the proof?"

"Send it to my home, and my computer will answer. The number is 555-4557. Please make absolutely sure it doesn't come here to Hamilton."

"I've got it."

After I hung up, I spent a few minutes trying to reorganize my office. Everything looked slightly out of place. I guessed the cleaning crew hadn't suddenly taken an interest in cleaning and that the changes in my office were more likely the result of Stacy's cleaning efforts before the Palimo trip.

It was quickly obvious to me that organizing my office was going to take more than a five-minute effort, so I abandoned that task, grabbed the invoice summary pages, and walked to the mail room. I filled out a cover sheet addressing the fax to David's secretary at Palimo. Then I waited while the pages fed through the fax. I decided deciphering the bill inconsistencies could wait until tomorrow.

The receptionist paged me for a phone call, so I hurried back to my office and put the bills in my briefcase before answering the phone.

"Maggie Connors."

"Hi, Ms. Connors. It's Stephanie Wolf from the Children's Hospice."

Oh, right, $30,000 worth of goodwill. I was never going to get any business done today.

"I wanted to call and thank you again for your generous donation and for helping to get the matching donations from the Goldberg brothers," she said. "I've been crying myself to sleep the last few nights, worried about what was going to happen. Last night I cried tears of joy before I fell asleep."

"I'm glad I can help," I said and started sorting through my in box. There was a notice that Malcolm Vandenberg had margined an additional seventy thousand from his uncle's account.

"You're so modest for a woman who just arranged for three donations of three million dollars each."

My heart seized. "I'm sorry, what did you say?"

"I said, 'You're very modest for a woman who arranged for three donations of three million dollars each.'"

"Three million?" I croaked.

"You're our guardian angel. The kids are making a special thank-you gift that I want to drop off to you tonight."

"Could you . . . could you hold for a minute please?"

"Of course."

A group of younger brokers were talking outside my office. I barged out and said, "Quick, how much is a wiz?"

"A thousand dollars," one of them replied.

"Are you sure? I thought a wiz was ten dollars."

"Nope, definitely a thousand," another one said.

"Holy shit, what have I done?" I asked the three, who of course had no idea what I was talking about. I went back to my office and stared at the blinking light on my telephone.

"Hi Stephanie, sorry to keep you waiting."

"No problem at all. So when would be a good time for me to come by and pick up your check? And would it be okay if I had a reporter join us to take some pictures of you giving me the check?"

"You know . . . I should . . . probably get clearance from my office manager before I have any pictures taken. Hamilton has a lot of public relations rules. Would it be all right if I called you back this afternoon?"

She said that was fine and gave me her phone number before hanging up.

I sat at my desk, shaking my head. Three million dollars. I couldn't afford that. Well, I could technically, but it was nearly half of everything I had. And the brothers had said if I tried to lower my donation, the whole deal was off. What the hell had I done?

My phone rang. I picked it up and then hung it back up. I needed to calm down. There had to be a way out of this, but I was too panicked to think creatively. My whole body was shaking, and I was starting to hyperventilate.

I needed a Pepsi.

I walked in a daze to the cafeteria for a late-morning snack. Actually, early-afternoon snack. Or possibly lunch.

When I returned with my Pepsi and Oreos, there was a piece of paper sitting in the middle of my desk with the words "Press Release" in huge, bold letters across the top. With my heart pounding again, I picked up the paper and read the announcement of Maggie Connors opening her new financial planning boutique in Clayton.

Shit. Shit. Shit.

I stood at my desk. I was afraid to move since spontaneous combustion was the only disaster that hadn't befallen me today.

Both of my telephone lines were blinking. My boss was probably on line one, calling me in to fire me before I vested in my stock options. Line two could have been anyone—my gyno with news my pap smear was abnormal, the Environmental Protection Agency letting me know there was a toxic waste dump under my condo I was responsible for cleaning up, or maybe just Psycho Phil asking me out. Whoever the blinking lights were, I didn't want to know. I grabbed the press release and my winter coat and walked to the front door.

"I'm gone for the day," I told Stacy as I walked by. The question was, was I gone permanently?

Chapter 5

I decided to take the Scarlett O'Hara approach to crisis management and think about everything tomorrow, which meant I needed a diversion today. I stayed on Highway 40 and drove past my exit. Two in the afternoon was too early to go home and pace the floor.

The snow had been cleared from the streets and replaced with grime and road salt. Everything looked dirty: The parking lots of the stores that dotted the landscape, the cars, even the people bundled up and walking from their cars to the stores looked dingy.

The Vandenberg Funeral Home popped into my mind. What better place to mourn my situation? For some reason I just loved the atrium in the middle of the home. It was so peaceful, without a fax machine or telephone in sight. Besides, I needed to talk with Stanley about his nephew draining his account and also ask if he would be interested in writing a testimonial for the hospital review committee.

I turned onto Highway 270 south and took the Manchester exit. Minutes later, I was in the funeral home parking lot, which was spotlessly clean but jammed with cars.

The sports guy's funeral.

I created my own parking spot and walked inside. My green silk suit was a little festive for a funeral, but I was hoping to sneak in, maybe have a few quick words with Stanley, and then park myself in the atrium and start brainstorming excuses to get out of my three-million-dollar pledge.

The crowd streaming in the front door wasn't part of my peaceful vision. I stood in the entrance being bumped and jostled by people passing me and wasn't sure what my next move should be.

"Maggie Connors," said a melodic voice with a British accent, "you just can't keep yourself away from me."

I looked up and saw the last person I wanted to see, pushing his way toward me.

"Hello, Malcolm. How are you?"

He stroked his goatee and gave me an appraising look. "Fine, just fine."

"Is your uncle around?"

"He's a little tied up with Tim Easton's funeral, but I'm sure he'd like to see you. Until he's available, might I steal you away for a moment?"

He took my elbow and guided me through the throng of people to Stanley's office. He closed the door behind us, and the noise dulled from the mass of people attending Easton's service. There was a white sheet draped over the birdcage, and I guessed Socrates had been retired for the ceremony.

"The viewing began an hour ago, and it's been a madhouse ever since." He sat down in the love seat, reached inside his suit coat, and pulled out a pack of cigarettes. "Mind if I smoke?"

I sat opposite him in one of the Queen Anne chairs. "Not if you don't exhale."

Malcolm put his cigarettes back in his pocket. He stretched out on the love seat, his long legs closing the distance between us. "I'm sorry I didn't have a chance to attend your Palimo deal last night. I would have enjoyed seeing your after-hours side."

I tucked my feet underneath my chair to avoid playing footsie with him. "You missed a great party."

"It's just as well. I spent the night sucking on cough drops and drinking cold medication."

"That does sound like a good time. Are you're feeling better?"

"I think it was just a twenty-four-hour bug. But you want to know what would complete my recovery?"

"Not really," I said. "How is your uncle feeling?" I added. "I didn't get a chance to talk with him last night. I guess he had a touch of the flu, too."

"He seems to be back on his feet, none worse for the wear."

I nodded and then looked around. Malcolm didn't say anything, and I wasn't sure what to say. "Was there something you wanted to discuss with me?"

Malcolm sprang to his feet and retrieved a briefcase from beside Stanley's desk. He dialed in a series of numbers and unlocked it. "I thought you might be able to take care of these for me."

He handed me a heavy manila envelope. I opened it and pulled out a thick stack of stock certificates.

"This time, I think it's over a million," he said.

I paged through and made mental evaluations as I went. He was probably right.

"Please sell them for me tomorrow," he said, "I'll need an evaluation for May 10th."

I wrinkled my face. I wasn't sure I was still going to be employed by Hamilton tomorrow.

"Is there something wrong, Maggie?"

"I should probably confess something to you."

He leaned forward and smiled. "Yessss . . ."

"Please keep this confidential."

He licked his lips and then pursed them together. "My lips are sealed."

"I'm serious."

He nodded to reassure me, but it didn't.

I let out a deep sigh. "The situation is that I am leaving Hamilton soon and opening my own financial planning firm. But there is a possibility this news may have leaked to my employer already, so I'm not sure if I'm still employed there right now."

He tilted his head and smiled wider. "And if the news hasn't leaked, then I guess it will be up to me to keep our little secret."

I didn't answer.

"Which means I think you need to have dinner with me to buy my silence, or I might accidentally give your boss a call. What did you say his name is?"

"I didn't. And I'm sorry, but I already have a dinner meeting planned for this evening."

"What time's your date?"

"Six."

"Where are you dining?" he said, tapping his fingers together.

"Why, are you planning on stalking me?"

Just then the door opened and Stanley walked in. "Maggie, how nice to see you. Did we have a meeting scheduled?"

"No, I was—"

"She was just dropping in to check on me," Malcolm said.

"Actually, Stanley, if you have a moment, there's something I'd like to discuss with you."

Stanley walked to his desk and reviewed some items on a clipboard.

His intercom beeped.

"Excuse me, Stanley," Grace said. "The new assistant needs some help in cosmetology. He's having a lip drift problem with Mrs. Stambaugh."

"Malcolm, would you mind making yourself useful and helping with Mrs. Stambaugh?"

A frown flickered across Malcolm's face and then disappeared. "I'm on my way, Uncle," he said. He excused himself and left.

Stanley looked up from his clipboard. "Wonders never cease."

I waited for Stanley to elaborate, but instead he walked over to the birdcage and lifted the sheet.

"Hello beautiful," the parrot said, coming to life.

Stanley opened the door and let the parrot crawl on top of the cage.

He turned back to face me. "So what's on your mind?"

"I don't mean to disparage your nephew, but I'm a little concerned about the advances he's taking on your account. He's borrowed about $170,000, and I wanted to make sure you were aware of that."

"Hmmm, that's a lot of money." Stanley continued to study his papers and then looked up at me. "Shall we go see what Malcolm is doing with all that cash?"

I didn't want to do that, but Stanley's statement had been more of a declaration than a question.

We left Socrates on his cage, and I followed Stanley out of the office. We walked down the hallway past the atrium, and then he opened a door to the left of Visitation Room One that I hadn't noticed before. We descended a set of stairs to what I realized was the body preparation area of the funeral home.

"Does death make you squeamish?" Stanley said.

"I guess it depends on if it is mine or someone else's."

Stanley nodded. "Most folks aren't allowed down here, but since Malcolm and Chris are just putting the finishing touches on Mrs. Stambaugh, I think your visit will be okay. Do you have any idea what lip drift is?"

"Not a clue," I said, following him past a sign that

read Preparation Room—Authorized Personnel Only. My curiosity was starting to rise.

Mrs. Stambaugh was laid out in the center of the room on one of the two stainless steel tables. Nearby was a mobile cart, which probably aided in her transportation. At the front of the room were cabinets containing lotions, potions, and a variety of medical instruments. With the tile, stainless steel, and antiseptic smell, the room could have passed for an operating room except for the casket against the back wall, which rested on some kind of hydraulic lift.

"Lip drift is one of our toughest challenges and requires quite a bit of ingenuity," Stanley said. "If the lips are too tight, the person looks anguished. Too far apart, and they look surprised. Our goal is for the deceased's lips to be slightly parted with the upper lip sticking out just a tad for a youthful appearance. But this isn't always easy to accomplish, and the lips drift apart."

Stanley approached Chris and Malcolm, who were huddled over Mrs. Stambaugh. I decided to wait by the door.

"I tried putting a couple of straight pins through the inside of the lower lip and then inserting them between the upper front teeth," Chris said, "but it just doesn't look right."

Malcolm and Stanley nodded. I closed my eyes.

"I think what you're going to have to do is dislocate the bottom jaw and then drill some holes so you can wire the mouth to the correct position," Stanley said. "Maggie, you probably don't want to be around for this."

"I'm not going to argue," I said. My curiosity was more than satisfied.

I was on my way upstairs when the door banged open, and Grace yelled down for Stanley.

"What is it?" he said.

"The media is getting out of control. I need you

now," she said. "And that damn bird is sitting on the casket!"

"We'll talk later," Stanley said to his nephew.

He turned to go upstairs, and I followed close behind him. I didn't want to get stuck in the basement with Malcolm, Chris, and Mrs. Stambaugh's uncooperative lips.

With Stanley's attention diverted to dealing with a zealous reporter photographing the bereaved, I snuck out of the funeral home and walked to my car. The testimonial request and relaxing in the atrium would have to wait for another day.

I climbed in my car, closed my eyes, and saw the big blue eyes of the baby in the photo Stephanie Wolf had handed me right before I so flippantly pledged three million dollars. I rested my head against the steering wheel and rubbed the stress collecting at the back of my neck. How could I tell that woman I had made a monumental mistake? Even with the money I'd made on Palimo and would make when they announced the vaccine trials, I wasn't ready to part with three million dollars.

And what about Palimo? I'd hardly had time to think about Tim's quick action against Richard Craig. I would have liked to think Tim was as obsessive as I'd accused him of, but now I wondered. And then there was that PR blunder that might cost me $300,000 in options. Of course, all of this paled next to my idiotic pledge to donate three million dollars—

A rap on my window caused me to scream. I turned to see Malcolm standing beside my car. I pushed the power window button and opened my window.

"You forgot these." He handed me the envelope of stock certificates I had left in his uncle's office. "Also, I forgot to tell you there's a check in there to repay the $170,000 advance I took against my uncle's account."

I opened the envelope, and there was indeed a check

for $170,000 at the bottom that I hadn't noticed before.

"You look a little stressed," he said. "Are you sure you don't want to blow off your dinner meeting and go out with me instead? You'll have a better time. I could offer you a menu that includes a Salisbury steak entrée with overcooked carrots, and Jell-O for dessert."

I frowned.

"I help serve dinner at one of the missions every Thursday night," he said. "I think it's good for the soul to help those in need. Kind of puts a perspective on your own life."

"Are you serious?"

"I should probably be offended by your shock."

"It's just—"

"It's just what?"

"Nothing." I shook my head. "You're full of surprises."

"I'll take that as a compliment. So, Maggie, if not dinner, why don't you surprise me and meet me for a late-night drink? What time do you think your dinner meeting will be over? Seven-thirty? Eight?"

"Probably, but I've had such a long day. A long week for that matter. How about another time?"

"I'll hold you to it."

He reached down and kissed my hand and then turned and went back into the funeral home.

This guy was too hard to figure out.

It was still a couple of hours before I was scheduled to meet Tim, and I didn't want to go home and stare at the walls. Besides, I was curious as to what he wanted to talk to me about. And what his hunches were about Richard Craig.

And whether the two were related.

Now that I thought about it, Richard Craig had originally been lured over to Palimo by the promise of more money. That kind of argued against Tim's trust-fund theory. I had both my fortune and reputation riding on Richard Craig's expertise. But I trusted Tim's expertise more. What was his hunch? What did he see? Why was he pursuing Richard so hard?

Tim probably wasn't going to share any details of Richard's investigation with me. That would be a violation of taxpayer confidentiality. Tim was more likely planning on interrogating me about Richard.

Perhaps I could do some investigating on my own.

I called Stacy on the phone.

"I need Richard Craig's home address," I said.

"Stephanie Wolf called again," Stacy said.

"Great, I'll call her later."

"Okay, hold on a minute and I'll get Craig's address."

I listened to the Hamilton on-hold music for a minute, and then Stacy returned.

"It's 322 Poinsettia Drive in Ladue."

"Thanks, I'll call you later. Oh, one more thing. I think Craig has his checking account with us. Would you pull his statements for the last six months? I'll call you back in a bit." I hung up.

In minutes, I was on Highway 40 headed to Ladue. My anxiety level rose as I drove. I took the Lindbergh exit and pulled into the first gas station I found. The more I thought about Craig's address, the more concerned I got.

"Do you know where Poinsettia Drive is?" I said.

The dazed attendant said she didn't. She didn't look like she knew what day it was, either.

"Do you sell street guides?"

My heart was starting to race, and I hoped the impatience in my voice might motivate the attendant to get off her fat ass and help me, but instead she simply nodded and pointed at the corner.

Iowa. Kansas. Missouri. There were state maps but no street guides.

"I need a street guide!" I yelled across the store. "Street! Guide! Where the hell are they?"

"Over by the magazines."

I grabbed the Saint Louis guide and returned to the register. It was $8.69, so I threw a ten at the clerk and left without getting change. As soon as I stepped outside I realized I could have saved ten bucks and some agravation by using the Palm Pilot in my car to get directions from the Internet.

I needed to calm down and think clearly.

I was sure returning a street guide was beyond the station attendant's abilities, so with shaking hands I ripped open the guide. According to the index, Poinsettia was on page 23, in the B-17 square. I searched the square once, twice, three times without seeing it. Then I noticed a listing in the middle of the page for streets that were so short there wasn't room to put the street name on them. Poinsettia was one of them. A little more deciphering, and I realized I was only a couple miles from Richard's place.

I screeched my tires as I pulled out of the parking lot. Maybe it was just latent anxiety from everything else, but the stress began to coagulate and choke my nerves. I didn't know how much time I had. Richard said he was meeting with Tim after lunch, and then there was the funeral, but would he come home first?

I turned into Greenbriar Estates, and my heart sank. Mansions dotted the rolling hillside, most set an acre or so back from the tree-lined street and boasting four plus car garages. There wasn't a pink flamingo or a piece of vinyl siding anywhere. This wasn't the neighborhood for Richard's salary.

Whatever Tim suspected, he was right.

A left turn here, a right turn there, and I found myself in front of Richard Craig's humble home, which was larger than my college dormitory. I parked my car next to one of the garages and got out. Craig's driveway and sidewalk had been scraped clean of snow. I walked to the front door and knocked. I wasn't sure what I would do if he answered, but it seemed like the best way to see if anyone was home.

I stared at the double cherry doors and waited. No one. Which made sense. Richard wasn't married and didn't seem to possess the social skills necessary to have a girlfriend. I tried the door. It was locked. I walked back to the driveway and found another sidewalk, which led to a mammoth brick patio in the backyard that overlooked snow-covered woods. I tried the back door. It was also locked.

Now what?

I could get back in my car, drive home, and wait for my dinner with Tim. Maybe enough alcohol would get him talking about Richard, but that was as likely as my tax return surviving an audit.

Or . . . since I was already here, I could take a quick peek inside Richard's home. With the millions of dollars my clients and I had at stake, it was probably my fiduciary responsibility to do a Nancy Drew.

The problem was, Nancy Drew never had to contend with things like electronic security systems. I let out a deep sigh, and my breath made a smoke signal in the cold air.

The security system would be the deciding factor.

If Richard had one, and all the signs posted around the property advertised that he did, I would walk my high heels back to my car and end my crime spree before it started. If he didn't have a security system, then it meant I was supposed to break in.

I peered in the back door's window to see whether or not I was going to jeopardize my securities license. There, on the adjacent wall, was the security panel, but it wasn't turned on. A green light was illuminated below a display that I think read: "Ready to arm."

Was this good news or bad?

I had no idea how to break into a house, and smashing in a window didn't sound like a good option. I needed a professional.

I returned to my car and retrieved my Palm Pilot from my purse. Thank God for Internet access on the road. A few taps later, I had a listing of locksmiths in greater Saint Louis. I used my cell phone to call the closest company.

"Myers Locks."

"Hi, I . . . I feel like such an idiot. I've locked myself out of my house. Do you have a way to get it open?"

"Yes, we can do that."

"What's the cost?"

"Where do you live?"

I gave the woman Craig's address.

"That should probably run about a hundred and twenty dollars," the woman said.

"I guess that's cheaper than breaking a window. How soon can you get here?"

"I can dispatch someone right now, but we're having a busy day. I'm guessing someone would be there within an hour."

"Oh, that would be great. I'll be waiting on my front steps."

I hung up and called Stacy back.

"Hi Stacy, did you get a chance to pull Craig's statements?"

"Yeah, I have them right here."

"What's his average daily balance?" I said.

"Looks like it runs between four and five thousand dollars."

"Hmmmm, any big deposits in the last few months?"

"Nope, only automatic payroll deposits."

"Okay, I've got to go. Thanks again for pulling the statements."

I hung up and reached for my purse. I took out my wallet and car keys and tucked them into my coat pocket. Then I stuffed my purse under the front seat of my car and walked to the front door to begin my vigil.

I watched a car drive past Craig's house and continue down the street. A few more cars came and went but no sign of Richard or my lock guy. About an hour and a half later, I had chewed off the ends of my fingernails and there was still no sign of my locksmith. I decided it was too late to risk standing Tim up again, so I stood up.

Of course, that's when a beat-up pickup finally pulled into Craig's driveway.

I walked around to the garages and watched the guy park next to my car. The magnetic sign on the side of the truck said Myers Locks. A man in his late twenties got out of the truck. He carried a black tackle box.

"Hi, I'm Maggie Connors, idiot extraordinaire. Thanks for coming." I flailed my hands around as I spoke to play the part of a flustered, new homeowner. "We just moved in last weekend, and I can't believe I locked myself out. I tried calling my husband, but he's in a meeting, and we haven't given a key to a neighbor yet."

"Don't worry ma'am. People lock themselves out of the house all the time."

He walked to the back door, and I followed behind him like an excited puppy. "That makes me feel a little bit better. Does this take very long to do?"

"Nope, I'll have you back inside in a snap."

He used a combination of small picks—the kind a dentist might scrape your teeth with—and had the lock opened in a few minutes.

"Wow, that was great. I'll go get my wallet."

The lock picker didn't follow me and instead returned to load his tackle box into the back of his truck. I stood in Craig's kitchen for a few minutes and then pulled my wallet out of my pocket before going back outside.

"What do I owe you?"

"A hundred and twenty."

I handed him six twenties.

"I need to get some information from you for our records." He reached into his truck and retrieved a clipboard. "Can I see your driver's license, please?"

I handed him my license.

"This has a different address on it," he said.

"Yeah, like I said, we just moved in over the weekend. I haven't had a chance to get my license changed."

He nodded and kept filling in information on the form.

"Okay, I need you to sign at the bottom of this form, which basically states that you are the rightful homeowner of this property."

Since I was going to be breaking and entering—or at least entering, since I now didn't have to break anything—lying on a security form didn't seem like such a big deal. I scrawled my name where he indicated, and he gave me a copy of the form for my records.

When the lock man left, I retrieved my purse from my car and stuffed the receipt in my purse to be filed later in the circular file. I wouldn't be writing off this expense on my taxes.

It was almost five-thirty when I walked back into Craig's kitchen. And what a kitchen it was. The floor was a deep, mahogany red, the cabinets were white with brass knobs, and the countertops were green granite. All the appliances were stainless steel. It was a beautiful combination, and I was surprised a scientist like Craig would make such great choices.

I stopped admiring the kitchen and did a quick walkthrough of the house. Off the living room were French doors that led to a small office area. I dropped my purse to the floor and decided to get started. While I waited for the computer to boot up, I searched the desk drawers. I was hoping to find something that would explain Craig's wealth. Something innocent. Something that would tell me not to sell every share of Palimo my clients and I owned. He certainly couldn't afford a shack like this on his income, or the yacht in the Mediterranean, for that matter. We'd talked about his financial situation enough times that if the source of these funds were legitimate, he would have mentioned them by now.

I opened a filing cabinet and fingered my way through the file folder names.

"Are you finding what you're looking for?"

I turned and saw Richard Craig standing in the doorway.

Chapter 6

"**R**ichard!" I slammed the filing drawer closed, as if that made a difference. "I didn't hear you come in."

"I'm not in a habit of knocking before entering my own house. But that's something you might try."

He looked like a lab rat after the kind of science experiment animal rights activists protest. He had dark circles under both of his eyes and one eyelid kept twitching.

"I was just—"

"Searching my office?"

I stood there speechless. What does one say in this situation? What the hell was I even doing in this situation?

"Why don't you have a seat right here," he said, and angled one of the office chairs at me.

"Richard, I'm sorry, this was a bad idea. I should have waited until you came home."

"Did you and your overzealous boyfriend plan it this

way? Was he supposed to keep me busy with his interview while you broke into my house?"

I raised my hands to a surrender position. "No, Tim doesn't know a thing about this," I said, for some reason feeling that protecting Tim's reputation was important.

"Who does know?"

"No one. I promise."

As soon as the words left my mouth, I knew I had made a mistake.

"Why don't you have a seat," he said again, his voice an ominous sweetness.

"Richard, you're obviously upset. I'll come back another time—"

He pulled a gun from his overcoat pocket. "Sit your skinny ass down in this chair. I'm not going to say it again."

I did as told.

"Did you find my stash of toys yet?"

I tried to keep my legs from shaking. "I don't know what you're talking about."

He kept the gun pointed at me and walked over to the filing cabinet. "Most people keep this stuff in the bedroom, but I like to keep a few items in here—for special occasions when I'm really feeling naughty."

I didn't know what that meant and wasn't going to ask.

He opened the bottom drawer of the cabinet. From where I sat, I could see all sorts of kinky sex props. I heard the sound of a metal clang, and Richard pulled a set of handcuffs from the bottom of the pile.

"Put these on," he said and threw them over to me. "Just your left hand."

The cuffs landed at my feet, the noise reverberating off the hardwood floor. I picked them up and placed the cuff over my left hand. They were heavier than I imagined.

"Now, both hands behind the chair."

I put my hands back, and the empty cuff clanked against a chair leg.

He walked behind me and grabbed my left hand, twisting it into a painful U. He pulled my right hand over, and I felt the cuff click around my wrist. When he let go, I realized he had threaded the cuffs through the metal backing of the chair before cuffing my other hand so that I was cuffed to the chair.

"Don't move," he said and walked out of the office.

I wasn't sure where he thought I could go, but I sat motionless. I heard more clanging, and he returned carrying a pair of cuffs that probably had three feet of chain between the cuffs.

"I use these for special occasions, but I think they'll do the trick for your situation."

He snapped one cuff hard over my left ankle. Then he pulled my chair over so I was next to the door. He snapped the remaining cuff around the doorknob.

"That's to keep you from doing a Lucille Ball and walking around with the chair on your back while you're cuffed."

I hadn't even thought about that. It would have been a good way to escape.

"Would you like to see what you were looking for?" he said.

I didn't move, and I didn't answer.

He lifted a briefcase that was sitting in the doorway. He must have brought it home with him, because it wasn't there when I came in. He set the case down on his desk, flipped open the locks, removed a file and a video from inside, and then pulled a chair up beside me and sat down.

He opened the file. On the top was a copy of a check made payable to Richard from David Chambers, the CEO of Palimo. The amount was for $100,000. The date was two years ago.

"It started off with this first check from David. He wanted to make sure our preliminary research results looked favorable so we could raise more seed money."

Damn, damn, damn. It was as bad as it could be.

Richard turned the page and revealed another photocopy of a check for $250,000 from David.

"This check was for doing such a good job with some angels who provided the seed money. By this time, I was more involved with faking research results than actually managing field studies. It was complicated, too. I had to transfer people between headquarters and Saint Louis so they never saw the big picture of what was going on. There were late nights where I had to go in and even alter test results. It was very complicated."

There would be no press release. There was no vaccine. It had all been faked.

He turned the page again, and I saw a copy of a $500,000 check.

"This is when things started getting more interesting. I decided that sucking money from David was more profitable than being a scientist, so I started blackmailing him. I'd say in the last few months, that fool has probably paid me close to two million dollars."

His voice seemed calmer, almost as if the confession had relieved him of the stress he had been carrying around. The calmer Richard became, the more upset I got.

"So the upcoming test results for the AIDS vaccine—"

"Made up. Every bit of it."

I hung my head. My clients and I had almost seven million dollars riding on a stock that had less value than toilet paper.

"How could you do this?" I said. "Do you know how many people are counting on this vaccine? Do you know how many lives this is going to affect?"

He shrugged. "There will be more lives affected before I'm done," he said.

"Why are you telling me all of this?"

"You'll find out soon enough."

Then I realized it wasn't as bad as it could get. It could be worse. He could kill me.

He walked to his desk and picked up the phone. "May I have the number for the CNN headquarters in Atlanta?" He scribbled a number down on a piece of paper and hung up. "Don't go anywhere. I'll be right back."

He packed his file and video into his briefcase, picked up his cell phone, and left the office. The house was so big that I couldn't hear a back door open or a garage door go up, but I assumed he was no longer in the house.

Now what?

I couldn't scoot to the desk to use the phone. Even if it were summertime and the windows were open, no one would hear my screams for help given the distance between the houses.

I pulled against the chair. No luck. This wasn't some office-supply-store chair. It felt solid and expensive.

Maybe this was God's way of telling me I should make that three-million-dollar donation to the Children's Hospice. On second thought, it was probably God's way of telling me to not break into houses anymore.

I needed to call Stacy and have her sell everyone's Palimo stock. I didn't care if my sell order was based on inside information. The SEC could jail me, but my clients would be safe. Richard's phone sat on his desk mocking me. There was no way I could reach it from where I sat, and I had left my cell phone in my purse, which was behind the desk. An overwhelming sense of doom descended upon me. The chair I was chained to might as well have been sitting on a train track.

Crying didn't help, but I cried anyhow.

Without anything to distract me, I spent the next hour sniffling and imagining the varying degrees of financial ruin my clients were about to suffer. My guilt increased with each client I thought about. Mr. Sherman had planned on selling Palimo next week to pay for his retirement home. The Kings needed their Palimo proceeds to pay for exploratory medical treatment their insurance wasn't covering. Gale Harris was going to take her Palimo profits and move to Florida once she recovered from her fall on the ice. This wasn't going to be a small blip in my clients' portfolios. It would devastate them and change the way they lived.

Tim had to have figured this out.

Why the hell hadn't he warned me? I would kill him if I ever got the chance.

"I'm baaaack." Richard came into the office. He still had his gun pointed at me, which seemed redundant. He flopped down in the chair behind the desk and put his feet up.

"Richard, I've been thinking. Perhaps I can help get Tim to call off his investigation. It's only been a day. He can't have gotten that deep into anything. Besides, I've got some money put away, and maybe if I make a donation to Tim's bank account he might look the other way." I knew from experience that Tim was more likely to push his grandmother under the wheels of a bus, but Richard didn't.

"Nice try, but I asked around. Tim Gallen has a reputation for not breaking the rules. Actually, what I've heard is that he won't even bend the rules."

Okay, he did know. "So what are you planning on doing with me?"

He smiled, which made the bags under his eyes look worse. "I'm going to destroy your life, since you destroyed mine."

"What did I do to destroy your life?"

"You brought Tim Gallen to the Palimo Party."

"That's it? You're holding me responsible for Tim's investigation?"

"Well, life's a bitch and then you die."

"Richard, killing me is only going to make things

worse for you." I tried to sound calm, but fear was gripping my vocal cords as badly as the cuffs were cutting into my wrists.

"Kill you? Don't be ridiculous. I'm a scientist, not a murderer. Besides, like I said, I want to ruin your life, and death would be too quick for you, my good buddy David, and all those greedy stockholders."

"Then what are you—"

He popped up to his feet and opened the double cabinet doors that were behind his desk and to the right. Inside was a small television. He turned it on and tuned it to *CNN Headline News*.

"Tomorrow morning there's going to be a story you won't want to miss." He took off his coat and sat back down in his chair. "I think I've timed everything pretty well. I'll empty all my brokerage accounts first thing in the morning, then I'm off to points unknown." He glared at me. "I'd hoped to cash the equity on the house, but your boyfriend moves too fast for that."

Tomorrow morning? "W-w-what about me?"

"Oh, don't worry. Your boyfriend will be here tomorrow, right around the time the market closes. He wanted to meet me here to do our second interview. I'll leave the back door unlocked and slightly ajar so he can rescue you when he gets here, but it's going to be just a little too late."

"What do you mean, 'too late'?"

"You'll see. I don't want to spoil the surprise."

He tapped his fingertips together and smiled. This was a side of Richard I had never seen before and never would have guessed even existed.

"Where will you be when Tim gets here?" I said.

"Somewhere anonymous and comfortable. Well beyond reach." He picked up the briefcase and tugged again at my chains. "Be seeing you." And he was out the door.

I glanced at the clock. On top of everything else, I was standing Tim up again.

Chapter 7

The musical jingle of *CNN Headline News* may be imprinted on my brain for the rest of my life. I quickly learned that CNN made most of their money by repeating the same mindless stories way too often. It was like listening to a broken record. But presently I found I had to really concentrate on the stories in order to ignore my fully expanded bladder.

The music finished again, and a CNN newsman began a report on new methods of manufacturing golf balls that were helping golfers improve their scores. I focused closely, trying to anticipate the next word. The next report was on bioengineered food, which wasn't captivating enough to keep my mind off of peeing. I started jiggling my one unshackled leg and tried to figure out what the protocol was for using the bathroom while handcuffed.

What do prisoners do in solitary confinement? They never show you in the movies. When the guy from *The Shawshank Redemption* goes into solitary, he doesn't get toilet paper or a bathroom. When he comes out a month or so later, he's grown a beard, but he's not covered in shit.

This situation sucked.

I tried lifting my butt off the chair seat. If I twisted, I could get my right hip up in the air, but that only gave me about three inches of clearance. I thought about tipping over the chair. That way maybe I could scrunch my suit skirt up and lie on my side and pee, which would offer some damage control. But I wasn't sure how it would yank my chained leg.

Finally, I took a deep breath and did something I hadn't done since I was two.

For a moment, there was an utter sense of relief followed by a warm, comfy feeling. That quickly faded once my wet clothes and seat turned cold. The only upside was that the front of my skirt wasn't wet. My panty hose seemed to contain it just to the posterior area, so it wouldn't be the first thing Tim would notice when he got here.

It was a very long night. I was hungry and thirsty and my underwear was cold and soggy. My arms were stiff from being restrained behind my back, I was tired of sitting, and the CNN music was driving me to despair. And utter disaster was yet to come.

Sometime around midnight, I must have fallen asleep. On the morning of Christmas Eve, the phone rang, and I woke from a dream of drowning. Tim was throwing me a life preserver, but it turned out to be a Palimo stock certificate, and it sank. Meanwhile, Malcolm and Richard sat in a rowboat next to me talking about how to deal with lip drift.

By the time the ringing phone stopped, I remembered where I was and why.

Shit.

I tried to stretch the kinks out of my muscles with little luck. Ten minutes later, the phone rang again, and then rang every ten minutes or so after that.

Who was trying so hard to get ahold of Richard? Probably that bastard David.

Over the noise of the phone, I discovered CNN was finally running a few new stories. A congressman had been caught with an underage girl, and that soaked up a lot of airtime.

My stomach growled, and I wondered when Tim would be arriving. According to the clock on the credenza, it was seven o'clock. I was in for hours of discomfort, alone except for the horror that was about to happen and CNN's music. As it turned out, I didn't have to wait long. A little before nine, Ketchum caught a break, and the news anchor announced CNN had a new, breaking story.

"We have an exclusive financial report concerning Palimo Technologies that you won't want to miss, coming up, right after this break."

This must be the story Richard had mentioned last night. But how did he know? Unless he arranged it himself. If he sent an overnight package with some of the incriminating evidence from his file, then the stock was about to tank. That might explain the ringing telephone, but why wasn't a reporter, or better yet, the police, knocking on his open back door?

I held my breath and waited for the end of a cruise line commercial.

"And now let's go to Bill McCollum for a CNN exclusive report on Palimo Technologies."

I stared at the small television screen.

"Thank you, David. I am standing here in front of Richard Craig's Jefferson City home. Craig is Palimo Technologies' vice president of research and development. This leading scientist is reported to have fled the country early this morning."

So that's why there weren't any reporters knocking on the door. This was his second home. Richard must have wanted me to sit here and suffer while I watched

Palimo's stock price wipe out my portfolio and those of my clients.

I tuned back into the report.

"Palimo Technologies was on the verge of developing one of the most sought-after medical breakthroughs in the world: a vaccine against the deadly AIDS virus. The AIDS epidemic started in the early eighties but gradually lost media limelight as creative chemical cocktails developed by the pharmaceutical companies removed patients from immanent death sentences and gave them additional years of life. But the AIDS epidemic gained media attention again when it was discovered that some third world countries now have more than a third of their population infected and no money or resources to treat the disease.

"According to inside information provided from Richard Craig, the lure of a vaccine's profitability became too much for the company." The reporter paused for dramatic effect. "Richard Craig tells us that Palimo Technologies has been falsifying research results to keep stockholders happy and raise research funding. I'm afraid Palimo stockholders won't be having a very merry Christmas this year."

My heart was pounding again.

Across the bottom of the screen, CNN ran a ticker tape of stock trading prices. There was Palimo at 74, then at 68, then 65½.

I tuned into the reporter again.

"Richard Craig has provided CNN with a five-page detailed account of how the company was able to falsify information without getting caught, even fooling many of the world's most renowned scientists."

A picture of David replaced the Palimo logo on the screen.

"We also have this exclusive footage. . . ."

A home video played showing David Chambers handing a check to Richard.

"Keep making Palimo research look good, and there

will be more where this came from," David said on the tape. "A happy stockholder is a stupid stockholder."

I closed my eyes. It was gone. My portfolio, my clients' portfolios.

"Palimo's president, David Chambers, who was shown on the tape allegedly paying off Richard Craig, could not be reached for comment. Additionally, officials who have been investigating the recent traffic accident of a Palimo scientist are now looking at the possibility that it was suicide. An official with the Manchester Police Department said Edward Kettner was killed Wednesday when he pulled his Volvo station wagon into the path of an oncoming tractor trailer. Kettner was pronounced dead at the scene. Kettner had been employed by Palimo for ten years and was under Richard Craig's direct supervision."

Next the newsroom anchor returned and explained that the New York Stock Exchange had temporarily suspended trading of Palimo Technologies pending comment from the company. In the seven-minute time period before trading was halted, the stock had fallen over 10 percent with triple the normal trading volume. Halting the trading of Palimo also protected uninformed buyers from buying during the sell-off frenzy.

My guess was it would take a few hours to find someone at Palimo to fess up to the mess. Since it was Christmas Eve, the market would close at noon, so Palimo might not open for trading until Monday morning. Whenever trading started again, it would be a bloodbath.

Shit!

For the next two hours, the Palimo story and the video played over and over.

I would have traded my firstborn for a telephone. I couldn't imagine the barrage of phone calls my assistant Stacy must be fielding from irate clients. I hoped they all planned on liquidating when the stock reopened.

My portfolio was being wiped out. My clients' portfolios were being wiped out. By now my boss had probably heard about the press release announcing the opening of my new office, but I no longer had a client base to transfer to a new office, and chances are that I wasn't going to have my old job, either. Then there was the sixteen-thousand-dollar party charges Palimo probably wasn't going to reimburse. And let's not forget about the three million dollars I owed the Children's Hospice and the matching six million dollars they were going to lose if I didn't pay up. Was I leaving anything out? Oh yeah, I was tired, sore, and soggy from sitting handcuffed in this chair, and tonight was Christmas Eve. And the only man I wanted to be under the mistletoe with apparently loved enforcing mindless IRS regulations more than he loved me, or he would have warned me about his Palimo suspicions.

Damn!

I concentrated on lowering my soaring blood pressure by perfecting the scathing speech I would deliver to Tim when he arrived.

At eleven-fifteen, CNN announced Palimo Technologies was holding a press conference at eleven-thirty. The minutes dragged by, and at eleven-thirty, the cameras switched to Palimo headquarters. I recognized the room from earlier press briefings. A Palimo Tech banner hung in the background behind a podium, and the room was packed with reporters and camera crews. The CNN reporter filled time by babbling about Palimo's history while everyone waited for a sacrificial Palimo representative to emerge from the inner sanctum of the corporate headquarters and face the hungry press.

At twenty-five before noon, a man I didn't recognize walked with his head down to the Palimo podium. His shirtsleeves were rolled up, and he looked like he had just been flattened by a tank. He adjusted his glasses, took a deep breath, and then looked up at the mob of reporters.

"My name is Robert Page. I am the chief financial officer for Palimo Technologies. Due to recent news reports this morning, Palimo Technologies will be working with authorities and the NYSE to investigate our research findings. We expect the findings to result in adjusted earnings, which we will release within the next few weeks—"

The room exploded with questions from the reporters.

I zoned in on the ticker tape running across the bottom of the screen. That's all the NYSE needed to hear. They would reopen trading, but where would the price be?

The market was up slightly for the day, and various stock symbols moved across the screen showing upticks of an eighth of a point or more.

And then I spotted the Palimo symbol.

It reopened at $13½ per share.

I heard someone in the house. The market would close in ten minutes. Maybe there was still time to salvage something.

"I'm in here! In here!"

I cranked my head around as far as I could and saw Tim and his partner coming down the hall. They both stopped in the doorway to absorb the scene.

"Get me a telephone!" I said.

"Maggie, what happened?" Tim said. "Are you all right?"

"I need a phone! Now!"

"You stood me up."

I started screaming loud and long, letting my vocal cords vent some of my financial anguish. My shrieking filled the small room and echoed off the wood floor. I launched into an audio meltdown that any tantrum-throwing two-year-old would have been proud of. I didn't stop until Tim took his cell phone out of his pocket, dialed my office, and then held the phone up to my ear.

When Stacy answered, I told her in a hoarse voice to sell all of my Palimo stock.

"Where the hell are you?" Stacy said.

"I'll explain later, just dump Palimo."

"But it's at eleven and three-eighths."

"I know where it's at. Sell it before it gets worse. Tell anyone who calls to do the same."

"The phones have been ringing off the hook here."

"Look Stacy, I've literally been handcuffed to a chair in Richard Craig's home since last night. If I could be at the office to deal with clients, I would be."

Tim shifted, and I couldn't hear what Stacy said.

"Tim, hold the phone closer!"

"Is Tim Gallen there? Did you say handcuffed?" Stacy said.

"Not now. Dump all the Palimo you can, and I'll be there as soon as possible."

"You might want to take your time, Mike said he wanted to see you when you got in."

In the background, I heard Tim's partner use his cell phone to call 911.

"Sell Palimo, and I will deal with Mike when I get there."

I said good-bye to Stacy, and Tim disconnected the call.

"Now, do you want to tell me what happened here?" Tim said.

My swollen hands trembled because I was so pissed off. "I've got nothing to say to you." So much for my scathing speech.

"Maggie . . . are you saying you want to speak with an attorney first?"

"No. I don't need an attorney. I need to get out of these handcuffs. I think the key is in the bottom of that filing cabinet."

"Who is she?" Tim's partner said.

"Forgive me. Dwight Buckley, this is Maggie Connors. Maggie, this is Dwight."

"I'm sorry I can't shake your hand," I said. "Now, will someone please get me out of these handcuffs?"

"Is she the same chick from the Cummings case?" Dwight said.

"One and the same," Tim replied.

"Excuse me, but please quit talking like I'm not here." My hostility was rising higher than I thought possible.

"So how exactly did you get here, and what happened to Richard Craig?"

"You happened to Richard Craig." I talked slowly, trying to keep my hostility from jumbling my words. "You have become a mindless government bureaucrat with a deep-seated arrogance that makes you a threat to society. Your IRS regulations have metastasized in your brain and eradicated any empathy you used to have for your fellow citizen. You arbitrarily use the power of the IRS to ruin people's lives, and your head is stuck so far up your ass that you don't have a clue about the destruction you so flippantly engineer. It is beyond me how anyone can be so evil and act so puritan at the same time. You caused my clients and myself to lose millions of dollars, and my guess is you don't give a shit."

Not a bad monologue, but it would have been better if I could have ended it by slapping him in the face and storming out of the room.

Instead, Dwight quietly left the room.

"You're holding me responsible for all of this?" he said. "What did I do?"

"Get me out of these cuffs."

"First tell me what I did."

Suddenly, it was all too much. My anxiety, anger and grief all collided, and I began to cry. "Tim, why couldn't you tell me about Richard?"

He was rooting around in the drawer for the keys to the handcuffs and stopped. "What about Richard?"

"That you suspected him of taking payoffs to fake his data."

"What! Is that was this is about?"

I blinked tears out of my eyes and stared at him. "You didn't know?"

He came over to me and wiped my eyes with his handkerchief, then bent over the handcuffs. "My hunch was industrial espionage, getting paid for passing results to competitors. It's a much smarter crime than data fraud. You don't have to flee afterward. I thought Richard was smart."

There was a click, and for the first time in almost twenty-four hours, I stood and stretched my sore limbs. My wrists were raw from the cuffs, and my hands were swollen. I desperately wanted a hot shower.

"Not very." I was suddenly conscious of my wet skirt. "Why'd you pursue him so hard?"

"He had a yacht in the Mediterranean. He had worked in England. That meant money, a valid passport, and contacts abroad. The textbook definition of a flight risk."

"Well, he has flown. At least you cost him the equity in his house."

"I may have cost him more than that. Can you call Stacy and check his account?"

I used Tim's phone and dialed my office. I expected to hear her tell me Richard's account was cashed out, except for his remaining Palimo stock, but she said his balance was $185,000. I thanked her, hung up, and shared the news with Tim.

"Good," Tim said, "it went through."

"What went through?"

"The freeze order against his account that I arranged for yesterday. I did the same for the four million dollars he had at BHN Financial Group. Did I mention he was a flight risk?"

It took a moment for the meaning of his words to sink in. And then, despite the near sleepless night, the loss of millions of dollars, and the beginnings of diaper rash, I began to laugh. After all the pain Richard had caused, at least he wasn't getting away with the money—money he had another broker investing for him.

Dwight poked his head in the door. "I got ahold of INS and the FBI. They've got a watch at all the border crossings."

"So he's not getting out of the country?" I said.

"Not if we can help it," Tim said. "We'll get him, Maggie."

The police arrived with an ambulance crew. I was checked out, fed, watered, and allowed to clean up a little. Then I spent the next several hours explaining to several different people what happened. I left out the part of my odyssey that involved breaking into Richard's house and instead explained that Richard and I had a meeting scheduled here.

By four o'clock, I had finished answering every question in triplicate and backed my wet ass out of Richard's house. Outside, the snow was falling in big, fluffy flakes. It was the kind of snow that wasn't serious about accumulating; it just wanted to twinkle down from the sky. This was the perfect time to be at home, celebrating Christmas Eve with loved ones, bundled up in front of a fire. Instead, I had a bad stain on the back of my suit skirt and was on my way to my office.

The Hamilton parking garage was vacant when I arrived. I parked my Corolla near the entrance and reached over to the passenger's seat to get my purse. Naturally, it wasn't there. I had left it at Richard Craig's house. I needed to get a security cord and surgically attach that thing to my body.

I stomped to the entrance of Hamilton Securities. The market had closed at noon, the office had closed at three. I unlocked the door, stepped inside, and then locked the door behind me. I flipped on the lights and trudged to my office. Along the way I noticed the Christmas decorations many of the secretaries had added to their desks. I quickened my pace to avoid a full-blown self-pity party.

When I got to my office, I found a chaotic mound of sell order confirmations mixed in with phone message pink slips. I glanced through them, scanning for the bottom line: 17¾, 14⅛, 9½. My voice mail light was blinking, and when I dialed into the system, I was told that I had forty-eight messages. I picked up a pen to take notes. The first message simply said: "Thanks for ruining my Christmas. I hope you burn in hell." At first I thought it was Psycho Phil's voice—I now remembered his entire portfolio was invested in Palimo—but then I realized it wasn't him. It was Father Kohler from Sisters of Hope. I was in for a long night.

I waded through the rest of the messages. Some were more informational, some were desperate, some were downright obscene. None of my callers seemed to have the Christmas spirit except, of course, for my parents, who called to wish me an early merry Christmas. They didn't have any idea their account was $45,000 lighter than it had been yesterday.

I noticed I didn't have a message from Psycho Phil. Perhaps he was already comfortably drunk for the holidays.

I turned on my computer and opened up my account management software. With a few clicks, I was able to get a listing of the eighty-three clients invested in Palimo. My clients had bought the stock from $17 to as high as $73 a share. Palimo's closing price was $8½. A few more clicks, and the computer gave me a summary of total Palimo losses. Combined, my clients had lost $5.2 million. I had lost $1.9 million.

I sat there and stared at the computer monitor.

From the moment I realized what Richard was up to, I had blamed him and hated him. Now that I had a moment to myself, I realized that I had my share of blame as well. I had overbought Palimo. I had hung onto it against my boss's advice. I had dreamed of the windfall when the trial was announced. Tim was right. I had gotten greedy. The painful cost of that greed flickered on my screen.

Maybe I wouldn't have so flippantly invested millions of my own money if it had been my own money and not some ludicrous IRS windfall. But the devastation over losing this much was the same as if I had slaved to earn every penny.

And my losses weren't over.

I spent the night going through the client list, account by account, to see what damage had been done. I made a list of those clients whose investment in Palimo had caused a loss of 20 percent or more of their portfolio; they were too heavily weighted in Palimo, and that was my responsibility. I also included any clients sixty years or older; they shouldn't have been in such a risky investment, and that was also my fault. And then I added another handful of clients who didn't fit either of the first two criteria but whose situation made their investment in Palimo imprudent.

My list totaled nineteen clients who had suffered combined losses of $2.1 million.

Never before in my life had I tried so hard and failed so miserably.

I opened up my word processing software and typed in a form letter addressed to my manager from a generic client. Thanks to the genius of Bill Gates, with another click of the button I sent nineteen form letters to my printer, now customized from each of the clients on my list.

While I waited for the letters to print, I leaned back in my chair and stared at my office mess.

The cleaning crew had already been and gone, but I still had a thin layer of dust on my credenza, except for the spot where my bronze piggy bank had been. A few days ago, my two girlfriends, pissed because I wouldn't take time off to join them for a ski vacation over Christmas, had barged in and kidnapped—or rather pignapped—my piggy bank. As I listened to the printer hum, I wondered what poor ski instructors my girlfriends were taking advantage of right this moment.

The bank was a gift from Cleon Cummings, my client who had the IRS problems that led to my seven-million-dollar reward. The bank had arrived a few weeks after I last saw Cleon with a note not to waste all my time chasing pennies. Back then, I had resolved to stop working so hard and enjoy life more, but one thing after another came up, and I found my resolution and my piggy bank collecting dust.

The printer motor quieted, and I realized the letters were finished.

It was past midnight and time for me to stick a fork in this day. I needed some sleep before I tackled the weekend, which would be filled with back-to-back client meetings. I shut down my computer and walked to the entrance. I turned off the main lights and stood at the front door in semidarkness. Light from the streetlamps shone in the windows and caused an occasional reflection off someone's tinsel-covered Christmas tree. I felt like someone had tricked me into stealing Cindy-Lou Who's Christmas feast. Once again I summoned my favorite Scarlett O'Hara mantra and decided I would think about it tomorrow.

I let myself out of the office and trudged through the snow to the parking garage. I made it to my car and locked myself inside. I looked at my watch. It was Christmas.

God, I just wanted to go to a Marriott and soak in a Jacuzzi. Instead I began the drive back to my condo.

Fifteen minutes later, I pulled into my driveway and remembered that I needed batteries for my garage door opener; it had been working sporadically for weeks now. I said a small prayer, promising abstinence—not a big sacrifice—if God would allow my garage door opener to work one more time. I pushed. I pleaded. I banged. I swore. I slammed. But of course the opener didn't open.

I let out a deep sigh and sat there listening to the ticking of the engine. I could either spend the night in my car or trek to my front door via the three feet of snow on my sidewalk. I had been wearing this same pair of underwear for almost two days and since it wasn't the wet and wear kind, it was time to seek fresh undies. Besides, the temperature in the car was descending its way to match the chill outside, so I left the comfort of my Corolla and tunneled to my front door.

When I got to the front door I was cold, wet, and miserable. I unlocked the front door and flipped on the living room light.

My mind couldn't make sense of the destruction I saw.

The door slammed behind me. "Ho! Ho! Ho!"

I turned and saw Psycho Phil standing behind me in a Santa Claus costume, minus the white wig and beard.

Chapter 8

Adrenaline is a terrific pickup, better than caffeine. From a standing start, I sprinted toward the kitchen, hoping to escape out the back door. But I never made it out of the living room.

Phil grabbed me by my hair and yanked me backward. He flipped me around and stuck his face in mine. Here was the missing link in human development. This Neanderthal could easily snap me in two.

"Where do you think you're going, my little Christmas elf?"

His voice was thick with an alcohol-induced slur. He had been drinking so much the smell of stale beer oozed out of his pores. I turned my head away to avoid the stench and the hatred in his eyes that was too terrifying to look at.

"Look at me when I'm talking to you!"

His hairy left hand backhanded me across the face. I fell on the carpet and rolled away, curled up in more pain than I had ever experienced in my life. My left eye was starting to swell shut. I coughed and gasped for breath. I could hear Phil laughing somewhere close by.

"Come on, get up. We're just getting started."

I stayed in a fetal position and didn't move.

He let out a long, low whistle. "With the money you have, you should get yourself a maid service. This place is a mess." I heard the sound of him smashing a lamp against the wall. "I guess one of the benefits of being so rich is you probably just sell your condo and move, rather than cleaning it. Am I right, little rich girl?"

Would that I could. But maybe a better investment would be a patrol with guard dogs and a security system, which I would keep activated.

"I wish I could buy shit when I wanted to, but no, everyone tries to screw poor Phil. Right now I should be sitting on a boatload of money. But no one ever does what they say they're going to, and its people like me that get shit on when that happens. But not anymore. Things are going to change, and I'm starting with you."

Evidently, having an opposable thumb was no longer enough for Phil.

He poked at me with his boot.

"Not talking? That's all right. We've got all night." He paused. "You know, before we get started, how 'bout we take a look in your refrigerator? I've been waiting all night for you to get home, and I'm hungry. Let's go see what's on the menu for your big, Christmas meal."

He grabbed my hair at the back of my neck and dragged me into the kitchen. He dropped me by a cabinet, then stuck his face into my refrigerator.

"You don't have shit in here!"

He started tossing things over his shoulder. A jar of pickles shattered on the floor. A plastic bottle of ketchup followed.

With my teeth gritted, I eased open the cabinet next to me and then pulled myself upright.

"The least you could do is keep some beer in here for unexpected company," he said.

He shut the refrigerator and turned back around. I clocked him in the side of the head with one cooking implement that had survived my cooking abilities: a cast-iron frying pan.

He fell to the floor, his bulk blocking any escape out the back door.

I stood panting for a moment. I decided not to stick around for a tearful good-bye and bolted for the front door. As I opened the door, I could hear Phil yelling from the kitchen, which obliterated any concern about improper shoe apparel for escaping through the wet snow.

I made it to my car without doing the prerequisite, horror movie, damsel-in-distress wipeout. My car keys were still in my coat pocket, and I managed to unlock the car, get inside, and hit the power door locks again. I was afraid to see if Phil was coming. I started the car, put it in reverse, and hit the gas.

I must have gone maybe ten feet when something slammed into the back corner of my car. The last thing I remember was hitting my head against the driver's window.

Chapter 9

Saturday, December 25

There was a faint beeping noise coming from somewhere behind me, but I couldn't convince my eyes to open and see what was causing it. I waited a few minutes to see if it would stop and it didn't. I reached for the snooze alarm.

There was an excruciating pain, and I made a note not to try that again.

"Maggie. Maggie, wake up. Can you hear me?"

It was a man's voice I had heard before.

Phil!

I opened my eyes and bolted up.

A burning pain shot through my side and I grabbed the bed rails for support. The man sitting beside me was Tim, not Phil.

Bed rails?

I looked around and realized I was in a hospital bed. On my left, the curtains were open, revealing a little too much light for my eyes. I looked to the right and saw that a curtain had been pulled halfway to separate my side of the room from my roommate's, but I didn't hear anyone over there. The rest of the room was a dingy, antiseptic green.

None of this made sense.

"What happened?"

"Merry Christmas, and welcome back." Tim bent down and gave me one of his popular forehead kisses.

I noticed he had a bandage on his cheek. "What happened to you?"

"I was in a car accident."

"Who'd you hit?"

"You. I was about to pull into your driveway last night when you came speeding out. I hit the back corner of your car and you got pretty banged up in the collision. You weren't wearing a seat belt."

My thoughts were slow and hard to organize. "You didn't do this. Psycho Phil did."

"Maggie, we had a pretty good collision. You really stomped on the gas."

"Didn't the air bag go off?"

Tim shook his head. "That's only for front collisions. I'm really sorry about what happened."

"No, you don't understand. You didn't do this. Phil—Phil Scranton, he's a client—attacked me in my condo last night and trashed the place."

"You think a client attacked you?"

"I don't think, I know. Psycho Phil owned a lot of Palimo . . . well, a lot for him. He was waiting for me inside the door when I got home. He was dressed like Santa Claus. I hit him in the head with a frying pan and he fell on my kitchen floor. That's when I ran out the front door and got in my car."

"Why the hell didn't one of your neighbors call the police? As I recall, the walls in your condo are pretty thin. Remember that guy's stereo that blared all night?"

"That guy now works the graveyard shift at Chrysler, and the retired couple who live on the other side spend December and January in Florida."

Tim pulled out his cell phone and made a call while I surveyed the damage to my body. My face felt swollen, and I got a stabbing pain when I lifted my left arm. But other than that—and the fact I had cost myself and my clients millions, lost my job, had a crazy man stalking me, owed a three-million-dollar pledge, and was being cared for by an ex-boyfriend who was taking someone else out on New Year's while I babysat his sister's kids—I was fine.

Tim finished his call.

"Who was that?" I said.

"The police. They want to meet you at your condo." Tim sat down next to me on the bed. "I'm sorry, it never occurred to me to check your condo. Things were so frantic—I couldn't tell how badly you were hurt—and it seemed like it took forever for the ambulance to get there."

I flopped back against my pillow, causing a small jolt of pain. I wanted to cry, but it wasn't worth making my eyes swell more. "What were you doing pulling into my driveway?"

"Returning your purse you left at Richard Craig's. By the way, an officer searched your purse. He . . . uh, found the Myers Locks receipt showing you had broken into Richard's, which you neglected to mention to anyone."

"Shit."

"It was pretty obvious from the crime scene that you were on the receiving end of all the aggravation, and Richard's not around to press charges, so I convinced the officer not to arrest you for B and E."

"B and E?"

"Breaking and entering. Anyhow, I was pulling into your driveway when we collided." He set my purse down beside me.

I pulled myself back to a sitting position. "Thank

you for your delivery, and now I'm leaving." I swung my legs over the side of the bed and stood up.

Tim came over to catch me if I fell. "I'm not sure leaving right now is a good idea. They've got you on Darvon for the pain, so you shouldn't drive."

"I'll just operate heavy machinery instead." I casually grabbed the bed rail again to stop the room from spinning. "By the way, where is my car?"

"Still in your driveway. The back end is pushed in, and I couldn't get the trunk to close, but I think it's still drivable."

"And my keys?"

He pulled them from his pocket and dropped them in my hand. "When did you last eat?"

I tried to think back, but it had been so long I couldn't remember.

"I thought so," he said. "Wait here."

A couple of minutes later, he was back with a tray of pale, bland, scrambled eggs, a hard piece of toast, and a fruit cup. And a cold Pepsi. I wolfed it down. When I finished, I pushed the call button for the nurse.

"May I help you?" came the crackly voice through the speaker.

"I need to check out," I said back to the intercom.

"I'll send a nurse in."

"Maggie," Tim said, "this isn't too wise."

"That's never stopped me before."

"In that case, mind if I stay and watch?"

"Suit yourself."

We waited in silence for the nurse, who showed up about ten minutes later.

"The doctor is scheduled to stop by this afternoon to check on you," she said and moved toward me, ostensibly to help me back into bed.

"I'm afraid that doesn't suit my schedule."

"You really need to give your body some rest." She spoke to me, but she smiled and looked at Tim. Watching the nurse flirt with Tim aggravated me more.

"How do I check out of this place?" I yelled each word as if the woman was hard of hearing.

"This isn't a hotel. You need to be discharged first by a doctor," she said and then stomped her little white shoes out of my room.

Tim was smiling an infuriating smile. "You do have a way with people."

I returned his smile. "Maybe I'll run for a political office." I hobbled to the doorway to look for signs of a doctor.

"Excuse me, Maggie," Tim said.

"What?" I turned halfway so I could keep an eye on any passing doctor-looking person.

"Before you make your break for the free world, don't you think you should put some clothes on?"

I looked down and realized I was wearing one of those sexy, backless hospital gowns that looks like a tent canvas. I grabbed the two back pieces to close up the view I must have been giving Tim.

"Sorry I said anything." He laughed, which pissed me off. After all, why was he hanging around if I was nothing more than his sister's baby-sitter?

"I assumed your condo was locked, and since the stores are closed for Christmas, I took the liberty of borrowing some clothes a friend had left at my place." He nodded toward a bag that was sitting on a chair. "You two are about the same size."

I went over to investigate and found a black bra, black thong underwear, a black turtleneck, and some jeans. I picked up the bag and went into the bathroom to change. I'd have stomped, but my head hurt too much. Inside I lowered myself down on the toilet and opened the bag for a closer inspection. I tossed the underwear into the trash can and chased it with the bra, but not before noticing it was several cup sizes larger than what I wore.

I tugged on the jeans and the sweater, which weren't a bad fit.

When I went to the sink to wash my face, I got my first look at myself in the mirror and almost screamed. My right eye was black and blue with mottled high-lights of purple, yellow, and green. But it was my hair that made me look like a bad Halloween mask. Al-though someone must have washed the blood off my face, there was still some of it caked into my hair. The crusted blood caused my hair to stand straight up from my scalp, giving me several additional inches of height and limiting my ability to ride in an open convertible under a low overpass.

My plan had been to go home, pick up some clothes, and then check into the closest Marriott. But I didn't want to go out in public looking like this, and I didn't want to take a shower at my condo with my recently developed Psycho Phil/Hitchcock syndrome. My lux-urious hospital bathroom sported a micro-shower but no shampoo or conditioner.

"Shit," I muttered to myself.

Given the state of my hair, I desperately needed my full ensemble of hair care products and a brush and comb or there would be no detangling this long mop of hair.

There were several knocks on the door. "How about I drive you back to your place? I can stick around while the police take your statement and wait while you get a shower so you don't have to worry about Phil showing up."

I dabbed water on my hair to try to deflate it, then opened the door. Tim stepped back and gave me a once-over.

"Thanks, but I'll be fine," I said. "Do you know where my clothes are from last night?"

"I think the nurse said she put them in the closet."

I limped over and found a plastic bag with my blood-soaked clothes. I pulled out my watch and the black pumps that were jammed on the side of the bag.

Tim leaned against a table with his hand in his pockets and a wry smile on his face.

"Thanks for the clothes, but I think I can take it from here."

"Uh-huh. What exactly is your plan?"

"I'm going to catch a cab to my place, meet the police, and then grab some of my clothes and toiletries. Then I'm checking into a hotel and taking a long shower. After that, I've got client meetings."

"On Christmas? Well, given what happened, I guess that shouldn't surprise me. But I don't think you're going to have much luck getting a cab today."

From the window, I could see the main intersection below, and there wasn't any traffic moving around.

"Let me give you a ride to your place," he said, "and stay while you get your stuff. Checking into a hotel is probably a good idea until they catch Phil."

I went out to the nurse's station and spent the next half hour trying to get checked out of the hospital. Everyone was deathly convinced that my discharge shouldn't happen without a physician's approval. I finally told them to bill me and left. Tim followed behind.

Tim called the police before we left the hospital to let them know we were on our way to my condo.

Outside, I waited while he retrieved his Volvo from the parking garage. I noticed it had only suffered a small dent in the front fender from our collision. During the ride to my condo, Tim kept asking me questions, which I answered with words of one syllable or less. It was probably unfair to be so pissed at him, but after everything that had happened, I had to be pissed off at somebody. He was handy.

He pulled into my driveway and parked next to my poor, battered Corolla. The front end and middle looked okay, but the trunk was popped open like an unzipped zipper. There was no sign of a police car.

Over my protests, Tim carried me to the front door,

which turned out to be a great way to travel since my sidewalk wasn't shoveled. He put me down on the front porch littered with newspapers. I opened the door, and we both froze at the sight of the mess.

Tim stood at my elbow, a somber look on his face. "Stay here and let me have a look around."

Tim unholstered his gun and searched the house. He returned five minutes later after checking all the nooks and crannies and said there was no Psycho Phil.

I walked into the family room and then through the rest of the house to survey the damage. Emptied drawers, overturned furniture, slashed curtains, and broken lamps. I felt so violated.

"It's going to take forever to clean up this mess," I said.

"I'm sorry, Maggie. Can you tell if he's taken anything?"

The TV was still there, as was the stereo system and my computer, but all had been massaged with a sledgehammer. My jewelry box was emptied on my bedroom floor, but it didn't seem as though anything was missing.

The police rang my doorbell about a half hour later. I'm glad I didn't wait for them to arrive when Phil was here.

"This was on your front doorstep," an officer said, holding a shipping tube neither Tim nor I had noticed. The return mailing label had Stephanie Wolf's name and the address of the Children's Hospice. "Would you mind if I opened it?"

"Be my guest."

He gently popped the end off, and nothing blew up or sprang out. He reached in and pulled out a poster. Tim and I watched as he unrolled the paper.

Across the top of the page was a hand-lettered message: "Thank You Miss Maggie." Below the words were eleven photos of children holding thank-you signs they had each made. My eyes immediately went to the

photo of the baby with the big blue eyes. It was the
same baby whose photo I had seen the other night. She
was being held by her mom and dad. There were tears
on the face of the woman. The bottom of the poster
read: "For Making A Difference In Our Lives With
Your $3,000,000 Donation. Love, Children's Hos-
pice." The children had also signed their names.

I collapsed in a chair and started crying.

"You gave the Children's Hospice three million dollars?" Tim said. "Maggie, that's . . . that's incredible."

I buried my head in my hands and cried harder. Between my demolished house and the faces of all those
kids thanking me for a donation I couldn't afford to
give, it was too much.

After a good ten minutes of flooding from my eyes,
I got myself under control.

Both the police officer and Tim were waiting for an
explanation, but I wasn't up to talking about it. Instead,
I gave the officer a quick tour of the destroyed condo
while I told him what I could about Phil, which wasn't
much: He worked as a maintenance man and a driver
for a retirement home, made about $24,000 a year, and
lived in South County. Then I filled the officer in on
what had happened to Phil's account, courtesy of Palimo Technologies. The officer took lots of notes, and
when he ran out of questions for me, he said he would
file a report when he got back to the station. It was
about eleven o'clock when he left.

Tim grabbed a couple of Pepsi cans from the refrigerator, and we took a break sitting on the fireplace
hearth.

"Can we talk about your donation to the hospice for
a minute?" Tim said.

"No."

"How can you afford to give them three million dollars? Especially after Palimo? You're not printing
money in the basement are you?"

"That's the problem," I said, looking down at the

floor. "I don't have three million dollars I want to give them." I filled Tim in on my confusion over the value of a wiz and the added problem of the Goldberg brothers matching pledge stipulations.

"Those little faces on the poster were pretty heartbreaking," he said. "What are you planning to do?"

I shrugged. "I can't write a check for three mil; that will almost clean me out. I'm going to have to come up with some creative excuse to get out of it. Any suggestions?"

He shook his head. "I can only tell you that at the Service we have a saying: It is better to give than to deceive. Every time someone lies about something, it always makes a situation worse. Doesn't matter if it's your taxes, or—"

"Great. Then you write the damn check." I stood up and took my Pepsi to the kitchen. I wasn't in the mood for a morality lesson.

A few minutes later, Tim joined me in the kitchen.

"Sorry about that," he said. "Do you want a hand with this mess?"

Tim wouldn't just straighten, he would want to really clean, and I didn't have the time or energy.

"No, I'll be fine."

From somewhere in the family room, a stack of CDs fell over, and I jumped at the noise.

"If you have some extra wood, and a hammer and nails," he said, "I could board up your garage back door so no one can get in."

"My garage door?"

"That's how Phil made his entrance."

We both walked out to the garage to inspect the door. The wood was split around the lock, and it was obvious I was going to need a new door.

"How could Phil have known I would go in the front door?" I said. "Because if my garage door opener would have worked, I would have pulled in, seen the door, and pulled back out."

Tim scanned the ceiling of the garage and then pointed at the housing for the garage door opener. "It looks like he unplugged the power to the opener."

Since I didn't own a stepladder, Tim retrieved a chair from the kitchen and reconnected the power to the opener.

"So what do we do about the door? I don't have any wood, a hammer, or nails."

"You don't have a hammer?"

I shrugged. "They're not advertised in Pottery Barn catalogs."

"We shouldn't leave your garage door like that. Too bad the hardware stores are closed. I could run to my place and get some supplies for you. I've got some extra wood from the deck I put on this summer we could use to board the door shut, and I'm sure I could scrounge up a hammer and some nails for you, too. Would you like to tag along?"

"But there's no way to lock that busted door."

"I'll prop a chair against it and then I'll just recheck the house when we get back."

I let out a deep sigh. I didn't particularly want to go back out, but I didn't want to stay by myself, either. "I might as well go with you. I could use a screwdriver, too."

"Come on, Bob Vila."

We locked the front door of the condo and wedged a kitchen chair under the doorknob of the garage back door. We didn't worry about the condo's back door, figuring if someone couldn't get into the garage, they couldn't get into the house.

I grabbed the garage door opener from my car and then climbed into Tim's car. He kept the conversation going during our ride to his place, which helped me keep my mind off of everything that had happened. When we got to his house, I waited in the car while he ran in to get what we needed. It was a wonderful opportunity to contemplate the evils of greed and the fleeting nature of wealth. Instead, I drifted off and only woke up when Tim slammed the trunk.

"Shit!" I said, as we pulled back into my driveway.

"What's wrong?"

"My garage door opener is almost dead. I should have borrowed some batteries from you, too."

Tim looked over at the deep snow covering my sidewalk he had traipsed through earlier. "Why don't you see if it still works."

I said a small prayer and pointed the opener at the garage. Nothing. I tried several more times, holding it at different angles, but got the same results.

"Here, let me try."

"Do you think I'm so mechanically challenged that I can't operate a door opener?"

"Do you want to walk this time? Those high heels aren't really the proper attire for a long, snowy trek to your front door."

I handed him the opener.

He held it between his hands for a moment, pointed it toward the door, and gently pressed on the button. The garage immediately opened, and he handed the opener back to me.

I glared at him. "You've never had a pimple, have you?"

"Batteries sometimes come to life if you warm them up a bit."

I shook my head but didn't say anything.

Tim checked the house one more time but didn't see anyone or anything unusual. Back in the garage, I watched as he put one of the scrap pieces of two-by-fours across the door about twelve inches from the top. He nailed it to the molding and then repeated the process two more times farther down. When he was finished, he yanked on the doorknob a couple of times, but the boards didn't give.

"I think that should hold you until you can get a new door."

We walked into the kitchen. I took off my coat and threw it on the back of a chair.

"Thanks for your help. I'll be okay from here. Unless my condo catches on fire and the only way out is through the door you just nailed shut."

"I think you could probably use a window if you had to." He paused and looked around the kitchen. Glass jars from the pantry holding spaghetti sauce, applesauce, and various other liquids had been broken on the floor along with all my dishes and glasses. "Are you sure you don't want some help with this mess?"

"It's getting late, and I have so many clients I need to track down. I just want to get to a hotel and get cleaned up. I'll deal with this disaster later."

"I think a hotel is probably the safest place for you right now, but in the interest of saving time, why don't you shower here. I can stay and clean while you get ready. Then you could pack a bag and take it with you and check into a hotel tonight after your meetings are over."

It was a faster plan.

"Do you have time to wait? I don't want to ruin your Christmas."

He knelt down and started picking up pieces of glass from the floor. "As long as I make it to my folks by five for overcooked turkey and soggy dressing, I'll be fine."

"Thanks."

I walked toward my bedroom and stopped when I realized Tim was following me. "Where are you going?"

"As I recall, Phil dumped your mattress by your bathroom entrance. I thought it might be easier for you to get ready if I put the mattress back on the box springs."

We walked to my bedroom, and Tim hoisted my mattress back to where it belonged. It felt a little strange to be alone together in my bedroom. A year ago we had spent so much time together here and then I had screwed up missing that date.

"I'm sorry, what did you say?" I said.

"Where would I find something to help with the kitchen floor?"

"Try under the kitchen sink," I said, and then watched as he left for culinary cleanup duty.

I was in and out of the shower before my hands started to wrinkle. It felt good to be clean. I dressed quickly and then grabbed a couple suits and other staples and threw them into a suitcase. I took a last look around my demolished bedroom and then joined Tim in the kitchen. He had cleaned all the splattered food off the floor and cabinets. There wasn't any sign of broken glass.

"You know, I was thinking," he said. "I'm staying with my folks in Columbia tonight. If you'd rather not go to a hotel, I could give you a key to my place."

If he didn't have a date for New Year's, I would have taken him up on his offer. "Thanks, but I'll be fine at the Marriott."

"You're sure? If you'd rather, I can tell my folks something came up and meet you back here tonight."

"Don't change your plans. I'll be fine. There's a mint on a Marriott pillow with my name on it—I promise."

On our way to the front door, I tried hard not to stare at the ruins of my condo. If I wasn't about to reenter the ranks of the working-class poor, I'd dump this place and go buy some big mansion in a gated community. So much for my brief life as a multimillionaire.

Outside, I used a belt to secure my trunk lid and then thanked Tim again for his help. It was time to start meeting with my Palimo victims.

Chapter 10

I knocked on the front door of a two-story brick co-
lonial and admired a picturesque suburban scene.
The neighboring houses all had Christmas trees in their
windows and lights strung on every external surface
possible. It was probably quite a sight at night. What
you couldn't tell by looking at this Norman Rockwell
setting were the stories behind the front doors.

Behind the door I just knocked on lived a sweet
couple in their eighties. He an avid golfer and she ac-
tive in numerous charities, until this summer. First
came dizziness and impaired mental abilities, then a
debilitating pain from atrophied muscles and nerves
that prevented her from moving. Eventually doctors
would give it a name: Strickley syndrome. They also
gave her six months to live. But this couple had been
through too many battles together to sit this one out.
As soon as the holidays were over, they were leaving
for Paris to try an experimental treatment. Insurance
wasn't going to pay for it. Their Palimo stock was.

That was before Palimo cost them $327,000.

I shook my head as I thought about our last conversation. Mr. King had called two weeks ago to liquidate his Palimo holdings because he didn't want to risk the money. I had talked him into waiting until the study results were published.

I heard the door open and turned and saw Mr. King. "Maggie, what happened to you?"

I touched my eye. "A traffic accident."

"Are you okay?"

"I'm fine. Would you mind if I came in for a few minutes?"

"Of course. Come in, come in. What are you doing here?"

I followed him inside. "I'm sorry to interrupt your Christmas celebration—"

He took my coat. "There's no celebration going on here. My daughter came and picked up Katherine. I didn't feel up to having everyone over."

"How did she take the news about Palimo?" I said softly.

"I haven't told her yet."

We stood in the foyer, and he didn't seem to know what to do.

"Maybe you won't have to. How about a cup of coffee? I'd like to talk to you about Palimo."

"You're welcome to all the coffee you can drink, but I'd rather not hear the words *Palimo Technologies* ever again."

I followed him to the kitchen and sat at the table while he tried to get the coffeemaker to work. It was a bright, cheerful kitchen with lots of windows and several skylights. The sun danced in and ricocheted off the copper bottoms of pans hanging above the center island. The kitchen table was a big oak number that must have comfortably seated the Kings' many kids when they were young. A two-sided fireplace separated the kitchen from the family room. There wasn't a fire in it, and the dark, cold spot seemed out of place but also mirrored Mr. King's mood.

"I never know how to get this thing to work," he said, still trying to load the coffee beans into the grinder.

"How about a Pepsi instead?"

"Now, that I can help you with."

He grabbed a can from the refrigerator and sat down across from me. "Maggie, it wasn't necessary for you to come out this morning. It's not your fault what happened with Palimo."

"Yes, in a way, it was. You were too heavily invested in it, and I should have sold your shares when you called a few weeks ago."

Mr. King looked down at the table, no doubt agreeing with me but too polite to say so.

"It's against the Securities and Exchange Commission's rules for me to personally reimburse you, because I can't commingle my money with yours," I said. "But if you give this letter to my boss, I will see that everything is taken care of."

I slid over the letter I had printed out the night before. He took his reading glasses out of his pocket and read it.

"This is a complaint to file an arbitration suit. Maggie, you can't do this. It'll ruin your record."

"I can, and I insist. Just give the letter to my boss, and I will make arrangements with him to settle the complaint by debiting my account."

"But how can you afford this?"

"I had some money set aside for a rainy day, and Palimo turned into a typhoon."

"But I can't take your money."

"Mr. King, look around you. The Christmas tree isn't lit. Your family isn't here. And you look like you haven't had much sleep. I took your Christmas away, which is bad enough, but with Mrs. King's health the way it is, you need to celebrate the holidays you have

together. Here's my chance to help you get some of
that Christmas spirit back."

"But—"

I reached my hand across the table and touched his.
"End of discussion. Now, promise me you'll join the
party at your daughter's. Isn't this your granddaugh-
ter's first Christmas?"

He nodded and pursed his lips together. He kept
nodding, trying to keep the tears at bay. Finally, he
squeezed my hand. "Maggie, although I'm retired, I've
still got lots of business connections. I'll make this up
to you."

"Mr. King, my guess is that Mrs. King is probably
pretty pissed off at you for ruining her Christmas celebration without telling her why. Am I right?"

"That would be kind of an understatement."

"Then go find her and give her a hug and a smile.
That's all the thanks I want."

He was still thanking me as I left.

I repeated this same offer with the other clients on
my list. Most gladly accepted. Some flatly refused.
Everyone appreciated my visit.

By eight o'clock, I had reimbursed over one million
dollars, with more on the schedule for tomorrow. I had
hoped that this holiday generosity would make me feel
better, but it didn't. Each claim would be filed on my
NASD record, and there was a good chance they'd pull
my securities license for so many complaints. Even if
it wasn't, my record would obliterate any career I
hoped to have as a broker, for Hamilton or on my own.

It was time to hang a Do Not Disturb sign.

I drove back into Clayton and the two-story canopy
entrance to the Marriott invited me to be a guest. The
lobby was buzzing with people coming from, or going
to Christmas celebrations. The front desk clerk noticed
me right away as I made my way to the counter.

"May I help you?" he said.

"I'd like a room, nonsmoking if you have it."

"Do you have a reservation?"

"No, this was kind of unexpected."

He wrinkled his face. "I'm sorry, but with the Christmas holiday, we're completely sold out. And I'm afraid every other hotel in Saint Louis is, too."

My shoulders sagged. I'd been so wrapped up in my Palimo and Psycho Phil drama that I kept forgetting normal people were going about their lives, enjoying the holiday.

The clerk tapped on his keyboard. "Most of our holiday guests are making a weekend out of it, so we'll have some vacancies tomorrow night. Would you like me to reserve a room for Sunday?"

I nodded and then mumbled my information for the reservation. Then I gave him my VISA to hold the reservation before I trudged back to my car.

I couldn't believe on Christmas that there wasn't any room at the inn. At least I wasn't about to give birth. But now what?

The snow was falling pretty intensely, so I started my car and began driving, hoping the movement and the defroster would help keep the windshield clear. I should have taken Tim up on his offer to crash at his place. I really didn't want to go home alone, but I couldn't keep circling Clayton in my wiperless car all night. I just wished I'd checked to see if Phil had found my second set of keys during his rampage. It was too bad the police couldn't deliver a security man for me to check out the place.

That's what I needed. A deliveryman.

I dialed the next phone number more often then I dialed my parents'.

"Domino's, please hold."

I listened to a message about their deep crust pizza and was in the middle of must-have information on bread sticks when a man came back on the line.

"Domino's, will this be takeout or delivery?"

"How long will it take for a delivery?"

"What's your telephone number?"

I gave him the number.

"You're at 845 Landis?"

"Yes," I said, nodding for no apparent reason.

"That's around the corner and down the street from us, but we're pretty backed up from the snow. I'd say about forty-five minutes or so."

"Great, could I have a medium hand-tossed, cheese pizza, please?"

The Domino's man said I could and asked if I wanted bread sticks with that, which I declined.

I drove home, stopping occasionally to impersonate my wipers and clear my windshield. When I got to my place, I drove past my condo and went down the street and turned around. Then I parked on the street across from my condo. I lived on a cul-de-sac, and this way I could watch anyone pulling onto my street.

No one came or left while I waited. But about an hour later, a little red Escort pulled onto my street with a familiar Domino's sign latched onto the roof. I flipped on my headlights, hit the garage door opener, and pulled into my driveway. The garage door didn't open. I pressed the button several more times and twisted it in different directions to see whether I could activate the opener. God, I didn't want to traipse through the snow to my front door. I popped the back off the door opener and pulled out the battery. I wiped off the ends to give any juice left in the battery a clearer shot at getting through. Then I reassembled everything, tried Tim's trick of warming it up, crossed my eyes for luck, and hit the button again.

The door opened, and I drove into the garage. The Domino's guy pulled into my driveway after me.

"I'm sorry the drive isn't shoveled yet," I said as he got out of his car.

"No problem. I'm dressed for deliveries tonight."

My deliveryman was actually a delivery boy who must have been in his late teens or early twenties. He was probably home for Christmas break, delivering pizzas to earn some extra money. I just hoped I wasn't about to get us both killed.

"I left my wallet inside. Why don't you come in out of the snow?"

He nodded and we cut through the garage. I ignored my boarded-up back door and hoped the delivery boy did, too. At the garage entrance to my condo there was a double light switch, one for the garage and one for the interior utility room lights. I flipped them both on, figuring the more light the better when it came to looking for stalkers.

I opened the door. No one with a butcher knife was standing there to greet us. We continued into the kitchen, and I turned on every light I could.

"Why don't you set the pizza on the table, and I'll go find my wallet."

The delivery boy walked through the kitchen to the eat-in area. When he wasn't looking, I grabbed the biggest knife I had out of my utensil drawer and tucked it next to my coat.

If the delivery boy noticed the general disarray of the condo, he didn't say anything. But he was a college kid, this was probably how his dorm room looked all the time.

"Have you been really busy tonight?" I yelled over my shoulder as I went into my bedroom. No one behind my bedroom door.

"Yeah, no one wants to go out in this weather and lots of people can't cook turkey."

I checked under the bed, in my closet, and in my bathroom. No Psycho Phil anywhere. I came back out of my bedroom. "How much do I owe you?"

"Ten forty-nine."

"I must have left my wallet upstairs. I'm sorry this is taking so long."

I climbed the stairs to the loft area that overlooked the family room. Luckily, the condo was open enough and the walls thin enough that the Domino boy would be sure to hear my screams for help.

"How late are you guys open tonight?" I said as I walked down the hall.

"Till midnight," he said, and I could tell by the sound of his voice he had walked into the family room to answer me.

At the end of the hall were two bedrooms that shared the same bathroom. I looked under the beds, checked both closets and the bathroom. Still no Psycho Phil.

The house was clear. The only area left was the unfinished basement.

I tucked my knife on the inside of my coat and returned to the kitchen. The Domino boy was back in the kitchen. He stood in a puddle created by the snow melting from his boots. He looked ready to bolt with his pizza.

"I'm so sorry. I can't seem to find my wallet anywhere."

He shrugged his shoulders. "I've got to get going. We're really swamped tonight."

I slapped my forehead with the palm of my hand. "I'm such an idiot. I left a twenty and some change in a bag from the hardware store downstairs. The basement door is right here. This will just take a second."

I opened the door and turned on the light. The stairs went straight down and were open on either side. I went halfway down the steps and could tell my nearly empty basement was empty of stalkers as well. I pulled some money out of my wallet before going back upstairs.

In the kitchen I gave the delivery boy the twenty and told him to keep the change. He handed over the pizza he had been holding hostage and thanked me for the tip. After he left, I closed the garage door and then locked the back door. I no longer had any confidence in my deadbolts, so I braced all external doors with chairs as well.

I returned to the living room and searched the piles of papers that had been in my desk and were now all over the floor. I found my second set of keys under a sofa pillow near the fireplace. That was one piece of good news. But then I remembered I had a second garage door opener. Had the spare opener been in my desk, too? Or did my parents still have it from their visit during Thanksgiving? I couldn't remember. I searched for another hour, couldn't find it, and gave up.

I tossed the cold pizza in the refrigerator, left all the lights on, and fell into bed. At this point, if Phil broke in while I was sleeping, it would be a mercy killing. I was so physically and emotionally exhausted that I was asleep before I could say "Nine-one-one."

Chapter 11

Sunday morning I got up, washed my face, did a few touch-ups on my hair, and added some fresh makeup. A shower would have been nice, but I couldn't shake my *Psycho* shower paranoia.

I was out the door by nine o'clock. I spent the day contacting the rest of the clients on my list. After I left the Hendersons in Ladue, I stopped by the Marriott to check in and drop off the suitcase I had packed yesterday. Then I was on my way to visit my last Palimo client, Stanley Vandenberg.

The funeral home parking lot was filled with motorcycles when I pulled in. Stanley's expansive black hearse towered over the bikes like a Russian wolfhound in a room full of pit bulls. I managed to create a parking spot without knocking over any Harleys. A greeter at the doorway told me Stanley was in the prep room and then excused himself to try to shut down the bar that had opened in the men's room.

I was going to wait in Stanley's office, but I was so tired I decided instead to go ahead downstairs and see if I could find him. I walked down the hallway and noticed that again several of the visitation rooms had been opened up and combined into one big room. Packed inside and spilling out into the hallway were leather-clad biker types. Although it was freezing outside, many of the more endowed women had opted for black leather halter tops. Interspersed among the bikers were businessmen in expensive suits and others who looked as if they had been living on the streets. It was an odd, mixed crowd.

I pushed the button for the elevator, but it never came. Disgusted, I found the door to the basement and made my way down. Halfway down, I could hear Stanley, Malcolm, and the parrot arguing, but I couldn't tell exactly what they were saying. I tiptoed my way closer to the entrance of the embalming area. The door was ajar, making my eavesdropping much easier.

From my vantage point, I could see Malcolm and Stanley. Lying on a table between them was a woman's body. When Stanley shifted, I caught a glimpse of her face, which looked vaguely familiar.

"Why didn't you tell me the crematorium broke when I called this morning?" Malcolm yelled.

"Uh-oh! Uh-oh! Uh-oh!" the parrot said.

I stepped back so I wouldn't be seen.

"It's not that big of a deal," Stanley said. He talked slowly like he was speaking with a lost child who was upset. Probably in his line of work, he was used to grief-stricken people losing control of their emotions, and I guessed it would take a lot to rattle him. "The guy will be out on Tuesday to repair it. We don't have any cremations scheduled before then, so why are you so mad?" Stanley said.

"The point, Uncle, is that this business is hemorrhaging money. Every time you turn around, there's a new repair needed. First it was the atrium ceiling at

$4,500, then it was $1,900 in hearse repairs. And your funerals are bleeding what reserve you have left. The sports anchor's funeral cost about $165,000 but you only billed them $157,000."

The parrot made a wolf whistle.

"Malcolm, this is my business, and I'll run it the way I have been running it for forty years and the way my father ran it before me. Nothing is going to change that. It was my decision to have the extra caterers and flowers, which I paid for. The family bought the Aegean Elite at full price. What we billed doesn't reflect what we netted. Besides, you've got to understand in a high-profile service like that, we're making an impression on thousands of people in a way that no advertising could. Did you see how much news coverage we got? And when the average person plans a funeral only once in fifteen years, big impressions make a difference." He paused. "I appreciate all the help you're doing with the bookkeeping, but you have to quit worrying so much about the finances. Things always work out, you'll see."

"You just don't get it," Malcolm said. I could imagine him pushing a stray piece of hair out of his eyes or perhaps stroking his goatee.

Stanley didn't answer, so I took this lull in the storm as my opportunity to enter. I put my hand on the doorknob, and the door was yanked back. Malcolm ran right into me.

"Uh-oh! Uh-oh!" the parrot said.

My coordination wasn't what it should be, and I toppled backward and landed on my ass. Malcolm tried to catch me but landed on top of me instead.

"Well, Ms. Connors, so nice to see you again," he said.

"The pleasure is all mine," I replied, but with his groin pushed against my thigh, I wasn't sure that was entirely true.

"My apologies for running you over, but you

shouldn't be down here. I didn't even hear the elevator come down."

"Maggie, is that you?" I heard Stanley ask from inside the prep room. His voice got closer. "For heaven's sakes Malcolm, get off the poor girl. Can't you see she's already been banged up? She doesn't need you causing more injuries."

Malcolm got to his feet and helped me up as well.

"What in God's name happened to you?" Malcolm said.

"A bit of a car accident," I said, copying his English accent. "I think I fared better than my car. I'm using a belt to keep the trunk closed. But, actually, the reason I'm here is that I need to talk with your uncle about one of his investments."

"What on earth would bring you out on a Sunday night during the Christmas weekend to discuss business?" Stanley said.

"Palimo Technologies."

"That dead horse?" Malcolm said. "Thank God I sold it before the news hit the fan."

"What?"

"Uncle, you bought it at $38 and we sold it Thursday morning at $71. It's been one of the few transactions lately we've made money on. I think it closed Friday around ten dollars."

I didn't correct his closing price.

"See?" Stanley said. "Now I can pay to get the oven fixed."

"We're in the money, we're in the money," the parrot said.

"You sold it?" I said. "Things have been so chaotic . . . I didn't—"

"See, Malcolm, all you need to do is follow something through for a change," Stanley said.

Just like that, the tension between the two men returned.

Malcolm glared at his uncle, who was now dancing

about. "Maybe I shouldn't have sold it," he said. "Uncle Stanley always seems to get bailed out of his financial woes."

"Now that we've got a little cash infusion, it looks like you'll be escorting one of our guests to Mexico after all," Stanley said, slapping Malcolm on the back.

Stanley was such an affable old gent that it was odd to see him intentionally aggravate Malcolm. I wondered what had transpired between the two.

"You're going to Mexico?" I said.

Malcolm ignored his uncle and turned to me. "It's to fulfill a last request. Would you care to join me? You look like you could use a few days in the sun."

"It sounds nice, but I'm pretty tied up the next few days." *I'm busy losing my job and all my money.* "You sold Palimo?"

"I was worried we were overextended, and the profits were good. You might want to rethink my Mexico invitation. You know, there are very few people on their deathbed who wish they would have worked more," Malcolm said.

"Come, Socrates," Stanley said. The bird swooped over and landed on Stanley's shoulder. "If you two will excuse me, I need to go check on Charlie Bankert's viewing."

"Previous owner of Hawg Heaven," Malcolm whispered in my ear.

Stanley and Socrates moved past us to the stairs, and suddenly I found myself alone with Malcolm.

"You look whipped," he said, "have you had dinner yet?"

I shook my head. "It's been a busy day. I was going to grab something after I talked with Stanley."

"Why don't you let me spend some of my uncle's Palimo profits and buy you dinner?"

I scrunched my face. I wasn't in the mood to be social.

"If you'd rather not," he said, "I'm sure we could

scare up some leathers and toss back a few beers with everyone upstairs."

"Nah. We'd have to get tattooed, and I've got a very low threshold for pain." I lowered my head for a few moments and massaged the back of my neck. "Actually, dinner sounds nice."

"What are you in the mood for?" he said.

"A couple of margaritas and some Mexican food. I'm staying at the Marriott in Clayton, and there's an El Serrano right next door."

"Why don't I follow you over to the hotel, and then we can walk to the restaurant. Then we won't have to worry about our alcohol consumption."

"You mean I won't have to worry. You're going to be driving home, my friend."

He smiled and said he would meet me out front.

Traffic on the highways was very light, and we made good time back to Clayton. The Marriott parking garage was relatively empty, so I was able to park right next to the elevator. Malcolm pulled in beside me.

The temperature dropped with the setting sun, and the snow that had melted earlier on the sidewalks now turned to ice. Malcolm and I made it to the restaurant without killing ourselves, but it was close. My high heels found all the ice patches, and Malcolm kept trying to help me balance, which made me lose my balance. We were both laughing when we opened the front doors of El Serrano and smelled the aroma of fresh tortilla chips.

I drained my first margarita so fast I got a brain freeze. Malcolm suggested the best cure was to chase it with another. I don't even remember him ordering the third . . . and that's when my real problems began.

Chapter 12

Someone was both shaking my shoulder and banging on the door, which didn't seem physically possible.

"Maggie, wake up."

I convinced my eyelids to separate and saw Malcolm standing over me. He had showered and dressed and looked ready to conquer the world. I peeked under my sheets. My clothes were missing, along with a little more of my dignity.

"I've got to get going," Malcolm cooed into my ear. "There's someone at the door, and evidently they can't read the Do Not Disturb sign."

I watched him walk out of the bedroom and then rolled over and closed my eyes.

Shit.

I jumped out of bed as fast as someone can with a death-defying hangover. I grabbed a fluffy bathrobe that had been carefully wadded up and thrown in the corner. I made it to the front door just as Malcolm opened it. I held my breath, expecting Phil to be standing in the hallway. Instead, it was Tim, holding a bag of Krispy Kreme doughnuts and a Pepsi.

Shit, shit, shit.

The three of us stood there in the doorway.

I tried to think of something to say, but my brain wasn't functioning, so I clutched my robe tighter.

"Excuse me, I was just leaving," Malcolm said and stepped past Tim, bumping his shoulder as he passed.

Tim gave me a long stare, looking as if I'd just run over his puppy. Then he turned and left, taking the doughnuts and my badly needed Pepsi with him.

I slammed the door and winced at the noise. Tim didn't play fair. Had he forgotten that he had a date for New Year's? And now I was supposed to feel bad for being with someone else? I had enough problems.

The most urgent one involved being vertical for too long. The effort and adrenaline it had taken to get to the front door was now catching up with me. I stumbled to the bathroom and flipped the toilet seat up before revisiting last night's Mexican dinner. My gag reflex was so intense that the bits and pieces I choked on ended up blowing out of my nose. Of course, not all of this blowing was done with marksmanship aim, and I spewed tacos grande on my robe and hair.

It was the perfect way to start a Monday morning.

When I finished erasing last night's calories, I dragged myself to the refrigerator and searched for a Pepsi. There was nothing left but caffeine-free 7UP. That meant a shower and dressing stood between me and the vending machine.

I returned to the bathroom and turned the taps on full blast, but the pounding water echoed inside my head, and I had to shut the flow down to a trickle. Once I had washed the Mexican dinner from my hair, I changed into a suit and checked my appearance in the mirror. My hair was having a good day, which would hopefully make up for the black eye, which was still very noticeable despite my makeup efforts. I had dabbed a ton of blush on my cheeks, but my face still looked pale and blotchy. I considered washing off the makeup and starting over, but instead I yawned and flipped off the light. There was only so much I could do given my circumstances, and no amount of makeup was going to disguise this hangover.

I grabbed a couple more Advil before I left my hotel room to search for a vending machine. Halfway down the hallway I noticed a familiar red glow reflected on one of the walls. I got closer and saw a gigantic Coke can illuminated on the front of the soda machine. Not my first choice, but it had sugar, caffeine, and phosphoric acid. It would do. I stuck my quarters in the machine, and when the can dropped down, I popped the top and swallowed my pills. I felt better after the first gulp.

I continued down to the hotel lobby. As I walked, I dug in my purse for my keys but couldn't find them. I was sure I had thrown them in there before we went to the restaurant. I stopped at a grouping of chairs in the lobby and emptied everything out of my purse.

The keys weren't there.

I returned to my hotel room and searched the obvious options: on the table near the door, in the bathroom, on the nightstand by the bed. I had given the hotel suite a once-over and a twice-over and was about to give up and call a cab when I caught a glimpse of the keys. They were on the floor by the door, poking out from under a table.

I bent down to grab the keys and almost lost the Coke. I managed to keep it down and then retraced my steps to the lobby and then out to my car. My Corolla was easy to spot with my brown, braided belt so tactfully holding my trunk closed. I really needed to find some time to get the trunk fixed. Maybe after I took some time off for my nervous breakdown.

Traffic was heavy and the motorists cranky in Clayton. Everyone must have been running late after the holiday weekend. I found a spot in the parking garage and made my way up the steps to the Hamilton office.

I had hoped to get into the office early so I could avoid explaining to all I passed what happened to my face. That obviously didn't work out. I entered the Hamilton reception area and saw the receptionists busy eradicating all signs of Christmas. It was time for investors to move on and start planning for the new year if they hadn't done so already.

"What the hell happened to you?" one of the receptionists said.

"I got mugged by Santa Claus," I said.

They both looked at me as if I had a contagious disease.

"Mike said he wants to see you as soon as you got in," the other receptionist said, trying to stuff some wreaths back into a box.

"He probably wants to give me my Christmas present," I said.

"I don't think so," the first receptionist said, still staring at my face.

I went back to my office to drop off my briefcase and coat before going to see Mike. When I got there, I found Luther Dodds waiting for me. Luther was eighty-something years old and frowned perpetually. His hair had receded long ago from his forehead, my guess in an attempt to distance itself from that cranky, old puss. He had about a million and a half invested with me spread over sixty-seven stocks. In that vast portfolio were one hundred measly shares of Palimo. The drop in the stock had cost him less then his weekly Viagra expenditure.

"Margaret," he said, "I've been sitting in your office since eight-oh-two. It is now half past nine. Your office opens at eight, and I should think you would be here."

"Normally I am here by eight, Mr. Dodds." I took off my coat and sat down behind my desk. Mr. Dodds returned to his chair. "This morning I had an early client meeting."

That was one way to describe what happened with Malcolm.

I moved some paperwork off to the side of my desk. "I'm sorry you had to wait. Would you like a cup of coffee?"

"No, what I would like is to know what the hell happened to Palimo Technologies?"

"Mr. Dodds, the news took me by complete surprise, as it did everyone else."

I looked around for Mike. Getting fired from him would be more enjoyable than dealing with this pain in the ass. My manager was nowhere in sight.

Mr. Dodds leaned forward and scowled. "Well, where the hell were you on Friday? I called every hour for you and never got a return phone call."

I decided to rearrange the events of the last few days. "I was unconscious in a hospital after getting rear-ended by a drunk driver."

"Maggie, your analysts should have seen this coming. Isn't that why you charge such outrageous commissions? So you can pay those guys to know what's going on with a stock?"

"Mr. Dodds, why would you expect our analysts to know Palimo was falsifying their research when the SEC didn't know?"

"Not my problem. My problem is a stock that tanks in a few hours."

"I think what is important now is determining a strategy for the future."

"The future is Jacobs and Riley Securities."

"What do you mean?"

"I'm transferring my account. You'll hear from my new broker in a couple of days."

I sat and watched him shuffle out of my office, apparently taking his money with him.

Stacy stuck her head in my office. "Mike called while you were meeting with Mr. Dobbs. He'll be out of the office until eleven, and he said when he gets back, and I quote, 'I want her ass in my office.'"

"Thanks."

"And you've got Mrs. Schwartz on line two, she's calling about Palimo."

The next hour and a half was a nonstop client bitch fest. The balance of my clients, comprised of those whom I didn't reimburse for their losses, called to critique my financial investment advice and my general worth as a person.

I came up for air about a quarter till eleven and decided to visit the cafeteria for a late-morning snack. I swallowed a bagel in the cafeteria and chased it with a Pepsi. It was time to face my boss. I had been working on my story, which was that the fax had been a big, practical joke.

I never got the chance to explain.

I opened my boss's office door and found him sitting with a police officer in the reception area of his office.

"Oh, I'm sorry for interrupting," I said. "I'll come back later."

"Now is fine."

This was said by a second officer standing behind me. He led me by the elbow into the office and shut the door behind us. His touch on my elbow was compelling without being harsh. It gave me the impression that getting fired was going to be the least of my concerns.

The officer motioned for me to take a seat across from my boss and the other officer.

"Are you Maggie Connors?" said the one who had been talking with my boss.

"Yes, and you are?"

"My name is Officer Barns and that is Officer Walker." He pointed at the other officer to avoid any confusion.

"Maggie," Mike said, "before the officers get started, I need your keys to the Hamilton offices."

"They're in my purse, back in my office. Why do you need them?"

My heart started pounding. Something was really wrong.

Mike stared at the floor and wouldn't look at me while he spoke. "Given everything that is going on right now," he nodded at the officers, "along with the complaint letters from your Palimo clients that have started coming in, and this—" He looked up at me. In his hand he held a copy of the press release announcing my new office opening. "I'm terminating your employment effective immediately. I can't tell you how it hurts me to say that."

Mike looked down at the carpet again, and the officers took that as their cue to start asking questions.

"Can you tell me where you were Saturday night between midnight and six in the morning?"

I crossed my legs, feeling defensive but not sure why. "I'm going to go out on a limb and guess that I was in bed, asleep."

"Can anyone corroborate that?" Barns said.

"Exactly why would my sex life be any of your business?"

"Can anyone corroborate that?"

"Who did you have in mind?"

Neither of the officers looked amused. Actually, they both looked rather pissed off. The first officer, Barns, was a beefy guy who didn't look comfortable sitting in a leather wingback chair. Walker was shorter and wiry, but I sensed he would be the first to jump into the middle of a bar fight.

"Were you at home, sleeping alone?" the second officer chimed in.

"Yes. Why?"

"Do you own a beige Toyota Corolla—" Officer Barns looked down at his notebook. "—license number EW9-S3Y?"

"I have a beige Corolla. I'm not sure what the plate number is. Why? What's going on?"

"Has your Corolla been out of your control in the last forty-eight hours?"

"You mean did I skid on the highway?"

"No, did anyone else have access to your car?"

"Mike, what the hell is going on?"

He shook his head sadly. "Maggie, you'd better answer their questions."

"I'm not answering anything until someone tells me what the hell is going on here."

The cop nearest me took my elbow and lifted me off my chair. Then he reached around to his back and produced a pair of handcuffs and proceeded to cuff me.

"Maggie Connors, you're under arrest for the murder of Eleanor Cosgrove."

"Who the hell is that?"

"The dead woman we found in the trunk of your car."

Although it was lunchtime, everyone seemed to be in the office and available to watch me being led out by police officers in handcuffs. We stopped at my office so I could get my purse—minus my office keys. I yelled to Stacy to get Tom Kimble on the phone and have him track me down.

I sat in the back of a police cruiser for the ride over to the station and kept repeating to myself that this was a bad mistake. Nice girls from the 'burbs didn't get arrested for murder. We preferred to keep murderers and those they murdered within the confines of the city limits.

My right leg started shaking and wouldn't stop. I was sure Tom Kimble—my client and now my attorney—would find a way to explain to the powers that be that a mistake had been made. He would probably just need my DNA or my fingerprints and this whole thing would be cleared up.

Assuming he would take my case. Tom had lost about $20,000 in the Palimo disaster.

I was taken to the county jail, where I was fingerprinted, photographed, and relieved of my personal items. Within a few hours, Tom arrived and managed to schedule my arraignment for tomorrow at eight-thirty in the morning and get my bail set at a million, which I was told was double the standard because of my wealth. They must not have seen my current portfolio balance. Now I just needed somebody to ante up $100,000 in cash or securities for my bond.

Although I knew lots of people with enough money to cover my bail, there were few that I wanted to know about my situation. This long list included my parents, my clients, and most of my friends. Tom was getting impatient, so I finally asked him to call Tim Gallen.

Monday afternoon stretched into evening and then night. No sign of Tim.

I was spending the night.

After dinner was served, I lay down on my lumpy bed and moped. Twelve months ago I was in love with a great guy, albeit an IRS agent. I had seven million dollars in the bank and the freedom to go anywhere, do anything, and buy anything. But I hadn't taken advantage of it. I didn't vacation or buy a big house or a cool car. Instead, I locked myself into my office and compulsively worked chasing bigger clients and better returns. Now, sitting in a cell with two women in for solicitation, two for drug possession, and another for drunk driving, I realized I had wasted a year of my life and sacrificed the one relationship I had ever cared about.

Sometime during this painful period of reflection, I managed to fall asleep to the sounds of thirty-three women talking and snoring. In the middle of the night, I woke up to use the bathroom, forgot where I was,

and knocked myself in the face when I ran into the cell
bars.

I cried myself back to sleep.

Tuesday, December 28

Early the next morning—I'm not sure what time since
my watch had been confiscated—we were served a
quick breakfast and then told to prepare for transportation. We were all dressed in unfashionable orange
jumpsuits, which made us look like escapees from a
psychotic pumpkin patch. With my long, red hair, I
looked particularly bad in orange, but I figured that was
the least of my problems right now.

Each prisoner's hand and foot was handcuffed to the
person in front and behind them. I ended up at the back
of the prisoner train. We shuffled our way onto a bus,
were driven to the Clayton courthouse, and corralled
into a courtroom.

When we entered, a man was pleading not guilty to
charges of agricultural vandalism. The judge asked the
prosecutor for clarification of the charge, and it was
explained that the man was caught by police in the
middle of the night having relations with a sheep at a
live Christmas nativity display. The prosecutor said
that since Missouri did not have a voluntary deviate
sexual intercourse statute, they charged him with agricultural vandalism.

I could not . . . believe . . . I was here.

Then each of my fellow bus passengers took turns
advising the judge that they had heard their rights and
were each innocent. Court dates were set generally in
seven to ten days. When my turn came, I repeated the
performance of so many of my orange comrades. My
preliminary hearing was set for the following Monday.
What a great way to start the new year.

Everyone was finished declaring their innocence in
about an hour. We were told to stand so we could make

our journey back to the bus, and that's when I saw Tim Gallen had come into the courtroom.

"Maggie, I'll get you bailed out as soon as I can," he yelled from several rows away.

I didn't answer him. I was too humiliated. I just shuffled along behind the big woman in front of me who seemed to pass gas with each step.

Back in my jail cell, I settled into my cot and waited.

The guard came and let me out of my cell an hour later. I was released and found Tim waiting for me.

"Would you like a ride home?" he said.

"That would be nice, since they impounded my car when they found the dead woman in it."

I followed him out to the parking lot. When we got into his car, he handed me the morning paper. I had made the front page, above the fold. There was a picture of me with my hands up, partially covering my face. It gave my horrible driver's license photo a run for the money. Next to me was a picture of Eleanor Cosgrove.

So that's who she was. The strange woman with the penchant for bizarre proverbs who came in with her bag of cash to open an account. I remembered she hadn't opened the account because Hamilton's fees were higher than her bank's.

I read the article, which gave me a few more details on the life of Eleanor Cosgrove. She was an eighty-four-year-old widow and former resident of the Autumn Oaks retirement home. That much I knew. Her husband had passed away thirty-six years ago from a traffic accident. She was not survived by any family members. She attended the Manchester Methodist Church and volunteered at the Water Street Rescue Mission. She was also a library volunteer and had been doing the children's story hour every Thursday at ten o'clock for the last fifteen years.

I stared at her photograph. She had a gentle, easy smile highlighted by pale eyes. The black-and-white photo didn't divulge the color of her eyes, but I thought I remembered them being a soft green. Her white hair was styled with gentle curls that flipped away from her face.

Police believed that the cause of death was a blunt blow to the head.

I shook my head. Why couldn't the woman they found in my trunk have been some child-abusing crack addict? The jury was going to love Eleanor and hate me.

"Do you want to talk about it?" Tim said.

"No, I just want to go home."

We rode to my condo in silence. I let the paper fall to my lap, and I stared at the landscape, the snow-covered trees, and the stores as if I hadn't seen them before. Being locked up for a day had definitely changed my perspective.

When we arrived at my condo, Tim asked if I wanted him to come in and check for Phil.

"I'd appreciate it if you would."

The sun had melted most of the snow on the side-walk, which made the walk to the front door easier. I wondered how long it would take to get my garage door opener from the place where they locked up naughty Corollas.

I unlocked my front door, and Tim went in first.

At first glance, I thought I had been robbed again. Everything was in shambles. Then I remembered.

"Damn, Phil."

"Actually, I think he had help," Tim said. "The police probably executed a search warrant while you were in jail."

I stayed in the foyer while he made his way around the place. Even though the condo was trashed for the second time—courtesy of the police—it felt good to be home.

"Maggie, did you leave water running for some reason?"

"No."

We both followed the noise of running water to the kitchen.

"The laundry room is behind that door, right?"

"Yeah, and that leads to the garage."

I stood behind Tim as he opened the door.

My laundry room was flooded, with water pumping from my washing machine, but that wasn't what we noticed first. Lying in the middle of the room was Psycho Phil. It was clear from the blueness around his lips that he was long dead, and from the look on his face, death caught him by surprise.

Chapter 13

Tim yanked me back. "Don't touch the water!"

Once the shock began to fade, I could see his point. The hose from the washer had been severed, and there was easily six inches of water in the small room. The ceiling light fixture had been removed, and a bare wire ran down to the crumpled mass formerly known as Phil. Had my kitchen not been one step up, it would have also flooded, causing Tim and me to get toasted as well. Instead, the excess water was spilling into a vent at the bottom of the wall.

Tim yelled at me to call 911, then he ran down to the basement to turn off the electricity. I went to the kitchen phone and called in our emergency. I was explaining our situation when Tim returned from the basement and ran to the laundry room. Evidently, he had managed to avoid the water in the basement and make it to the breaker box.

"Nine-one-one wants to know if you can get a pulse," I yelled after him.

Tim appeared a few moments later. "No pulse. This guy's fried."

I relayed Tim's information to the 911 operator and was assured that help was on the way. I know it wasn't appropriate, but I almost laughed when I hung up the phone. The entire Marine Corps couldn't give me enough help.

Tim was doing something in the laundry room, and I didn't want to know what. As it was, I would be having barbecued Phil nightmares for a long time.

I made my way to the living room and tried to pretend there wasn't an electrocuted psycho in my laundry room, that my house hadn't been trashed, and that I hadn't been arrested for murder. Oh yeah, and that I hadn't lost millions of dollars and my job. And my boyfriend. I picked a chair cushion off the floor and put it back where it belonged before flopping down on it.

What had I done to deserve such industrial grief? Okay, so I promised a bunch of dying kids three million, but other than that, my conscious was clean. Too bad my karma seemed to have developed cancer.

I could hear the sirens wailing as they came down my street, and I got up and met the police and an ambulance crew just as they were getting to my door.

"He's in the laundry room," I said, pointing to the kitchen.

They filed through, except for one officer who stayed behind to question me.

We stood in the living room while he wrote down my full name and took detailed notes as I described how we found Phil. He then excused himself and went to check on the situation in the laundry room. I flopped into my chair and waited.

About twenty minutes later, the officer returned. Rather than picking up a cushion for the other empty seat, he sat on the chair's arm so he could look down at me.

"I have a few more questions for you," he said.

"Am I going to have to buy a new washer?"

"That I don't know." He flipped open his notepad and removed his pen from his shirt pocket. "What was your relationship to the deceased?"

"I was the stalkee."

He didn't respond.

"If you'll talk to a Detective Duckett at the Clayton station, he will tell you that Phil attacked me. That's how my face got so banged up."

"And why do you believe he was stalking you?"

I explained the Palimo situation.

"The front door wasn't pried open, and the back door to the garage is still nailed shut," he said. "Any ideas how he got in?"

"He might have found my spare garage door opener when he broke in the first time."

The officer nodded and kept writing in his notepad. "We're a little confused as to how this guy fried himself. It looks like he had already cut the hose from the washer and he was in the process of running an electrical line from the overhead light. I think his plan was for you to get juiced when you came in from the garage and flipped on the light. But somehow our boy genius electrocuted himself, which doesn't make a lot of sense. Only an idiot would flip on the lights with all that water around an exposed wire."

"I don't know if I would describe Phil as the sharpest tool in the shed."

The officer paused for a moment, and then leaned closer. "Where have you been for the last twenty-four hours?"

"I was out buying a stepladder and some wire strippers so I could trick Phil into electrocuting himself in my laundry room."

"This isn't a joking matter, Ms. Connors."

"You can't even imagine."

"Please answer the question."

"I was out." I was also tired of being questioned and having uninvited men in my house.

"Is there someone who could corroborate your whereabouts?"

"You could check with the concierge at the Saint Louis County lockup."

The officer gave me one of his many blank looks. His sense of humor must have been mopped up at the last crime scene.

"I was arrested yesterday morning because a dead woman was found in the trunk of my car."

"Yep, that will do it," he said, making some more notes. "But at least it gives you a pretty tight alibi."

"Then that makes the whole thing worthwhile."

I waited while he scribbled some more.

"How long before fried Phil is out of my house?"

He didn't bother to look up. Apparently, I was less interesting when I was off the suspect list. "Not long. We're waiting for the coroner to get here."

Eventually, the police finished doing whatever it is they were doing in the laundry room, and they began to evacuate the area, taking Phil with them.

Tim found a garden hose and siphoned the water from the laundry room floor out the back window. He said there was at least an inch of water in part of the basement and that luckily the breaker box was in the dry section. I didn't care about the basement lake, there wasn't anything important down there.

While Tim put the garden hose away, I surveyed the laundry room for the first time since Phil's departure. At least I had enough clean underwear to get me through a few days until the washer could be fixed. The cops had taken Phil's toolbox with them for evidence, and someone had put the ladder away in my garage.

A severed washer hose for a stepladder? I guess that was a fair trade.

Everything in the laundry room was back to looking

like it usually did. I turned to join Tim in the garage and noticed a set of keys on the shelf by the laundry detergent. I picked them up and held them in my hand. They didn't look like Tim's keys. Phil's?

I tucked them in my pocket. If one of the cops had left them, I'm sure I'd hear about it soon, otherwise, it might be useful to have access to Phil's apartment.

I found Tim in the garage, checking the boarded-up back door. With Phil now out of the picture, I wasn't as concerned about break-ins. I figured I had statistically reached my limit.

Tim offered to help with the latest mess. I declined again, thanked him for his help, and sent him on his way.

By two o'clock, I had my condo to myself.

I climbed into my shower to boil for a while and devise a plan of action. I was losing faith in the police, especially since it seemed—even to myself—that I was in the middle of a one-woman crime wave. But more than that, I had lost nearly everything I had, and I needed to understand why. It was time to start doing something for myself.

I figured I had until my preliminary hearing on Monday to prove my innocence. According to my attorney, at the preliminary hearing the prosecution would present evidence and witnesses to justify probable cause existed to prosecute me. If by some miracle, I could prove by then who Eleanor's real killer was, the prosecution would have to drop the charges against me. Otherwise, I would get railroaded into a trial that would probably result in me having to engrave numbers on license plates for the State of Missouri.

When my fingertips reached the prune stage, I climbed out of the shower and got dressed. Since my Corolla had been impounded, I called a rental car company that delivered. A blue Escort arrived an hour later. After returning to the rental office and completing the necessary paperwork, I was off, to, of all places, the beauty salon.

The Face & Body was my spa of choice, but it usually took several weeks to get an appointment. My plan was to loiter in the lobby until the guy who did my hair took pity on me.

Surprisingly, I didn't have to loiter long.

After ten minutes, Stephen came out to see me.

"Maggie, love, I'd ask what you've been up to, but it's all over the papers."

"Stephen, please help me. I need a new look, fast."

He looked at the receptionist. "Carol, call Mrs. Grenich and tell her I have to reschedule her. If she gives you any grief, tell her to find a new stylist."

Carol turned to her computer to retrieve Mrs. Grenich's phone number.

"Thank you, Stephen. I'm so sorry to do this."

"Not a problem. That woman has been coming into my salon every month for the last six years. Every time she says, 'Stephen, I want a completely new look,' so I give her some suggestions and then she invariably says, 'No, just trim it up, instead.' She's been making me crazy and wasting my time, and this is a good excuse to get rid of her. Besides, love, I'd much rather hear the 'butt on what you've been doing. Let's get you back to the shampoo bowl, and you can tell Uncle Stephen all about your killer days."

I followed him back to the shampoo area. He gave me a black robe to slip on over my clothes and then scrubbed away at my just-shampooed hair. He tried to ask me a few questions, but with the water rushing around my ears, I couldn't hear him.

He toweled off my hair and then led me back to his station. I took a seat in his chair, and we looked at each other via the mirror.

"So, what are we doing today?"

"Whack everything off and change the color."

He tilted his head down and looked over the rim of

his wire glasses. "Are we preparing to flee the country?"

"Not a bad idea, but they confiscated my passport. I need to do some investigating, and I think it will be easier if I don't look like my perp walk photos."

He ran his fingers through my long hair. "Oh, but Maggie. This hair is so gorgeous. Are you sure?"

"It's just hair. It will grow back."

"You're absolutely right. Let's give you a complete new look." He spun my chair around so I faced him. He crunched my hair up, pulled it to the side and then bunched it back. "I think you need chic. Something with some style and not so traditional."

I nodded.

"Since you have such thick hair, let's cut it first and then color it. I'm thinking a soft, ash brown. How does that sound?"

"It sounds like you're a genius. All I ask is that I don't watch the amputation."

"How about this? I'll braid your hair before I cut it and then, with your permission, I'll send your hair to this company that makes wigs for children in chemotherapy."

"That's a great idea," I said.

Stephen kept my back to the mirror and proceeded to work his magic. Two hours later, I had a completely new look. My hair was blunt cut just below my chin. He had layered the top, with soft bangs around my forehead. The brown color made me look average and wasn't as memorable as my long, red locks were.

Now it was time to put my new look to the test.

My first stop was Kinko's. I posed for a passport photo with my head turned slightly so my black eye wasn't noticeable. While that developed and was cut down to size, I rented some computer time. My computer skills weren't that advanced, but I knew enough to open a word processing application and type the words "Press Pass" in large, bold type. I made the words about two inches wide and a half inch high. Below that I typed *St. Louis Post-Dispatch* and centered the words. Next came my new name and employment title: "Shelly Culbertson, Special Features Reporter." In smaller type below that I wrote: "This press pass is the property of the *St. Louis Post-Dispatch*. It is issued to provide this reporter journalistic access to news events. At the termination of employment, this press pass shall be immediately surrendered." I checked the Yellow Pages and typed the *Post-Dispatch*'s address and phone number at the bottom.

I had no idea what a press pass looked like, and I was assuming the people I was about to interview didn't, either. This one looked convincing.

I printed out a copy. It wasn't quite right, so I made a few changes to the type size and printed out another copy. Perfect.

My passport photo was ready, so I pasted that to the left of my press pass information. I cut the paper out and it came to about the size of a business card. Next I had skippy boy behind the counter laminate my creation and, voila! I was an official *Post-Dispatch* reporter.

It had taken less than an hour to make my pass, and I handed the kid my credit card to pay for the computer rental time, photo, and lamination, which totaled $42.70. He ran the card through the credit card terminal. It was declined.

I asked him to try again and he got the same result. Shit.

The charges for the Palimo trip must have maxed out the card.

I fished around in my wallet and dug out the necessary funds, with four dollars of it in change. He gave me my press pass, which I tucked into the front window compartment of my wallet. It was a little before six o'clock and time to begin my new life as a roving reporter by roving over to the Autumn Oaks retirement community, former home of Eleanor Cosgrove.

And, I suddenly realized, former workplace of Psycho Phil Scranton. Hmmm, that was a lot more coincidental than I liked.

The single homes in Autumn Oaks seemed to be a retirement version of Smurf Village. All the tiny homes were ranch style and looked big enough to have a kitchen, living room, and one bedroom. There must have been a sale on white, maintenance-free vinyl siding, because every home had it. Some homes had a porch peak to the left of the garage, others to the right, but otherwise there wasn't much variation. All the driveways and sidewalks had been shoveled, probably one of the services included by Autumn Oaks. Overall, the neighborhood had a sense of orderly routine, which was probably reassuring to the residents.

I drove up to Eleanor Cosgrove's home and assessed the homes on either side. The one on the left had a wooden snowman figure on the front porch and a single string of Christmas lights draped across an evergreen bush. The one on the right was dark and void of Christmas cheer.

I decided to try my luck with the dark house. I still wasn't sure what I was going to say, and knocking on the door to an empty house seemed like a good way to stall for time and work up my nerve.

I pulled into the driveway and walked to the door. I knocked three times and waited. I could do this. I was used to getting information from people I didn't know. How tough could some nice, elderly people be? Compared to some of the CEOs I dealt with? Pussycats.

I rang the doorbell and the door flew open.

"Do I know you?" the little man demanded.

"No—"

"Do we have an appointment?"

"No, the reason—"

The door slammed.

Well, that was certainly a confidence builder.

I walked back to my car with my head hanging, giving the searing wind a chance to frostbite my neck. Who was I trying to kid? I wasn't a private detective. I was an unemployed, almost broke murder suspect who owed the hospice three million dollars.

I started my car and backed out of the driveway, put the car in drive, and debated whether to pull into the driveway of the other neighboring house or to find a cliff and put myself and this Ford Escort out of our misery.

I let out a deep sigh and decided it was worth risking a little more humiliation if I could find some evidence linking someone else to Eleanor's death. I pulled into the driveway of the other house and made my way to the front door. I knocked and then braced myself for battle. From inside, I could hear a shuffling noise, then the door opened.

"Lordy, child, it's cold enough to freeze the balls off a pool table. Get yourself in here before you catch your death," the woman said.

She looked to be in her eighties or nineties. She stood by her walker with her mouth in a wide smile. Her voice was heavy with a Southern drawl, and she shared Eleanor's gift for memorable phrases.

Things were looking up.

She moved back to give me room to enter. I stepped inside the compact home and was greeted by what I can only describe as old-person smell. A combination of overwaxed kitchen floor, Ben-Gay, disinfectants, and something else I couldn't quite decipher. While she bolted the door closed behind us, my eyes adjusted to the dim lighting.

"Hello, my name is Shelly Culbertson, and I'm a reporter with the *St. Louis Post-Dispatch*." I showed her my newly created press credentials. "I'm doing a profile piece on Eleanor Cosgrove, and I was wondering if I you had a few minutes to talk with me."

"Sure, sure. I just finished my dinner and was sitting around watching my toenails grow. Come in, come in."

I walked into the living room, with her doddering along behind me.

"What on earth happened to you?" she said. "You look like you've been run down, run over, and wrung out."

I rubbed my cheekbone. "Traffic accident. I'm sorry, I didn't get your name."

"Ida Parker. Here, sit a spell."

I sat on a floral couch whose color combination hadn't been popular since the sixties. She dropped into a gold velvet chair that swiveled back and forth as well as 360 degrees. From the look of the worn spot on the front of the chair, it was Ida's seat of choice.

"From everyone I've talked to," I said, "Eleanor Cosgrove was a wonderful woman. Were you very close?"

"Like two fleas on a frozen dog."

"I'm not sure I know what that means."

"We were as close as can be. Eleanor was my sister-in-law."

"I didn't know that." I scribbled that down on my notepad—not that I didn't know, but that Ida was Eleanor's sister-in-law. Odd analogies evidently ran in the family.

"Yeah, we knew each other since Moby-Dick was a minnow."

"That sounds like a long time. Did she know anyone who would want to harm her?"

Ida leaned back in her chair and shook her head sadly. "Eleanor was somebody that would lend you a hand if you had two broken arms and your nose needed pickin'."

Where was my *Hee Haw*-to-English translation guide when I needed it?

"No one ever had a complaint against that old gal.

I'm sure going to miss her." Ida pulled out a tissue that had been tucked in her sleeve by her wrist and dabbed at her eyes. "We've been through some terrible times together. Betcha didn't know our husbands were killed within a few days of each other."

I shook my head.

"Eleanor and J. J.—"

"J. J.?"

"Jonah John. He was Eleanor's husband."

"Jonah is kind of an odd name."

"That's why he went by J. J. His momma named him Jonah because when she was pregnant with him, she felt like she had swallowed a whale."

I knew from my few years of Sunday school that Jonah wasn't the whale's name, but arguing that now seemed rather pointless. "I'm sorry I interrupted you. You were about to say that Eleanor and J. J. . . ."

"Oh yeah, they were down visiting Earl and I— that's back when we lived in Memphis. Anyhow, the boys were on their way from the grocery store—we were out of cornstarch—and a drunk driver hit them head-on. J. J. was killed instantly. My Earl walked away with just a few bruises. After J. J.'s funeral, everyone gathered at our house, and we ended up running out of beer. So we sent Earl to get some. He was going a might too fast when he went over the top of a hill and didn't have time to avoid a fat cow that had wandered into the road. Next thing you know, my Earl's dead, too."

"How awful. How old were the men when they died?"

"I think J. J. was about forty-seven, and my Earl was forty-two."

"Did you or Eleanor have any children?"

"Nope, both of us never got around to it. Fact is, Eleanor didn't have any other family and not much money, so after the accident, she moved down to Tennessee to help me work the farm." She paused and looked down at the carpet. "Those were some hard years."

"How did you both end up in a retirement village in Saint Louis?"

"Well, 'long about ten years later, we were having some money troubles. The weather hadn't been kind to our crops, and the bank wanted to take our farm. About that time, this attorney who had been pestering us about J. J.'s death shows up with a hundred thousand dollars as some sort of settlement. The sheriff finally anted up, and it nearly flipped our skirts over our heads!"

"What did the sheriff have to do with this?"

"His reckless kid was the drunk driver that killed J. J., and the kid wasn't even legal drinking age."

"Eleanor didn't know they were prosecuting the son?"

"Eleanor, God bless her soul, didn't keep much of a mind when it came to business things."

"What did Eleanor do with the money?"

"Well, that old girl says to me we should take the money and get ourselves some retirement villas where we wouldn't have to do no yard work ever again."

I made a few more notes. "How did you pick Saint Louis to retire to if you were from the South?"

"I was from the South, but Eleanor grew up in the Midwest. Her and J. J. spent a few years in Chicago before he transferred to Saint Louis. J. J. was a salesperson for a big machine company that sold, oh, I forget what they called it, I think it was computer storage systems. This was back when computers were just getting started."

"Did you know many of her friends?"

"We've had a group of twelve women who played bunko every week for the last six or seven years." She paused and gripped her tissue tighter. I noticed that arthritis had taken its toll on her swollen knuckles.

"It's just not going to be the same bunko game without Eleanor."

I looked down at the floor. I felt guilty for putting this poor woman through my questioning, but not guilty enough to stop.

For the next hour and a half, Ida droned on about her adventures with Eleanor. From their hairstylist who scrubbed too hard when she shampooed, to the best restaurants for senior discounts, I heard it. All this chatting was making two more deaths quite imminent: mine from boredom and Ida's from old age. I needed to interrupt this hobble down memory lane to get some answers to the questions I had. I didn't have a graceful way to redirect the conversation, so I just jumped into the middle of her hip replacement story.

"Speaking of doctors, do you know if Eleanor ever mentioned a scientist by the name of Richard Craig?"

Ida leaned toward me. "Why would she know a scientist?"

I shrugged. "No reason."

"Lordy child, I'm sure you have a reason for asking such a bizarre question."

I guess I didn't have Barbara Walters's smooth technique. "This man was responsible for the deaths of several elderly women," I lied.

"Well, Eleanor didn't know him, because I knew everyone she did."

So that was a dead end. "What about Phil Scranton?"

"Oh, he was the dearest man. I understand he was electrocuted trying to fix some woman's lights."

Fix, put out, whatever. "Did you and Eleanor spend much time with Phil?"

"He was one of the only maintenance men who would actually come when you asked him to and fix what you needed. And he fixed it right the first time. Some of the young kids they hire around here are as sharp as a pound of liver."

Phil a skilled craftsman? The man who accidentally fried himself?

"If you want to know more about Phil, you should talk with the Alzheimer's patients in the main building. They loved him to pieces." Ida shook her head sadly. "But they could also tell you they never heard of him— if you know what I mean."

"Do you remember what the last thing was Phil fixed for Eleanor?"

Ida let out a long sigh and looked to the corner of the ceiling for help. "I'm not sure. It might have been the toilet in her bedroom." She drew out her words, trying to coax a memory forward. "I think it was leaking or running, or maybe both. I remember there was some complication, and it took quite a while to get it fixed."

The toilet. I'm sure there was a good, detective follow-up question I should pursue, but I had no idea what that was. "I know I'm jumping around a bit, but was Eleanor much of a coupon clipper?"

"No, she canceled her newspaper subscription. Said the news was too depressing."

"So money wasn't a problem for her?"

"No more or less than for the rest of us."

"A hundred thousand wouldn't go far. How did she pay for both villas and her bills?"

Ida leaned back and crossed her arms. "In addition to the settlement, there was J. J.'s life insurance money and the proceeds from the sale of Eleanor's house. We didn't get much for the farm. That pretty much paid for the villas, and our social security covered our monthly bills." She paused for a few moments. "Perhaps it's time to cool these chairs a spell."

She pulled herself up, and I guessed that was my cue to get going. I thanked her for her time and wished her a happy New Year before leaving.

I'd spent two hours with Ida, and all I had to show for it was the accumulated detail of everyday life in an old folks' home. Detail that made me want to die young more than ever. No connection between Eleanor and Richard. No connection between Eleanor and Phil, except that he'd fixed her toilet. And fixed it well, which seemed out of character, given what I knew of him.

And what was the connection between Eleanor and me, except that she had stopped by and almost opened a Hamilton account? I couldn't believe she was a victim of random violence and my Toyota was only a convenient place to stash her body. There had to be a thread tying it all together. But what?

I checked my watch. It was almost eight o'clock. I had to hurry. I had a date to be locked in a room full of trash.

Chapter 14

One of the benefits of being a compulsive worka-holic rather than enjoying a real life was that I knew the cleaning crew would start their Hamilton office disinfection at about eight o'clock. They took a less-than-methodical approach to ridding Hamilton of the day's discarded information and other assorted trash, followed by a halfhearted effort of dusting and vacuuming. The lead cleaner, who probably had a more official title I wasn't aware of, would unlock locked doors as the crew moved through the offices. These doors were eventually relocked before the cleaning crew left. To clean the Hamilton office took five cleaners about two to three hours, depending on the day of the week; for some reason, cleaning never seemed to take as long on Friday nights.

There was a room just behind the Hamilton mail room, about ten by eighteen feet, with no windows and no furniture. It was kept locked during the day and was only opened by the cleaners, who filled it with trash bag after trash bag of documents destined for shredding. These account papers, client statements, and other confidential information waited patiently for the shredding company that came to pick them up. At that time, with the drama of Brink's security guards, the shredders would come in, remove all the bags, give the receptionist a receipt, and disappear with glimpses or entire financial profiles of Hamilton's 32,000 clients.

I needed to get myself locked into the shredding room.

I left my coat and purse in my car and walked to Hamilton's front doors. From outside I could tell the lights were on and the cleaning crew was working—well, what they called working.

Luckily, my talent for losing keys, wallets, and purses—and then finding them at a later date—meant I had accumulated about four or five keys to the Hamilton offices. My boss had relieved me of the office key on my key ring and apparently the spare I kept at the bottom of my purse, but it hadn't taken long for me to find a backup office key at my condo. I used that key to unlock the front door and slipped inside.

It would have been nice to saunter through the halls with a Pepsi in my hand and pretend I was a broker on a break from an evening of paperwork. But since I was no longer a Hamilton employee and not allowed on Hamilton property, I didn't want to risk running into one of my former coworkers. Instead, I made my way as fast as my little heels could carry me to the mail room. I didn't see any cleaning people or any of my coworkers. I was feeling pretty happy with my undetected trespassing ability when I turned to go into the mail room and got run over by a trash can being pushed by a trash guy.

"I'm so sorry," he said.

He quickly uprighted the can and then darted around to help me to my feet.

"What'd you do to your face?" he said, with all the tact of a trashman.

"I got run over by a trash can a few days ago," I said and smiled.

"You must be getting good at it."

I let him pass and then continued to the back of the mail room on the pretense of looking for some Hamilton letterhead. Once at the back, I listened to see if anyone was coming. Everything was quiet. I took a deep breath and went in through the open door to the shredded paper room. I dashed to the back of the room, feeling like a secret agent who could be shot in the back at any moment. The reality was that the cleaning crew probably wouldn't have cared less what I did in there as long as I didn't create a mess they would need to clean up.

I made a quick fort out of trash bags and tucked myself inside. When my breathing calmed down and the boredom of sitting among trash replaced the thrill of breaking in, I didn't feel like such a secret agent anymore.

Then it was time to wait.

And wait.

And wait.

A professional trash room breaker-inner probably would have had the foresight to bring some reading material to pass the time, but I was a rookie. So I spent the next hour reading and rereading the same client statements showing through the clear plastic trash bags. I determined that Ed Weinstein, whoever he was, had suffered the biggest portfolio drop, losing $182,000 compared to his account value thirty days ago. Poor guy. Then I remembered the thrashing my own account had suffered and decided old Ed could suck it up.

I looked at my watch again. Not much had changed since the last time. The little hand was still on the nine and the big hand had moved a few tick marks to the right of the number four. I was a compulsive multitasker, and without anything to occupy my mind, I felt like my gray matter was going to seep out of my cranium and ooze onto the linoleum floor.

Another hour dragged by like a load of bricks across my last nerve. I began to think about the possibility that the cleaning crew was long gone and had forgotten to lock the door to the paper shedding room. Then I began thinking that perhaps the building was on fire and the crew had abandoned ship, leaving me to go up in flames with all this trash. I was pretty well consumed with this paranoid delusion when I heard a trash cart bump against a doorway. I sucked in my breath, and a few seconds later, the light to my room was turned off.

Just as I heard the door about to close, my cell phone rang.

I grabbed at my pants pocket, pulled the noisemaker out, and shut it off as fast as I could, but not before two full rings escaped.

The lights went back on.

"What are you doing?" said a female voice from out in the mail room somewhere.

"I heard a cell phone go off in here," said another voice, coming from the doorway to the shredded paper room.

"Who gives a shit if some dumb-ass broker threw his phone away? We're outta here."

The body belonging to the closer voice must have agreed, because the lights went back off, the door closed, and I heard the scraping of the deadbolt being locked.

Alone, at last, in a dark room filled with trash.

I stayed in my hiding spot for a while to make sure one of the cleaning crew didn't decide to come back and investigate the cell phone noise. While I waited, I checked my cell phone to see who had called.

Malcolm Vandenberg had left a message inviting me out for a late-night drink, no doubt hoping for a replay of Sunday night. I still wasn't sure what had happened the first time around and didn't feel the need for a repeat performance. I left the phone on but turned it to vibrate.

I checked my watch. Ten minutes had passed. Time to go to work.

I turned on my pocket flashlight, made my way back to the door to examine the door frame. This room had originally been used to house client deposits, so the door sealed solid against the frame. No one outside would see any light creeping out from under or around the door. It also meant I didn't have to search this whole room of trash using my flashlight. I flipped on the overhead light.

The other good news was an inside release to the deadbolt, obviously installed with foresight to protect Hamilton employees from themselves. Now I could stop worrying about being trapped in this room and sucking the last remaining hint of oxygen into my burning lungs before I suffocated to death. Not that I was obsessing.

Time to focus on the task at hand. I had put Eleanor's driver's license in my shred box Tuesday afternoon, which meant the cleaners would have dropped it in here Tuesday night, making it part of the oldest trash in the room. It would make sense to me that the oldest trash would be in the farthest corner.

I grabbed a bag from the back corner and emptied it on the floor. From the dates on the correspondence, this bag looked like it came in here sometime Friday. So much for my theory on chronological stratification of trash.

I sorted through bag after bag. To maintain some sense of order, after I emptied the first bag of trash on the floor, I filled that empty bag with the trash from the next bag. I was working on my eighth industrial-size bag of trash when it became obvious to me that my coworkers weren't very discriminating in deciding what needed to be shredded. There were old coffee cups and copies of the *Wall Street Journal*—typical items that would threaten national security and client confidentiality—in every trash bag to be shredded. The stale coffee that soaked through the papers or spilled on me made the whole scavenger hunt that much more enjoyable.

My phone vibrated, and I gladly took a break to answer it. The caller ID came up as a private name, private number. Probably Tim.

"Hi Maggie, I'm just checking in on you," Tim said.

I sat down on one of the trash bags and rubbed the back of my neck. "I'm doing okay."

"What are you doing?"

"Sorting through some old paperwork."

"I thought you'd be deep into the search for Eleanor's killer by now."

I was deep, all right, but I wasn't sure in what. "Well, actually, I am following up on a few leads."

"Just promise me one thing," he said.

"And that would be?"

"I know you're under a lot of pressure right now. I talked with Stacy earlier, and she told me about you getting fired. Please promise me you won't do anything stupid to get yourself into more trouble."

"I'm not sure that's possible, but what did you have in mind?"

"I'm serious. Please don't break any laws while you're out on bail. You can't help yourself if you get tossed back in prison, and you look awful in orange."

"I'll take that into consideration."

"That's not quite the commitment I was looking for."

"I didn't think you were interested in commitments," I said.

"Maggie, my boss has suggested to me that it would be a bad career move for me to get involved with your situation. I've decided what I do on my own time is my own business. But I can't help you if you break any laws. Understand?"

I let out a deep sigh. "I understand."

"How about if we get together tomorrow to discuss everything? I've got an annual firearms class that will run late, but we could meet afterwards."

I agreed and said good-bye.

I tucked the phone back in my pocket and continued my search, only now I felt more guilty and paranoid.

Sometime before midnight, I lifted a stack of familiar client statements and found the driver's license of Eleanor Cosgrove resting innocently and pristinely below. I picked it up and scrutinized it. Other than not having Eleanor's picture, it looked perfectly normal to me. Hopefully, a careful inspection at home would reveal some clue as to where it came from, who was looking for it, and why.

It was time to get out of here. I closed the opened trash bags and tidied up. Everything was back to looking pretty much the way I had found it.

I cracked the door open to take a peek. The office was dark, and I didn't hear anyone. I stepped into the mail room and closed the door to the paper shredding room behind me. I didn't have a way to lock it. Maybe someone would notice, maybe not. If they did, it was unlikely anyone would think it was crime-related, and more likely they would blame the cleaners.

I tiptoed to the front door and made my exit. Outside, the weather had gotten serious about being cold, and I regretted leaving my warm coat in my car. I hurried to the parking garage. Once in my car, I started the motor, flipped the heat on full blast, turned on the dome light, and examined my ill-gotten gains.

It looked like an ordinary driver's license. Date of birth, social security number, expiration date—all looked in order. Except for that awful picture.

That awful, familiar picture. It certainly didn't look like Eleanor, but it did look like someone I'd seen around lately. I held it closer to the light. Maybe if the hair was different? I put my finger over the woman's gray hair, which was done up in a bun, and recognition hit like a truck.

It was Phil Scranton, in drag.

The makeover was incredible, but there was no camouflaging that big, flat nose.

Okay, none of this made any sense, but it had to mean something. I really should take it to the police, but that would involve explaining where I'd gotten it. And Tim was right; committing a crime while out on bail was not smart. At least, not if you got caught.

And with my luck, even if I did go to the police and they didn't mind how I got the license, there was a good chance they would use this evidence to strengthen their case against me. After all, Phil was killed in my laundry room and Eleanor was found in my trunk. I'm sure the police would find a way to use this license to establish a motive for me killing both of them.

No, it seemed I was on my own here.

I pulled out of the garage. I had two more B and Es on my schedule.

Chapter 15

My next stop was at my good friend Phil's. Since he had thoughtfully left his keys for me, I didn't think this technically qualified as breaking in.

His apartment was located in a complex of about a dozen buildings, all four stories. The wood exteriors had turned a dull gray, and the whole complex looked like it needed a cash infusion and remodeling. I drove around to the back of his building to a parking lot filled with domestic pickups, a few old Mustangs, and a sprinkle of rusted jalopies for added flavor. This was a working-class neighborhood, and most of the occupants were sound asleep, waiting for alarm clocks that would shrill before dawn and signal the start of another shift. I pulled into his spot marked #45A. I took it as a good sign that his space was empty.

The snow removal wasn't as meticulous as the job at Autumn Oaks. There were piles of it everywhere. I crunched through the wet stuff to the front door and was grateful the entrance didn't require a pass code. I would have been surprised if it did. This wasn't the kind of community that needed protection from an aberrant manual laborer looking to relieve an executive family of their wealth. If Phil was any indication of the resident type, these apartments were where the aberrant manual laborers lived.

The paint on the bottom of the front door had disappeared, and by the looks of the splintered corner the popular way to open the door was to kick it. I opted to use the doorknob and pushed it open. The metal tension bracket at the top of the door was broken, and the door fought against opening. That probably explained all the kicking.

Inside, a single, bare lightbulb illuminated the dirty, brown carpet in the hallway. Even the areas next to the wall, which probably didn't see much foot traffic, were grime covered. To overcome my bug paranoia, I convinced myself the cold weather had frozen the cockroach population. As breaking and enterings go, I much preferred Richard Craig's place over Phil's.

I pushed the button for the elevator and was happy not to find a drunken or dead body in the compartment when the doors opened. There was some kind of sticky goo that looked like old bubble gum all over the elevator buttons. I took off my shoe and used the heel to push the number four button.

The hallway on the fourth floor was comparable to the entrance. I followed the numbered doors until I found #45A. I rang the doorbell and waited. No answer. I rang again and knocked, just to make sure.

I stuck my key in and was relieved that it fit but a little unhappy, too, since it meant I now needed to go in. I opened the door, found the light switch, and whisper-yelled, "Hi Phil, I'm home."

No one answered.

The living room and kitchen were combined, and empty. I walked to the door that probably led to the bedroom. "Phil, are you home? I'm back from skiing."

Still no answer. I turned on the light to the bedroom and let out a sigh of relief when I saw that the unmade bed was empty as well. The bathroom was dark, but I turned the light on and looked in the shower and saw more caked dirt than I thought was possible in something that saw water every day. Or maybe it didn't see that much water, who knew? Either way, the shower was empty. There didn't seem to be any evil, psycho twin brothers, relatives, or girlfriends sitting around sharpening axes.

I went back to the front door, put the deadbolt across, and surveyed the room again. If someone came in, there weren't any other escape options, because I wouldn't be able to go down the icy fire escape without killing myself. I started to feel like a trapped rat.

It was time to begin my search.

From the job the police had done on my condo, I got an indirect education on how to search for stuff. Their method seemed to have been to start at one point and work their way around the room, opening everything, looking in anything, and tossing what they could over their shoulders once it proved useless. I didn't plan on being as destructive, but I was going to be as thorough.

I started in the kitchen. I checked the freezer and even emptied the ice cube containers into the kitchen sink. I'm not sure what I was looking for, but frozen ice cubes would be a great way to hide diamonds. Then again, if Phil had diamonds in his ice cubes, he probably wouldn't be living in this kind of dump.

The refrigerator had cans of Schlitz beer and all sorts of Styrofoam containers that had managed to grow green mold on the contents despite the temperature. After the first container of furry burritos, I wasn't as thorough searching the rest.

Next it was onto the cupboards and the pantry. Nothing much there to search and nothing to find.

I found his mail on a countertop. There were overdue subscription notices to *Maxim* and *Hustler*. Overdue bills from all the utility companies except his cable bill, which had been paid on time. And a credit card statement showing a $4,500 balance. Apparently, he really had put every cent he had into Palimo. I reviewed the itemized charges from the past month. Nothing enlightening. A couple of bars, lots of nine hundred number charges, and some gas. I tucked the credit card bill into my pocket for future reference.

His telephone didn't have a caller ID display, and his phone service had been disconnected.

In the living room was a vinyl sofa that might originally have been white. The cushions were covered with wadded-up White Castle hamburger wrappers, and there was an empty bag of potato chips on the floor. I checked under the cushions; behind and under the sofa; in the side tables, under the side tables; in, around, and under the television; behind the curtains. Nothing. Then I checked the sides of the carpet for lose edges to see if something was tucked underneath. Again, nothing.

I stood and looked around, taking in the squalor in its entirety. How could anyone who lived in a dump like this ever be a decent handyman? Then I noticed a couple of things. Someone—probably a creditor—had once kicked in the door. The wall next to the deadbolt had been neatly patched. The avocado-colored lamp had been rewired. A broken slat on a kitchen chair had been splinted. Evidently, Phil was good at what he did but just didn't care about hygiene. A sort of idiot savant, emphasis on the *idiot*.

On to the bedroom. I held my breath and looked under the mattress. Nothing there. I used my foot to poke through the dirty clothes that had accumulated around the bed. My only discovery was that Phil wore really big underwear and must not have had many pairs, because they looked like he lived in them for a while before dropping them on the floor.

The dresser drawers were basically empty, which made sense since most of the clothes seemed to be on the floor. A search of the bathroom didn't turn up anything else of value unless you counted a pile of men's magazines.

I walked back to the living room and surveyed the apartment again.

There was no computer or photography equipment to make fake IDs. There were no hate letters to or about Eleanor. In fact, there wasn't a reference to Eleanor anywhere in the place. No bloody clothes. No bloody blunt objects. No weapons. There was nothing to identify this guy as Eleanor's killer.

From the looks of things, he went to work, picked up takeout on the way home, ate in front of the TV, took a dump in the bathroom while enjoying some stimulating reading—or at least, some stimulating picture-viewing—avoided the shower, and then dropped his clothes on the bedroom floor and flopped into bed.

This had been a complete waste of time.

I reached to unlock the front door deadbolt when pounding from the other side stopped me cold.

"Whoever's in there, come on out."

I remained frozen and didn't say a word. The pounding seemed to reverberate off the door and straight through my heart, which was beating at the rate of a cricket, assuming, of course, that crickets have fast heartbeats.

"I know you're in there, and I'm not going anywhere. You might as well come on out and pay up."

Pay up? Now what?

I fumbled in my purse for my mace and tucked the small cylinder in my hand. I shoved the lock back and opened the door right as a man was preparing to pound on the door again.

He looked to be in this late thirties. Oblivious to the weather, he wore a muscle T-shirt covered with brown and orange stains. His worn shirt revealed a mass of black chest hair, which comically contrasted with his balding head. He stepped inside the apartment, and I backed up. I pretended not to notice the threatening stance he took.

He leaned his face into mine. "Who the hell are you?" he said. His breath had the distinct smell of someone who had just eaten a bag of Doritos.

"Who the hell are you?" I replied.

"I'm the super for the building. Now, once again, who the hell are you?"

"My name's Debbie Dean. I'm looking for Phil."

"Phil is no longer with us, but he owes me money."

"Where'd he go?" I said, acting as stupid and non-threatening as I could.

"To the big ice rink in the sky."

I put my hand to my mouth in shock. "He died?"

"He kicked owing me three months' back rent. How 'bout you make good on that for him?"

My knee was positioned so that a quick thrust upward would find his nuts, and I still had the mace hidden in my hand. But I wasn't especially confident of my ability to pull off either move, so instead I decided to take a commiserating approach.

"That dumb-ass drunk owes me two thousand dollars in hospital bills plus another fifteen hundred for the damage he did to my car." I gently tapped my still-swollen eye as proof of my claim. "I guess he screwed us both."

The hostile man laughed, and the tension in the room eased.

I moved past him into the doorway, and he didn't try to stop me.

"Does he have any relatives I can sue?" I said.

"None that I've been able to find."

I nodded in shared disappointment. A horn honked from somewhere outside.

"Well, Larry's waiting for me, so I better run."

"You're not going to run very fast with those shoes."
He laughed, and a shiver went up my spine.

"Good point. I'd better be going." I turned and
didn't look back. I went to the elevator and was glad
to find it waiting at the fourth floor. I got on and
stabbed through the gum goo to the main floor, and
the doors closed without another sign of the hairy, bald
man.

Outside, I almost wiped out when my right shoe
found the center of an ice patch. I regained control and
basically skated back to my car. I got inside and hit
the automatic door locks and then sped out of the complex. I got back on the highway and slowly eased my
speed down from seventy-five to the speed limit. Once
I was sure I didn't have a new psychopath following
me, I took the Sunset Hills exit and pulled into a well-
lit 7-Eleven parking lot. I put the car in park and waited
for my adrenaline to slow.

This detective work was a lot of work. That
wouldn't be bad if I was coming up with something,
but so far, all I had were no answers and new questions.

I stared at the digital clock in the car. It was almost
two in the morning. I should probably go home and
get some sleep, but I was so pumped up I knew I would
end up staring at a dark ceiling.

I put the car in reverse and left the parking lot. Time
for my last breaking and entering of the day, which
would actually require some breaking. But first I
needed to stop at home for a change of clothing and
some supplies.

Chapter **16**

At two-thirty, I was back at Autumn Oaks. I drove past Eleanor Cosgrove's home. There weren't any lights on, naturally. Ida's house and the rest of the neighboring houses were dark as well. I circled around and drove past Eleanor's again for another look, parked my car a few houses down and turned off my lights. I cracked the windows a bit and listened.

Nothing.

No barking dogs because they probably weren't allowed in the community. No drunk teenagers speeding home after curfew because they weren't allowed in the community either. Everyone seemed to have finished watching Jay's monologue and tucked themselves in their beds. My guess was that the majority of the hearing aids had been turned off for the night.

I turned off the interior light switch before I opened my door. I wore black sweats, a black coat, and black gloves. My snow boots were a dark green, but I was hoping no one would notice the fashion faux pas. Before I left my car, I packed the front and back license plates with snow. It wasn't as professional as stealing a getaway car, but I was proud of myself for thinking to do it.

I was ready to jeopardize my bail again.

I ambled back down the street to Eleanor's house. In my enormous purse I carried—courtesy of Tim—my newly acquired, high-tech breaking and entering tool: a hammer. This delicate instrument was accompanied by a flashlight, a screwdriver, duct tape, and other burglary necessities such as tampons, lipstick, and my video rental card. I still had my mace and my cell phone in my coat pocket.

I left the snow-plowed streets and crunched my way around to the back of Eleanor's house. The snow had melted some, but it was still about six inches deep on the side of the garage. The roof probably shaded this part of the yard from the daytime sun, allowing the snow to linger. The moon was high in the sky, and in the silence of the night I could hear the occasional sound of ice melting off the garage gutters and hitting the drain spouts. I hoped my footprints would also be melted by morning.

When I reached the back door, I stopped to catch my breath and wait for my courage to build. I surveyed Eleanor's backyard. Her home backed to a common area surrounded by about a dozen houses. I hoped everyone was sleeping soundly, enjoying post-Christmas visions of sugar plums, or at least the melodic sound of their teeth fizzing in the glass next to them.

I took the duct tape out of my purse and taped long strips across the back window. Next I grabbed the hammer out of my purse and tapped the back door's window. It made a soft thud against the cushion of the tape, but the window didn't break. I gritted my teeth and swung harder. The sound of splintering glass shattered the silence, and the middle chunk of the window fell onto the floor inside. I held my breath and waited for a helicopter to appear overhead with a searchlight.

Everything remained peacefully quiet.

I reached my arm in to unlock the door.

Problem.

There was a deadbolt lock that required a key, and there was no way I could climb in the small window without cutting myself to pieces.

Time for Plan B, which was to come up with a Plan C.

Beside the back door was a walk-out bay window. I looked around one more time for signs of anyone stirring, but all remained quiet. I applied my duct tape to that window, gritted my teeth again, and swung my hammer.

More large pieces of taped glass fell inside Eleanor's home, and the sound seemed to echo back and forth across the open area. I couldn't imagine how loud the noise would have been if I hadn't used the tape. I got set to run as soon as a light came on.

Nothing. Didn't this place have any security?

I used the hammer to knock out the jagged edges of glass that remained around the window framing. When I was done, I had created a nice little opening that I could easily get through.

Inside, I was met by the fragrance of cinnamon. I turned on my flashlight and took a look around. The home was impeccably clean, except for all the broken glass.

I went first to the telephone in the kitchen and hoped for a caller ID display. No luck. I hit the last number redial and got a recording that the West County library branch was closed for the evening. I searched the desk area in the kitchen for old mail, new mail, address books, anything that might hint of a connection between Eleanor and Phil. There was stuff in the desk; a Yellow Pages, some coupons, and old AARP magazines. But nothing personal.

I searched the rest of the house and found absolutely nothing of use. There was no checkbook, no tax returns, no old letters. It was as if somebody lived in the house but there was no evidence of who.

What I did find was a zillion of those old-fashioned dolls, the kind they sell on the cable shopping network. These creepy dolls were everywhere. On bookshelves. On nightstands. On the counter in the bathroom. Everywhere I searched were sets of beady little eyes staring blankly at me. It was unnerving.

I walked back to the kitchen and leaned against the counter. My detective ability sucked. Why did it look so easy on TV?

Maybe the police had already taken all the personal papers. Though if they did, they'd done a much neater search job here than they had at my place.

I flashed my light around the kitchen to see if I had missed anything. The light reflected off the broken glass on the floor. Maybe I should sweep it up before I left. It seemed disrespectful to leave such a mess. I decided I would do another walk through the house and then begin cleanup.

In the living room, my flashlight found the edge of a manila envelope sticking out slightly from the top of the bookcase. I hadn't seen it before.

I tried to pull it down, but I was too short. I stepped on the bottom shelf and reached up for it. I was still a few inches shy. I stretched as far as I could. My fingers brushed the envelope. I tapped at it, easing it out on the shelf until it tilted and dropped to the floor.

The bookcase came with it.

I fell backward and landed on my back, the contents from the bookcase pummeling me. Then the thick oak shelves landed on top of the books and dolls, which were on top of me.

I lay there for a moment to catch my breath. Then I wiggled my hand down to my side and pulled out *Gone With the Wind*, which was jabbing into my ribs.

I took a deep breath and pushed up on the shelves.

Nothing happened.

I tried several more times with the same results. I was at the wrong angle to get any leverage to maneuver this thing off of me.

Would someone please cue the serial killer?

For the next ten minutes, I struggled in vain to get the bookcase off. The only thing I was accomplishing was a hernia, on top of my other problems.

It was time to call for help.

I reviewed the list of possible rescuers, which took all of two seconds. My two girlfriends were still on vacation, and it didn't seem appropriate to call any of my close clients. Stacy's home number was unlisted, and I couldn't remember what it was. My only choice was the man I had promised I wouldn't do something like this.

I managed to get the phone out of my pocket and dialed Tim's number. As the call rang, I silently prayed that whoever he was dating New Year's Eve wasn't about to pick up the phone.

"Gallen," he said.

I couldn't tell from his voice whether he had been sleeping or cleaning his gun.

"Tim, it's Maggie. Are you alone?"

He paused. "Are you calling in the middle of the night to check on my love life?"

"Well . . . no. I've got a small problem and I need some help."

"What's wrong?" The edge in his voice remained.

"I'm stuck under a bookcase, and I can't get up."

"Wasn't that a commercial from the seventies?"

"This isn't funny. I need help."

"Fine. I'll be over."

"That's . . . part of my problem. I'm not at home."

Another pause. "Do I want to hear where you are?"

"Eleanor Cosgrove's house."

"I'm going back to bed."

"Please, Tim, I don't know who else to call."

"Let me get this straight. I'll assume you broke into Eleanor's house, since a dead woman doesn't often invite visitors over for a late-night cup of coffee. And in the process of unlawfully searching her house, you managed to pull a bookcase over on yourself. Or did Eleanor's ghost push the bookcase on you? You know what? It doesn't matter. Either way, you promised me you would not do anything stupid. You promised, Maggie."

"So, are you just going to leave me here?"

There was a long pause.

"Help is on the way," he said and hung up the phone.

I lay there and worked on my apology speech. A cuckoo clock sounded for the third time to let me know forty-five minutes had passed. I revised my apology speech to include some sarcasm for making me wait. Fifteen minutes later, there was another cuckoo, and I lightened the apology and added indignation. After all, he hadn't even asked if I was hurt. What if I had internal bleeding and was hemorrhaging to death? Another cuckoo, and I dumped the apology speech and replaced it with a hostile soliloquy.

Over my shoulder I spotted the manila envelope I had been trying to reach. I contorted my right arm and was able to reach it and open it one-handed. It was filled with cooking recipes.

With renewed aggravation, I was polishing the finer points of my speech for Tim, when red lights flashed around the living room walls. I craned my neck to see that the lights were coming in through the bay window. Tim's car didn't have flashing red lights, which meant there must be a patrol car parked in the driveway.

Chapter 17

There was a knock on the front door.

"Police, open up."

I didn't move. Didn't say a word. Everything was quiet except for my heart, which was beating out of my chest.

The flashing red lights stopped.

Maybe they were going away. I closed my eyes and prayed to Saint Ignoria, Patron Saint of Delusions.

"This is the police. Please come out with your hands up." It was a man's voice, coming from the kitchen window I had broken.

I stayed where I was. I assumed I wasn't violating a police order if I wasn't physically capable of following it.

"This is your last chance. Come out now with your hands up."

I continued my impression of driftwood. Maybe petrified wood would be more accurate.

Next I heard pieces of glass breaking as someone

came in through my broken window. I could see a flashlight moving around the kitchen, and then it slowly worked its way into the living room, followed by the officer who was holding it. The light hit my eyes and I squinted to see who was going to determine my demise.

"Maggie Connors?"

"Yes," I said and closed my eyes.

"Are you hurt?"

"No, I don't think so."

"Do you have any weapons?"

"I have some mace in my pocket. Does that count?"

"That counts."

I waited for him to remove the bookcase and put me in shackles, but instead of coming closer, he remained in the doorway.

"We have two broken windows," he said. "One is a window in the back door, the other is part of a walk-out bay."

"Are you talking to me?" I said.

He didn't answer and walked back into the kitchen. I realized he was talking on a cell phone, but I couldn't hear what else he was saying. A few moments later, he came back into the living room.

"Do you have any personal belongings here?"

"My purse is in the kitchen."

I listened in the dark as he returned to the kitchen. I could hear the jingle of my car keys as he took them out of my purse. This was followed by the sound of him stepping on broken glass and going back out the window.

Had I just been robbed by the police?

I waited in the darkness in utter confusion. In my purse was Eleanor's duplicate license. If the cop stole my purse, how exactly would I file a complaint to get it back?

Another cuckoo interval passed, and then the cop returned.

"I assume you know that breaking and entering someone's house is a violation of your bail and grounds for reincarceration."

I began to sob. Of course I knew that. It had been all I had thought about. How the hell was I going to prove my innocence sitting in a jail cell? My life was officially over. Why couldn't this bookcase have snapped my neck when it fell? It seemed I couldn't do anything right anymore.

"But I guess before I can book you, we need to unbookcase you," he said.

Just what I needed. Police humor.

"Ms. Connors, I'm going to lift this bookcase off of you. When I do, I want you to remain on the floor, and don't move a muscle until I tell you to. If I see you move, then I'll drop the bookcase back on top of you. Are we clear?"

I meant to say, "Clear," but the stress of my situation caused the word to stick in my throat and it came out more like "Beer." Apparently, he understood my meaning because he proceeded to upright the bookcase.

I stayed right where I was, although some of the books shifted around a bit.

His flashlight had been tucked in his back pocket, and he pulled that out and shined it in my face. "Okay, now I want you to get up slowly. No sudden moves."

"I really don't think I'm capable of sudden moves. That bookcase hit me pretty hard."

"You're lucky you didn't break your neck."

With the grace of a rhino, I managed to get back on my feet. He patted me down and removed the mace from my pocket.

"Okay, let's go," he said.

He led me into the kitchen, and we both exited through the window I had broken. While I walked, he kept a tight grip on my elbow. I wasn't sure if he was concerned about me slipping on the ice or if he was trying to prevent me from making a break for it while my hands were cuffed behind me. When we got to his squad car, he opened the back door and helped me inside. I was too scared to ask any questions and simply sat there during the long car ride and tried not to hyperventilate.

I couldn't believe I was going back to jail. Where the hell had Tim been when I needed him? I couldn't decide which I was more pissed off about.

The officer abruptly put the car in park, and it jolted me back to the reality at hand. I looked up and realized we weren't at the police station. We were in front of Tim's house. The officer left me in the back of the car and knocked on Tim's door.

Had they traced my cell phone call somehow? Was he going to arrest Tim for offering to help me? Holy shit, I was in trouble now. Knowing how much Tim's integrity meant to him, I would never be able to forgive myself for making so many bad decisions in one night.

I watched as Tim answered the door and the two men talked. Tim remained at his open door as the officer returned to the squad car. He opened the back door, helped me out, and then unlocked the handcuffs.

I stood there trying to understand what was happening, while the officer got in his car and drove away.

So I wasn't going to jail? I looked around, not sure what to do next. Then I spotted my car parked in Tim's driveway.

Time to find out what was going on. I trudged up to Tim's doorway and followed him inside.

"In case you didn't figure it out, you're not going to jail," he said and slammed the front door. "A buddy of mine owed me a favor, and so he picked you up for me."

"Oh, I see. Your hands are too pure to get a little dirty so you have—"

"A cop on the scene has some legal leeway. I don't. And it's my job to enforce the law, not to break it.

Can you get that? Or has your new brown hair dye affected your brain?"

I had never seen Tim this angry. He was breathing hard, almost snorting, and his jaw muscles kept clenching.

"Tim—"

"I've got to get up in an hour and go to work. We'll talk later."

He left me in the living room and went upstairs.

Now what?

I noticed there were blankets and a pillow piled on the sofa. I guess this was my bed for the night. I briefly considered traipsing upstairs to get my car keys from him so I could go back to the hotel, but I didn't have the energy for another verbal assault.

Instead, I pried off the snow boots, collapsed on the couch, and spread the blankets over me. Tomorrow was going to be a busy day, and I needed some sleep. I had a nine o'clock appointment with my attorney to discuss my case and strategize my defense. Then I also had the little matter of proving my innocence. I just didn't know how I was going to do it.

Perhaps I should add finding the cure for cancer to my to-do list.

Chapter 18

"**R**ise and shine, Maggie."

The intrusion into my ear was way too early for my brain's liking, so I kept my eyes closed.

"Come on, I don't have much time. Wake up."

Next I heard the sound of a soda can being opened.

I separated my eyelids and saw Tim standing in front of me, dressed and ready for work. He held a can of Pepsi.

It took a few moments for the activities of last night to reenter my short-term memory.

"Can we talk about last night before I leave?" he said.

"Which part did you want to talk about? The part where you left me stranded under a bookcase for over an hour? Or the part where you sent one of your cop cronies over to fake arrest me and scare the shit out of me? I take it while I was stuck under the bookcase, he gave you my keys to drive my car back here?"

"I was trying to make a point."

"Point made. Now, if you'll give me my car keys. I'll be leaving."

"Maggie, being your friend is like trying to hand-feed a pet crocodile. Sometimes it's just too much work."

The tears burned at the edges of my eyes.

"Do you know what it is I do for a living?" he said.

"Ruin peoples' lives?"

"That is one interpretation. But I conduct investigations. I figure out who isn't paying their share of taxes and build a case to prove it. And I'm good at it. It would seem to me that if you are innocent of killing this old lady—and I believe you are—that I might be a good ally for you. Perhaps it's time for you to realize that asking for help is not a sign of weakness."

I looked down at the floor.

"Here, take a sip of this, and you'll feel better."

I took a long, cold drink. The caffeine in the Pepsi definitely worked its magic.

"Would you like to talk about this case for a few minutes?"

I nodded.

"Why don't you tell me exactly what you did last night and what you know so far?"

"Eleanor came in to see me last week to open a new account. She had a new driver's license with someone else's photo on it. She said the Department of Motor Vehicles had sent it to her, even though hers wasn't due to expire."

"What happened to the license?"

"She gave it to me to shred. I went to Hamilton last night and retrieved it. The license was in my purse that the cop took."

"Your purse is right here." He lifted it from beside the sofa and handed it to me.

I dug in and pulled out my wallet. I found the duplicate license and handed it to Tim.

He scrutinized the printing on the card. Then he ran his finger around the edges and corners. Finally, he held the ID at the left and right edges and bent the card so that the center deflected about an inch. First in one direction and then in the other. Both times, the ID slowly returned to its original position.

"This is interesting," he said.

"What? What is it?"

"Did you see how long it took for the license to get back to its original position? Now look at what happens when I do the same thing with my license."

He demonstrated, and his license bounced back immediately.

"This duplicate license of Eleanor's is a fake. A really good one but still a fake." He handed the license back to me.

"You can tell that just by twisting it?"

"Desktop computers and specialty color printers have made the duplication of licenses easier to do and harder to detect. But the average forger still hasn't mastered the printing of holograms. That's not a big problem if you're a college kid using a fake out-of-state license to get into a bar. But if you're using a fake ID to fool a government official, then you've got to have a real hologram on the ID. The only way to do that is to take a real license and soak it in acetone. The acetone eats away the glue and allows the lamination to separate. Then, it's just a matter of removing the hologram and putting it on the fake ID. But this can lead to other problems, one of which is the additional layers can cause the ID to lose its elasticity."

He smiled like a two-year-old who's just done number one in the potty for the first time. I smiled, too. Knocking his ego down a notch was a great way to start the day.

"Actually, I knew it was fake. It's got Phil Scranton's picture on it."

"What?" he grabbed it back and stared. "Well, I'll be . . . What else did you find last night?"

"That was it." I leaned back on the sofa. "I spent all night searching Phil's apartment and Eleanor's house and found absolutely nothing."

"How thorough were you?"

"Extremely."

"Okay, let's look at this thing logically. Assume Phil killed Eleanor. What was his motive?"

"No guesses. She seemed like a harmless old lady."

"How about hiding her in your trunk?"

I shrugged. "To frame me?"

"Maybe. You certainly have a way of pissing people off. Who was mad at you besides Phil?"

"Recently, just Richard and Phil."

"But why would Phil frame you and then go to the trouble of trying to electrocute you? As for Richard, killing a stranger to screw up your life seems a bit extreme. Besides, I'd think Eleanor would have wound up in my trunk."

"But your trunk lock worked. Any news on Richard?"

"We don't think he's left the country. His checking account and credit cards are frozen. We'll get him. Anyone else who was mad?"

"I've got a list of people pissed off over their Palimo losses. Besides Phil."

"Let's take another approach." He sat down beside me on the couch. "There are usually only a few reasons a person is murdered. Either they're an innocent bystander—for instance, killed while their house is being robbed, or shot during a gang war, something like that—or the murderer is mad at the deceased for some reason—could be for revenge or a crime of passion— or the murderer wants something the deceased has."

"I talked with Eleanor's sister-in-law yesterday. According to her, everyone loved Eleanor."

"Assuming she isn't lying, that leaves Eleanor as an innocent bystander, or Phil wanted something she had."

"What could she have been an innocent bystander to?" I said.

"Maybe she witnessed Phil commit a crime."

I drank more Pepsi. "Again, the sister-in-law says Eleanor and Phil got along fine."

"I already checked with the police, and there weren't any crimes committed around Autumn Oaks recently. So perhaps Eleanor was murdered because Phil wanted something she had."

"I searched her house. There weren't any rare art collections, stamp collections, or anything like that. Just a bunch of those old dolls. And when Eleanor came in to open an account, all she had was about two thousand dollars. That's not really a fortune to kill someone over."

"You'd be surprised. But maybe Phil wanted something Eleanor didn't know she had."

"Look, Tim, I haven't had much sleep the last few days, so I'm not up to games of mental agility. Why don't you just tell me what you think happened?"

"I've been doing my own checking on Eleanor, and I agree; she was a sweet old woman who didn't have much that anyone would want. I frankly didn't have any ideas until you showed me the fake ID this morning. Someone went to a lot of trouble to make this license. It wasn't some teenager with a digital camera and some desktop equipment. The motor vehicle department isn't backlogged on sending out IDs, but a company that manufacturers fake ones might be. And they might just be screwed up enough to send the license to the address supplied on the license rather than to the person who ordered it."

"So all I have to do is look in the Yellow Pages

under fake identification, find the company who made it, ask them if Phil bought it, and that proves Phil is the murderer?"

"I don't think it's that easy."

"That didn't sound easy to me."

"You might have better luck trying to figure out why Phil would want to borrow Eleanor's identity."

Light was beginning to dawn. "To cash a check made out to her?" I said.

"Then the check would probably have been mailed to her, too."

"Phil could have intercepted it."

"True, but where would she get a check big enough to be worth the trouble?"

"Well, maybe the ID was for gaining access to something like a safe-deposit box?"

"Could be."

"Shit, who knows what it means. Maybe my attorney will come up with something." I took another sip of Pepsi. "Besides, how does having a corpse in the trunk of my car prove I killed her?"

"Stranger cases have been made. I wouldn't count on the judicial system to guarantee your innocence."

I looked down, and my hands were trembling. At least if I was in jail, I wouldn't have to worry about dodging the Children's Hospice woman in her quest to collect my three-million-dollar pledge.

"Now don't flip out on me," he said. "I'm just saying, I think if we work together on this we could come up with something."

I drained the rest of my Pepsi and tried to relax. "So what did you have in mind?"

"Well, a safe-deposit box or intercepted check are both possible, but . . . I prosecuted a company one time for not turning over unclaimed assets to the state of Missouri."

"You mean like stuff from their lost and found departments?"

"No, unclaimed financial assets. In Missouri, if a person hasn't made a deposit or withdrawal in five years or had any correspondence with the bank during that time, the account is declared an unclaimed asset. The same rules apply for stock certificates, dividend checks, insurance settlements or proceeds, and utility deposits. When a company holding an unclaimed asset can't find the owner, then the asset by law has to be turned over to the Unclaimed Property Division of the Treasurer's Office. There are billions in unclaimed assets nationally."

"How in the world can people not know they have money somewhere?"

"When someone moves, they can forget to notify everyone. Doesn't Hamilton ever get client statements returned as undeliverable?"

My eyes widened with understanding. That had happened with a couple of my clients.

"The company I was prosecuting wasn't turning over stock certificates to the state," he said. "A taxpayer complained that his deceased parents never got their stock certificates, and the company wouldn't give the certificates to him. An audit of the company's records showed they were sitting on about four million dollars that had been unclaimed for fifteen or more years. They were mysteriously forgetting to distribute the dividends on these shares as well. They were saving a boatload of money and claiming the assets on their balance sheet."

"Who was it?"

"Central Farming Utilities."

"I think I remember seeing that in the news."

"My point is, perhaps Eleanor had money coming to her that she didn't know about."

"Ohmygod! One of the things Eleanor mentioned at our meeting was that she had gotten a check—I think it was for about a hundred dollars—that the government had sent her from her husband's old bank account. So maybe—"

"Maybe if she had one unclaimed asset returned to her, then there are others out there as well."

"My crystal ball is in the shop, so how do I find out where this money is coming from?"

"It's a lot easier these days, thanks to the Internet. There's an organization called the National Association of Unclaimed Property Administrators. They have a web site that links to each state's unclaimed property division. You click on the division, input a name, and seconds later, it lets you know whether the person has an unclaimed asset. Some states will tell you the dollar amount of the unclaimed asset, others just tell you there is an asset. And it's free of charge. I'll give you NAUPA's web site address." He took out a pen and scribbled it down on the back of one of his business cards. "I've got to get going. I'll call you later to see how you're making out."

"Usually on my back."

It took a few moments for him to get my bad joke, and then he smiled.

"Mind if I grab a shower before I go?" I said.

"Help yourself. When you're done, you're welcome to use the upstairs bedroom that I turned into an office. There's a computer in there that might be helpful, since Phil put a sledgehammer through yours. Just click on the Internet icon on the desktop, and it will connect automatically." He took a key out of his pocket and handed it to me. "Here's an extra key. Don't lose it. Lock up when you're done."

I watched him leave. When the door closed, I was amazed at how we had gone from wanting to kill each other to working together. It seemed as though he sincerely wanted to help me and not just keep me out of jail so I could baby-sit his sister's kids Friday night.

While I had his place to myself, I was tempted to poke around, just to find out who his date was. Instead,

I willed myself to walk straight to the bathroom without any recreational snooping.

I turned the shower on full blast and submerged myself under the water. Muscles I didn't know I had, ached from my bookcase collision. Right when the pulsating water began to ease my knotted muscles, I remembered I had a nine o'clock meeting with my attorney to discuss my defense.

I bolted out of the water and ran wet and naked to Tim's bedroom phone. I dialed information and requested the law offices of Coppinger, Neil and Kimble. A recording returned a phone number, and I pushed the button to have the call automatically connected.

Tom Kimble wasn't happy that I forgot our appointment. He gave me a tongue-lashing, saying that if I didn't care about proving my innocence, he wasn't going to, either.

I begged and pleaded with him to reschedule. He was booked the rest of the morning and then he was going out of town for a long holiday weekend. We agreed to meet an hour before my hearing on Monday. He made it clear that I wasn't to be late.

I hung up and wanted to get back into the shower, but it was already nine, and I needed to get going. I shut the water off and dried off. I wasn't particularly excited about putting on yesterday's clothes, so I opened Tim's closet to see what my options were. I found a big sweatshirt and put it on. The arms were about eight inches too long, so I rolled them up. Pants were going to be a problem. Then I remembered the pair of green sweatpants I had been missing. I left the closet, opened the bottom drawer of his dresser, and got lucky. This was the drawer Tim always put the clothes I left behind, back when I was leaving clothes here. I slipped the sweats on and felt warm and snugly.

I mopped up my wet footprints with a towel and tried to return the bathroom back to its spotless condition. I came pretty close and even remembered to put my wet towels in his hamper. I brushed out my short hair and checked myself in the mirror. My new hairstyle was very wash and wear, which would come in handy in prison. Then I started getting depressed, so I flipped off the light and walked down the hall to the other bedroom.

This was the cleanest office I had ever seen. I still had paper clips on the floor in my home office that I dropped about a month ago.

The computer took a few minutes to warm up. When it finished loading, I clicked on the Internet icon, and the home page for Netscape came up. I typed in the web address Tim had given me and was instantly connected to the NAUPA home site. A few clicks later, I was at the Missouri Unclaimed Property site. I typed in Eleanor Cosgrove and hit the Enter button. I closed my eyes and prayed that it would come back with something. I looked at the screen. The hourglass was still working. I waited a few more minutes, and nothing happened.

The number for the Missouri Treasurer's office was listed at the top of the web page. After ten minutes, I gave them a call.

"Unclaimed Property, may I help you?"

"Yes, I've been trying to access your web site for the last ten minutes, and I can't get it to work."

"I'm sorry. They've been having a problem with the web server, and it won't be fixed until tomorrow."

"Could I give you a name and have you check for unclaimed assets?"

"I'm sorry, we can't take phone requests. You are welcome to come in and use our in-house computers to do a search."

"Where are you located?"

"We're on the corner of Federal and Oak in Jefferson City."

Jefferson City was a three-hour drive from St. Louis.

"How late are you open?" I said.

"Someone is here until five."

I thanked her and hung up.

Should I waste six hours of round-trip driving to look up Eleanor's name? I decided I would first check the other states to see if Eleanor had unclaimed assets someplace else.

I clicked on the browser's Back button until I was at the NAUPA home page again. I spent the next hour or so checking the other forty-nine states for any unclaimed assets in the name of Eleanor or her husband Jonah. I didn't come up with anything.

I told the computer what I thought of its abilities and then shut it off by pushing the Off button instead of shutting down the applications like you were supposed to.

Screw it.

I turned out the lights and went back downstairs. Halfway down the steps, my cell phone started ringing, and I almost fell the rest of the way trying to get to my purse.

I got to the phone on the fifth ring. The caller ID said it was Malcolm Vandenberg, and I swore for almost killing myself for no good reason.

"Maggie, where have you been?" he said. "I've been trying to get ahold of you everywhere,"

"I've been busy chasing my tail."

"Chasing your tail is my job," he said, his voice a chocolate-coated murmur.

Some other time that remark might have been funny, but I wasn't in the mood. "What do you want?"

"Do you have plans for lunch?"

"It looks like I'm driving to Jefferson City, unless you know a good cliff I can jump off."

"Now, now. It can't be that bloody bad. Why are you going to Jeff City?"

"To do some research."

"When do you think you'll be back?"

I looked at my watch. It was ten-thirty now. Three

hours to get there, figure a half hour of research, three hours back. "I should be back around five or six at the latest."

"Perfect. Meet me for dinner, and I promise to cheer you up. I have a few ideas that might even improve your legal situation."

There was something about his English accent that offered hope. Right now, I was ready to try anything. "Such as?"

"I think you should join me for a little adventure."

"What did you have in mind?"

"My Mexico trip, remember? I'm leaving tomorrow night for my uncle so I can deliver a guest to his final resting place. Why don't you leave this awful mess behind you and join me?"

"I can't really travel out of the country right now. There's the little matter of a hearing on Monday I need to be here for."

"Why? So you can be prosecuted for something you didn't do and spend the rest of your life sitting in a jail cell teaching other inmates how to invest their cigarette proceeds?"

Somehow my mind turned to what Tim would think of my skipping bail rather than facing my problems. For once, I agreed with him.

"Thanks, but no thanks."

"Margaret, you deserve a little pampering. The stress you've been under has probably been playing havoc on your nervous system. You know it takes three days to get an adrenaline rush out of your system? You need to meet me at the Blue Moon Spa for a fabulous dinner and a massage. Then I can tell you my delicious plans for our escape."

That actually did sound good. Not escaping, but a dinner and a massage. The Blue Moon was the country club of spas. You had to be a member for the privilege of shelling out several hundred bucks for a gourmet meal followed by a full-body massage. And membership to the swanky joint cost an initial $20,000, with monthly dues that ran from $1,000 to $2,000. As far as I could tell, the main reason for joining was to prove you could afford to.

"Are you a member?" I said.

"Recently joined."

"How the hell did you pull that off?"

"Fees from those estates you've been liquidating for me. I'll tell you all about it over a candlelit dinner. So, will you meet me? I have a dinner reservation for six and a double massage room reserved for seven-thirty."

"Malcolm, I can't tell you how much I'd like to do that, but I can't meet you."

"You are way too focused, and I think you need to relax."

"No argument there," I said. "But there's no way I can relax with everything that's going on. How about a rain check?"

"I'm not giving up so easily. I'll talk to you later."

Next I called Tim's cell phone and got his voice mail. I explained that I didn't turn up anything in my Internet search and that the Missouri web site was down for a few days. I told him I was driving to Jeff City to search their office database and would be back later.

I went home first and changed out of my sweats and snow boots so I would look more presentable for the bureaucrats. Then I began the long drive to Jefferson City. The roads were clear, and the traffic was light. I found a radio station still playing Christmas music and listened for a while, but it only made me more depressed. I wasn't in the mood to count my blessings when so much of my life had been screwed up in the last week.

The miles passed under the tires, and I found myself trying to imagine what life would be like if I skipped the country, taking my last three million with me. Life in a foreign country certainly sounded more appealing then a gray jail cell, but running away would only convince people I was guilty. And then there was the little matter of skipping my bond, which Tim had posted.

I shook my head, hoping to clear the temptation from my mind, and my right tires plummeted into and back out of a deep pothole. The jolt messed up my alignment somehow, because I now had to keep the steering wheel turned about fifteen degrees to keep the car pointed straight. Next, the little red light warning popped on advising me to check my engine. The way my luck was going, if I pulled over right now and asked a mechanic to check the engine, they would probably discover it had fallen out a few miles ago. At least it was a rental.

At two-thirty, I took the Jefferson City exit from Highway 70 and turned south. Twenty minutes later, I was parked outside the Missouri Department of Treasury.

I entered through the Federal Street entrance and spent five minutes trying to decipher where the Unclaimed Property Division was on the huge office map. I finally located it in the bowels of the building.

I took the elevator to the basement and followed a gray hallway that seemed more like a tunnel. I walked all the way down one side of the building before taking a sharp right and following that to the end, which brought me to a mail center. I was surprised that one of the few government offices that actually provided a service for taxpayers and existed only to help people get their money back, would be relegated to this dungeon. How typical of our government.

"Excuse me," I said to a man wearing coveralls, "could you tell me where the Unclaimed Property Division is?"

He pointed to a small sign, probably five inches by five inches, that had "Unclaimed Property Division" hand lettered on it and an arrow pointing to the right.

I thanked him and continued to the right.

Thirty feet later, I was standing at the office entrance to the Unclaimed Property Division. I opened the door, and a woman greeted me with a cheery "May I help you?"

"Yes, I called earlier. Your web site was down, and I'm interested in doing a search."

"I'd be glad to help you with that. Do you have a claim number or a person's name?"

"A person's name: Eleanor Cosgrove."

I spelled *Cosgrove* for her, and she typed it into her computer.

"No, I'm sorry, we don't have anything listed under that name."

"Would you try Jonah Cosgrove?"

She typed again and then shook her head. "I'm sorry, nothing under that name, either. Is there another name you'd like to try?"

"How about Maggie Connors?"

Again she tapped on the keyboard. "Here we go, there is an unclaimed bank account in the name of Maggie Connors."

"Really?"

"The Bank of Kirksville."

"I went to college in Kirksville," I said. "How much is it?"

"If the assets are under $25 I can tell you; otherwise, it's not available. Let's seeee," she said, drawing out the word. "There is a balance of eight dollars and fourteen cents."

That would pay a lot of my legal fees.

"Would you like to fill out a claim form? After it's verified, we can disburse a check in four to six weeks."

She held up a form that was filled with lots of little blanks to be completed. For eight bucks and change, it wasn't worth my time.

I had wasted the whole day.

I was so upset, I couldn't even answer the lady and simply turned and left the office.

The drive back to Saint Louis took an eternity. At least on the way down to Jeff City, there had been the hope of finding out something that would help me. Some small clue that I could build upon to prove my innocence. Now I had nothing. No ideas to pursue. No clue as what I should do next.

My cell phone rang, and according to the caller ID, it was Malcolm.

"How did the research go?" he said.

"It didn't."

"I took the liberty of maintaining our reservation for dinner and a massage. Why don't you take the night off and join me for a little pampering?"

I hesitated. If I had garnered some information, I might be able to justify the spa outing as a celebration, but given the circumstances, it didn't seem right.

"I'd love to, but I'm afraid I wouldn't be good company. How about another time?"

"I insist that you meet me. It sounds like you've had a rotten day, and you need a change of pace to refresh your mind. Right now, you don't sound capable of finding your way out of a paper bag, much less the mess you're in. Give yourself a break and meet me."

I let out one of my many deep sighs. "You're on."

"Splendid. I'll meet you there. What are you driving these days?"

"A blue Escort."

"I'll see you at the spa."

I agreed and said good-bye.

My cell phone rang, and I checked the caller ID before answering it. It was Stephanie from the Children's Hospice. I let the call go into my voice mail.

I couldn't imagine things getting any worse, which would only prove I didn't have a very good imagination.

Chapter 19

Since my exhaustive research took all of five minutes in Jefferson City, I was back in Saint Louis with enough time to go home and freshen up before my spa/dinner date with Malcolm.

Back at my condo, I checked my messages. Tim had called. He had something Service related he needed to do tonight and said he would meet me at my place around ten to review the latest events. This was followed by several messages from Palimo clients who said Stacy had been giving them the runaround about where I was, and they wanted to know what was going on. Then there was the daily message from the Children's Hospice lady who was sounding quite desperate. And my parents called to find out why I hadn't called them lately.

Just what I needed before a massage: another twelve-message helping of anxiety. I hit the Erase button and went to the bathroom to wash my face and put on a clean layer of makeup.

When I came back out of the bathroom, the message light on my answering machine was blinking again.

I hit the Play button.

"This is the pignappers calling to see if you received our package."

The rest of the message was an incoherent mix of screams and laughter. My two girlfriends were obviously having a good time on their ski vacation.

I went to the front door to check for a package and found an overnight box tucked discreetly in the corner of my porch. I brought it inside and ripped off the packing tape.

Inside was my pignapped piggy bank.

There was a note attached to the bank written on the Colorado resort's letterhead. It said: "Here's what I did on my Christmas vacation. Hope you're having as much fun."

Wrapped inside the letter were a series of Polaroid pictures. The first showed the piggy bank on a conveyor belt, coming out of the airport's x-ray machine. In the next picture, the bank was relaxing in a first-class leather chair, wearing blinders and he had a pair of the airline's wings attached to his chest. That was obviously staged; I knew my two friends were flying coach. In the next picture, the piggy bank wore ski goggles, a scarf, and was positioned on a pair of skis at the top of a slope. His adventure continued to the next picture, where he was sitting on the edge of a steaming, bubbling hot tub with a glass of champagne beside him and a beautiful snowy backdrop. But it was the final picture that put the others to shame. My piggy bank was resting on a fluffy pillow. On one side, a cigarette burned in an ashtray. On the other side was a sleeping Adonis—my guess was a passed-out ski instructor who had no idea he was involved in a photo shoot.

I couldn't believe it. This stupid pig had a better Christmas than I did. I badly needed that massage.

I decided in the interest of trying to destressify that I would leave early for the spa so I could have a peaceful ride and not rush. Maybe this massage would give me the energy I needed to start chasing another windmill and find a way to prove my innocence.

I pulled into the Blue Moon Spa parking lot and saw Malcolm waiting for me at the entrance. I parked in a corner under a big tree and was thankful that when I slammed the Escort's door, the snow from the tree didn't plunge down on me.

"You're early," Malcolm said, greeting me at the door. "We'll have more time to drink before our rub-downs."

I followed him inside and felt as if I had stepped into another world. The lobby entrance of the Blue Moon Spa was decorated in pastels and filled with fresh flowers. Soft instrumental music floated around from hidden speakers. The receptionists were busy answering calls, but there were no ringing telephones. I guessed a flickering light probably alerted them to an incoming call and then chastised myself for even giving it a thought.

A beautiful blond woman without makeup greeted us.

"Mr. Vandenberg, I'm so glad you and your guest could visit us tonight," she said, her hands wrapped around his. "If you'll please follow me, we have a table prepared for you, by the fireplace as you requested."

The woman led us to a cozy little table that was indeed right in front of the fireplace. Through the use of flower arrangements and privacy screens, each table enjoyed maximum privacy.

We sat down, and a waiter appeared with a bottle of red wine and two glasses.

"Monsieur Laraquet sends this with his compliments," the waiter said as he poured a small sampling into Malcolm's glass.

Malcolm approved, my glass was filled, and then

Malcolm's. The waiter explained the night's specials, how they were each prepared, and what the Blue Moon Spa chefs did to make them extra special. We both decided on the veal without bothering to look at the menus.

"So, tell me about your day," Malcolm said, leaning in to sip his wine. "I spent the day reviewing estate inventories. I could use some vicarious excitement in my life."

"Well, you won't get it from me." I told him about my wasted trip to Jefferson City in search of unclaimed assets for Eleanor or her husband.

"Unclaimed assets," he said. "How did you ever come up with such a hypothesis?"

"My friend Tim Gallen. He's a special agent with the Internal Revenue Service. He has all sorts of ideas on what people will do for money."

"But what led him to the idea?"

"When I met with Eleanor a week or so ago—she's the one they found in my trunk—she had a fake driver's license that someone had mailed her. Tim and I thought that one of the reasons for faking an identity might be to claim some of Eleanor's assets."

"I guess that's possible. Do you know much about Eleanor's family?"

"I talked with her sister-in-law, who said Eleanor never had children."

"What about other relatives; a mother, father, uncles, cousins, etc.?"

"I got the impression that the sister-in-law and Eleanor were the last of the clan. Why do you ask?"

"One possible reason for stealing someone's identity might be to claim an inheritance. Sometimes when a person dies, the only remaining family member is a distant cousin who has no idea Uncle Larry was loaded to the gills."

"That's a great idea. I'll check in to that tomorrow." Maybe I hadn't wasted the day.

"Of course, your other option is to bag all this cops and robbers stuff and run away with me to Mexico. Starry nights, warm ocean breezes, mariachi music . . ."

"It's tempting, but I think I need to clear things up here," I said. "Could we talk about something else?"

"Sure, pick a subject."

"Your uncle told me you're still a licensed mortician. That was a surprise."

Malcolm shook his head. "It's my father's and my uncle's biggest disappointment that I didn't follow in the family footsteps. Maintaining my license seemed like a good way to appease them both and keep a finger on what's going on with the business. But I really do hate the industry."

"I can imagine dealing with grieving people would take its toll."

"Oh, its not that at all. It's the deception that gets me."

I frowned. "What do you mean?"

"This really isn't dinner conversation material, so tell me when you want me to shut up, but the funeral business is one of the biggest rackets ever."

"I have no idea what you're talking about."

"Well, did you know embalming is not required by law?"

"I thought embalming was done as a health precaution, so you couldn't contract anything from the corpse."

He shook his head. "Doesn't make a bit of difference. And you wouldn't believe how many people agree to have a body embalmed before it's cremated. Absolutely astounding the decisions people make when they're an emotional wreck."

"So why do funeral homes insist on embalming?"

"We charge about $275 to embalm someone, and it's profitable for a lot of reasons. A body will only keep for about twenty-four hours if it's not embalmed. If you don't embalm the guest, then you can't have a viewing. If you don't have a viewing, it's a lot harder to sell an expensive casket. Caskets are usually marked up about five times the wholesale cost and make up almost half of the funeral expense. So if you think about it, the body is the whole center of focus for the funeral. Take away that, and you lose on other funeral expenses that can be marked up from three hundred to eight hundred percent." He paused. "Rather than deceiving poor widows, I'd rather prey upon innocent, young women." He smiled and refilled my wineglass.

"I guess the apple doesn't fall far from the tree. How is your uncle doing?"

"He's an odd duck. He doesn't bat an eye at the expenses of his beloved high-end caskets, but when I told him we were meeting here, he thought my membership was an extravagant waste of money."

I raised my wineglass. "A toast to financial extravagance during life and afterward."

We clinked glasses, drained the wine, and ordered another bottle.

The rest of our dinner conversation was a cat and mouse exchange filled with double entendres. I laughed all evening, which was a great to relief to my constant worrying. When dinner was through, we were escorted back to the main lobby area and greeted again by the same blond woman.

"Did you enjoy your meal?" she said.

"The veal was perfect," I said, "and just the right amount of food to feel full without being overstuffed."

Malcolm agreed.

She led us down a hallway. "Here is the men's changing area, and the women's is on the right. Inside you should find everything you need, but if you don't, use the phone inside. It's a direct line to my portable phone. Also inside are robes we would like you to change into before your massage. When you're ready, exit out the green doors, and you'll find yourself in another hallway. There will be a spa associate waiting there for you, and he or she will escort you to your massage room. Any questions?"

We both shook our heads.

"Enjoy your massages," she said.

I went into the women's changing area and was greeted by another woman who offered to help me disrobe. I thanked her and told her I could handle it myself. She went to check on something and then magically reappeared once I had changed into my robe.

"Do you have any valuables you need to place in a safe?"

"Only my purse, I guess."

"If you don't have anything valued at over a thousand dollars, then I'll place all your items, including your purse, in this locker. We have kind of a valet system for the lockers, and I assume complete responsibility for your items. I will not return the key to anyone but you."

"What if your shift ends before my massage?"

"I'm here as long as you're here," she said with a smile.

So customer service was still alive and well. It just cost a small fortune to enjoy it.

The woman escorted me out the green door, where Malcolm and an associate named Marsha were waiting for me. Marsha led us to a private room with two tables and two masseurs. The bottle of wine had eased my nervousness about the whole massage-naked-exposure thing in front of Malcolm, but that wasn't a problem. We were each draped with so many towels it was hard to tell who was who.

The next hour evaporated as every inch of my body was kneaded, rolled, pushed, and rubbed. When it was over, I looked up, and Malcolm was standing beside me.

"How do you feel now?" he said.

"Like melted buuudddar."

"Would you like to go another fifteen minutes?" Malcolm whispered in my ear.

"Could I?"

"I thought you might, so I scheduled you for a longer massage. I'll wait for you in the bar."

There was something about Malcolm I still didn't completely trust, and rather than risk waking up tomorrow with company, I decided to avoid the possibility.

"Actually, could I just call you tomorrow?" I said. "It will take me forever to get dressed because I know after this I'm not going to be moving too fast."

He smiled and nodded.

After Malcolm left, my masseur resumed his work, and it was almost like an out-of-body experience. For once I wasn't worried about my life. I felt like a happy mass of warm Play-Doh.

When my additional fifteen minutes were up, I thanked the masseur and went to the changing room. As expected, I got dressed in slow motion and made it to my car. An icy snow had started falling again, but I didn't care. I felt too good.

I sat in my car and retrieved my cell phone. The best way to maintain this state of relaxation was to cancel my meeting with Tim. I dialed his number.

"Hi Tim, it's Maggie."

"I've been trying to get ahold of you. How did your day go?"

"Actually, it was awful. I spent the morning checking every state's web site for unclaimed assets in Eleanor's name and her husband's and found nothing." I started the car and backed out of my parking space. "The Missouri site was off-line, so I drove to Jefferson City to check their in-house database. That turned out to be a wasted trip." I left the parking lot and joined the slow-moving traffic on the icy streets.

"I'm sorry you didn't have any luck. I really thought

the unclaimed assets might have been it. Are you doing okay? You sound out of it."

"I confess that I stopped and got a massage. It completely erased my stress. The way I feel right now, you'd never suspect how shattered my nerves are."

The traffic light turned red, and I slid to a stop.

"So where are you now?"

"I'm in Ladue. I'm just getting ready to get on the highway."

"I'm glad you're taking a stress break. You deserve it."

"That's why I called. Could we reschedule tonight?"

Tim answered me, but I didn't hear him. Something tugged at the edge of my mind. A car horn honked behind me, but I didn't move. My stress was gone, but it was still there. Maybe Eleanor's unclaimed asset was gone but still there, too.

"Maggie, are you there?"

"Tim, I am such an idiot. The reason I couldn't find an unclaimed asset in Eleanor's name is probably because it's already paid. The state most likely deleted it from their on-line listings."

I stepped on the gas, and my wheels slid slightly, but I corrected and turned onto the top of the entrance ramp for the highway.

"You may be on to something there," he said.

In my excitement, I touched the gas a little too hard and went for the brake to slow down. My car was evidently feeling the same sluggishness I was, because there wasn't any resistance to the brake pedal. My foot went right to the floor.

I was speeding down an icy highway entrance ramp without any brakes.

Chapter 20

Thursday, December 30

The only thing worse than waking up in the hospital is waking up in the hospital with déjà vu.

My body hurt from nose to toes. I had no idea how I got there. Tim was sitting in my hospital room, as usual, although this time he was hunched over a table with his laptop while he talked on a phone.

"Do you know of any other states that have recently paid out a large claim?" he said.

I looked at the window to get an idea of what time of day it was. The shades were shut, but around the edges, a bright sun leaked through. I heard Tim hang up.

"What happened this time?" I said.

"Your brakes gave out." He bent down and kissed me on the cheek. "It's nice to have you back with us. I thought I was going to lose you this time."

I gripped the bed rails. "Was anyone else hurt?"

"Just an old oak tree you smashed up pretty bad."

I relaxed in my bed, thankful that I hadn't killed a van loaded with a family on their way home from the holidays. It would have fit with the way things were going. "What day is it?"

"Thursday; the accident happened last night."

I nodded. For some reason my first thought was that my stuff for the hospital's account review was due today. But that was another lifetime. "So, did I break anything new?"

"You have a bad bump on your head. The Escort was totaled."

"At least I don't have to explain to the rental company about driving into a pothole and screwing up the alignment."

"When did that happen?"

"On the way to Jeff City." I closed my eyes. "The engine light came on, too; I must have done something to the brakes then."

"Maggie, I called a friend at the Missouri Treasurer's Office to see if an unclaimed asset for Eleanor or her husband had been paid in the last twelve months. I'm sorry, but they didn't. I also called a half dozen other states, but I didn't have any luck."

"What about Tennessee?" I mumbled. "Eleanor moved down there after her husband died."

"Yeah, I think I checked that one." He flipped through his paperwork, looking for something. "I take that back. I called them and their director wasn't in yet. I'll try again."

He picked up his calling card and punched in a series of numbers on the hospital room's phone. "May I speak with the director, please? My name is Tim Gallen, and I'm a special agent with the Criminal Investigation Division of the IRS." This was one of those times when having a long scary title had its benefits.

"I called earlier. I'm conducting an investigation and I'd like to speak with . . ." He paused and looked down at his notes. "Rick Killian. Is he in yet?" Tim paused. "Well, maybe you can help me. I'm trying to track down some information on a claim you recently paid on behalf of Eleanor and Jonah Cosgrove." There was another pause. "You're sure there hasn't been a claim in the last year or so under either name?" He nodded a few times. "Thank you for checking."

He put the phone back in its cradle and came to my bedside.

"Sorry, no luck." He pushed a strand of hair out of my eyes. "The nurse said the doctor should be in any minute to check on you. Would you mind if I keep making calls until he gets here?"

"Doesn't matter to me," I said.

Tim dialed away, but after hearing the outcomes of several calls, it was too painful to keep listening. I diverted my attention to the room's barren, gray decor. Tears filled my eyes, and I tried to blink them away. A glimpse of my future wrapped around my heart and squeezed the remaining hope out of my soul.

I closed my eyes to keep the bleakness of the situation from invading any more than possible. I must have drifted off to sleep, because some time later, I woke to Tim shaking my shoulder. I thought perhaps the doctor had arrived, but instead Tim was shoving the bedside phone in my face and motioning me to be quiet. He went back and picked up the phone on the table.

"Thanks for holding while I changed phones," he said. "As I was saying, I'm calling for information on a claim you paid out on behalf of Eleanor Cosgrove."

"That was one of our biggest claims in a long time," a woman said on the other end of the phone.

I bolted up in bed. It hurt. A lot.

"Exactly how much was paid out?" Tim said.

"We didn't actually cut a check. The claim was for five hundred shares of IBM. The stock certificates were in the name of Jonah John Cosgrove. He was a former

IBM employee. The stocks were found in a safe-deposit box that had been abandoned about thirty-five years ago."

"IBM trades around a hundred bucks, doesn't it?" Tim said.

I nodded, and the woman said yes.

"So the claim was worth about $50,000?"

I shook my head no.

"Oh, no," the woman said. "There have been numerous stock splits and such since then. Currently those shares are worth about two and a half million and change. It was quite a party around here when we issued the certificates."

Tim was smiling. "And who were the shares sent to?"

"That you'd have to talk with my director about, and as I said, he's in a meeting until this afternoon."

"Could you just confirm for me that it was Eleanor's brother that filed the claim?" From the sound of Tim's voice, you wouldn't have known he was guessing.

"No, this claim wasn't filed by a relative."

"Then it must have been filed by her attorney," Tim said.

I listened, but the woman didn't answer.

"Can you confirm for me that it was Eleanor's attorney who filed the claim?" he said.

"I'm sorry Mr. Gallen, but I can't give out that information over the phone."

I watched as Tim looked down at his notes.

"Mrs. Pench, were you aware that Mrs. Cosgrove is deceased?"

"Yes, as I recall she passed away some years ago."

"No, she was murdered earlier this week. I believe this claim was the motive for her murder."

"Oh my God, that's terrible," she said. "It was her attorney that filed the claim."

"And the attorney's name?"

"Please don't tell anyone I told you this, because I could get in a lot of trouble," she said.

"This is an IRS investigation. I promise, you won't get in any trouble."

"The attorney's name was Philip Scranton."

"I knew it!" I mouthed.

"But I can't give you any more information than that," she said. "I'd like to help you, but I don't really have any proof of whom I am talking to or if what you said about Mrs. Cosgrove is true."

"Is there some way I could get ahold of your director at his meeting?"

"No. I don't know where it is."

"What about his cell phone?" Tim said.

"He keeps it turned off unless he's making a call."

"Mrs. Pench, thank you for what help you've been able to provide. I realize there is a protocol you need to follow. I really do appreciate your assistance. Just one last question: Do you remember how long ago the certificates were sent out?"

"About two weeks ago."

"Thanks again for your help. Would you please have your director call me when he returns?"

Tim gave the woman my hospital phone number, his cell phone number, and his office phone number before hanging up.

"What state was that?" I said as soon as he put the phone down.

"I'm not telling you until you promise once and for all to baby-sit my sister's kids New Year's Eve." His smile was contagious.

"Fine, I'll watch the kids. What state was it?"

"Illinois."

"I am such an idiot. Eleanor's sister-in-law said that Eleanor and her husband spent some time in Chicago before moving to Saint Louis. She said J. J. worked for a big machine company that made computer storage disks. I never guessed she meant IBM. And thirty some years ago, IBM would have been the only player in the computer industry. Eleanor must not have known or remembered that J. J. had a safe-deposit box." I let out a deep sigh of relief. "So what's next?"

"I'll catch the next flight to Chicago and wait for the director to return from his meeting. It might be helpful to talk to him in person so I can get photocopies of the claim and things like that. If we can get all this put together, maybe we can get the state to drop the charges Monday."

"I knew it was Psycho Phil! Ida had said he was doing some maintenance work at Eleanor's—fixing her toilet, I think—and he probably found out from her about the claim."

"I'm happy for you, but it still doesn't make a whole lot of sense to me. Blue-collar handyman as high-level con artist?"

"Uneducated doesn't mean stupid." I flung back the covers on my bed. "I'm coming with you." I tried to pull myself to a vertical position, but the spinning room forced me back against the bed.

Tim helped me lie back. "I think you need to sit this one out. You've been through a lot in the last week, and I don't think running to the airport to catch a plane is a good idea."

"You can't expect me to just sit here and wait to hear from you. I'll go nuts."

"I'd rather you stay put. With the luck you've been having, the flight will crash and burn before it even taxies onto the runway."

I smirked at him to let him know that wasn't funny. "When did this become an IRS investigation?"

"It's not. I happen to have some unused vacation time I need to burn by year end." He packed up his laptop. "Look, Maggie, they'll discharge you soon. Why don't I leave my car for you, and I'll catch a cab to the airport? Then maybe you can relax and try to stay out of the hospital for a while. I'll call you as soon as I know something."

Tim didn't wait for another one of my arguments. He told me where his car was parked, handed me his keys, and left. He was gone a few moments when he reappeared in my room and said he forgot something. Then he kissed me on the cheek and left again.

Although I tried not to get my hopes up, it was impossible not to. For the first time since my catastrophic financial losses and arrest, I had a real reason to hope.

A half hour later, a doctor came in. He checked my chart, checked my eyes, and asked me how I felt. Other than a pounding headache, I was in good shape. He wrote out a prescription for six painkillers and said I was good to go.

Tim's car was where he said it would be in the parking lot. By the look of it, you wouldn't know it was winter; every surface gleamed as though it had been hand washed in the summer sun. I climbed in and started the car. Nothing blew up or fell off. Maybe my luck was changing.

On my way out of the hospital's parking lot, I drove past a billboard advertising the hospital's maternity ward. Pictured was a sweet, blue-eyed baby who reminded me of the hospice baby in Stephanie's picture. Would blue-eyed babies haunt me for the rest of my life? And forever remind me of the nine million dollars in donations I had cost the hospice?

I let out a deep sigh. I had survived Phil's attack, survived crashing into Tim, survived my icy car crash last night, and now Tim was following up on a $2.5 million motive for Phil to kill Eleanor that was sure to give my attorney evidence to create reasonable doubt.

As I drove, I chewed on my thumbnail. I kept thinking about a box of Chiclet gum I had taken from a grocery store when I was about three or four years old. I put the gum in my pocket when my mom wasn't looking and took it home. I kept it hidden inside my

Easy Bake Oven. My guilt over taking the gum kept me up nights as I imagined the grocery store's Chiclet police were minutes away from surrounding my house and taking me to someplace where they punished little girls who stole stuff.

Eventually, I forgot about the Chiclets, and when I went to use my Easy Bake Oven a few weeks later, the gum box caught fire. Black gum lava oozed all over the oven's heat source—a fifteen-watt lightbulb. The guilt over what I had done returned as if I had stolen the gum that very day. When my mom discovered what happened, she took me and my piggy bank back to the grocery store. I can still remember standing in front of the manager, trying to apologize for taking the gum. I was crying so hard the words came out in spits and coughs. Then I handed over my life savings to reimburse the manager. I can't remember how much the gum was, but my piggy bank was empty when I went home.

That night, I went to bed penniless and with a sore butt from getting spanked. But I didn't have another nightmare about the Chiclet police.

Since then, had I led a completely moral life? Not even close. I was in sales, for God's sake. But this hospice pledge gnawed at me like those stupid Chiclets.

One way or another, it was time to resolve the three-million-dollar pledge.

I pulled off the road and picked up my cell phone. Stephanie Wolf had called so many times it didn't take long to find her number in my log of missed calls. I punched in the number, and hit Send.

Chapter 21

"**H**ello?"

"Hi, Stephanie, this is Maggie."

"Maggie, it's so nice to hear from you. I can't thank you enough for your donation."

"That's why I called. I'm sorry it has taken me so long—"

"You don't need to apologize. I know you've had other things on your mind. I saw the story about Eleanor Cosgrove, and I don't believe a word of it. I'm just so proud that with everything going on, you're still honoring your pledge. You're going to make such a difference in the lives of so many children."

I nodded. "I've got some free time now, so I thought perhaps I could meet you to give you the check." I said the words slowly, like I was pulling off a Band-Aid one skin cell at a time.

Stephanie didn't answer.

"Stephanie?"

"I'm a little confused. Your attorney said you asked

him to drop off the check to me today. He's supposed
to be meeting me here at my house any minute."

"My attorney?"

"Yeah, I met him at your condo."

"What? When?"

"The day after the Palimo party, of course. Didn't
he tell you?"

It took me a minute to recall the events of the last
week and remember what had been going on when
Stephanie delivered her poster. I'd been chained to a
chair in Richard Craig's house, peeing my pants. She
had to have seen Phil. Jesus, he'd been out to get me
even then.

"Stephanie, that wasn't my attorney you saw. It was
this Phil guy who broke into my place and was trying
to kill me. I'm glad you weren't hurt."

"I don't believe it. He seemed like such a nice man."

"It's true. He attacked me and gave me a pretty good
shiner. It scares me to think what could have happened.
Did you talk with him very long?"

"Actually, no. I didn't get a good look at him, either.
Your electricity was off, and you know how early it
gets dark these days. He was using a flashlight and told
me he was there as part of the insurance investigation.
When I—"

"Wait a minute. Insurance investigation?"

"Sure. Your place was trashed. Vandals. He said you
were tied up at work and had asked him to help with
the inventory, or something like that. Anyway, he was
really busy, and things were such a mess, so he asked
me to leave the poster on the front porch."

"Well, the good news is, Phil electrocuted himself
at my condo on Monday, so neither of us need to worry
about him again."

"Then it can't be that Phil guy. The attorney called
me this morning. He said you didn't want any publicity
over the donation, so he asked if he could meet me at
my home."

Phil was stalking me because Palimo collapsed. That news didn't become public until the following morning, two days after the Palimo party and the day after Stephanie delivered the poster. Stephanie was right; it couldn't have been Phil. It did explain why Phil bitched about the condo being messy; someone had trashed it before he got there. But why would someone trash my condo when Palimo was still trading at $70⅜ a share? Looking for something? But what?

"Maggie, I know it's the same man. I'm sure of it. I recognize his English accent."

Suddenly my heart began to race. It all fell into place. Who was liquidating millions in stock certificates? Who was smart enough to control Phil Scranton? Who had told me there was no such thing as an unclaimed death, only unclaimed assets? Who had an English accent?

Malcolm Vandenberg.

"Maggie, please tell me the truth. I know you've been under a lot of stress, but are you saying all of this because you've changed your mind about paying your pledge? This is the last day I have to fax a copy of your check to the Goldberg brothers so I can get their matching donations. Frankly, I'm desperate for your money, but I'm tired of playing games." She paused. "Hold on a minute, there's somebody at the door. It's probably him."

"Stephanie, listen to me very carefully. Can you see who's at your front door without letting them see you?"

"No, my front door is open but the storm door is locked."

"Where do you live?" I tried not to sound too excited because I didn't want to scare her.

"Off of Brentwood, behind the Starbucks in the Chapel Forge neighborhood. Why?"

"Okay, here's what I want you to do. Very quietly, use your back door and get out of the house now. Run

as fast as you can, and I'll come pick you up at Starbucks."

"You've got to be kidding. I'm not running through
a bunch of snow-covered yards to avoid your donation
check. He keeps ringing the doorbell. I better go let
him in."

"Stephanie, that is not my attorney. If you open the
door to him, I think he's going to kill you because you
met him at my condo. Get your butt out of that house,
and don't stop running until you get to Starbucks. I'll
meet you there with my checkbook."

"He's pounding on the door," she said. "I'm leaving
now."

Chapter 22

I pulled a U-turn and skidded Tim's car into a snowbank. I backed up and stepped on the gas, then sped through town, running red lights when it was safe to do so.

As I drove, more and more pieces fell into place. Malcolm had access to all the Vandenberg files. Since insurance often picks up part of funeral costs, the files probably included the deceased's social security number, previous place of employment, as well as home and work addresses. All the stuff you need to be able to file a false claim.

I had no idea what Malcolm had been doing while I was passed out in my hotel room on our night of supposed passion. He could have easily been shuttling Eleanor's body from his trunk to mine. And I suddenly remembered the extra fifteen minutes of massage he so generously gave me. Was it so he could go out in the parking lot and tamper with my brakes?

I shuddered and drove a little faster.

And he had sold his uncle's Palimo stock before it tanked. How had he known? Was Richard Craig involved, too?

Now, that put a new wrinkle in things. After all, Richard had reason to hate me. Actually, he had real reason to hate Tim, but Tim probably wasn't as accessible. The home addresses of IRS Special Agents are among the most closely guarded secrets on the planet. Richard may have arranged with Malcolm to dump the body on me. But what was the connection between them? And Phil?

Before Richard joined Palimo, he had been working at a biotech in England. Malcolm had lived in England, too. Could they have met there?

I dialed Tim again. Still no answer.

When I got to Starbucks, I left Tim's car in a no parking zone and ran inside. I found Stephanie standing by the front door, sobbing. She wasn't wearing a coat, and her pants were wet to the knees.

She ran to me and wrapped her arms around me. Nonprofits types evidently weren't used to this much excitement. I pried her off like a wet swimming suit and convinced her she was safe.

A manager approached and asked if there was something he could do to help.

I apologized for the scene, put Stephanie in Tim's car, got on the highway, and drove west. I wasn't sure where we were going, but we were going fast. I tried Tim several times on his cell phone without luck.

"Stephanie, how about this?" I said. "Let me check you into a hotel until we get this figured out."

"Wouldn't it be safer for us to go to the police?"

"My experience has been that unless the police have the bad guy in custody, you're not safe. I can't believe Malcolm was stupid enough to open the door when you knocked."

"Actually, when I walked up to your door, I thought it was you I saw through the front window. I couldn't imagine who else would be walking around your living room with a flashlight. I assumed your power had gone off because of the snowstorm, not that you were getting robbed. I'm sure the man knew I saw him, too. I just kept knocking until he answered the door."

A Residence Inn sign loomed ahead. I pulled into their parking lot and stopped at the entrance. I took the still-shaking Stephanie inside and got her settled in a room. I told her I would call once I found out something but as a safety precaution not to tell anyone else she was there. I said good-bye and turned to leave.

"Maggie? Aren't you forgetting something?"

I turned around to look at her.

"Your check for three million dollars?"

Oh, yeah. It was time to empty my piggy bank.

I retrieved my checkbook from my purse and carefully filled in the information. It was the slowest signature on a check I had ever signed.

"God bless you for saving my life and for helping to ease the pain of so many children," Stephanie said.

She gave me a warm hug. I wish I could say it felt good to do the right thing, but it sucked. With my luck, the financial pain of writing that check would probably stigmatize me to the point that I wouldn't be able to write with my right hand anymore.

As I walked back to Tim's car, I tried several more times to reach him on his cell phone but still didn't have any luck. I climbed in behind the wheel and debated what to do next.

My phone rang, and I grabbed it.

"Tim?"

"What's wrong?"

"Where are you?"

"At a pay phone in the Saint Louis airport. I'm on standby for the next flight to Chicago. It leaves in ten minutes, and I thought I would check on you before I go."

I told him what happened with Stephanie and tried to sketch out my theory.

"You think Richard is involved? And who the hell is Malcolm Vandenberg?"

"Malcolm is the guy you saw Monday morning at my hotel room. His uncle is a client and owns the Vandenberg Funeral Home."

"Does every man who sleeps with you want to kill you?"

"Funny. But during the last week, every time something has gone wrong, Malcolm has been around." I took a deep breath to calm myself, then filled him in on the details. And as I did, more came to me.

"When I went over to the Vandenberg Funeral Home Sunday night, I overheard Malcolm and his uncle arguing because the cremation oven was broken. Maybe Malcolm was so upset because he had already killed Eleanor and was planning on cremating her and didn't have a way to dispose of the body. Then, when he and I went out for dinner afterward, he loaded me up on margaritas. Sometime during the night, he could have moved Eleanor from the trunk of his car to the trunk of my car." I paused as a horrible thought occurred to me. "Tim, what if Eleanor wasn't the only person Malcolm killed?"

"Why? Who else is missing?"

"No one that I know of. But he's been liquidating stocks for the last week. Plus, he's a licensed mortician in a funeral home, which is an ideal position to get rid of bodies."

"My you do have a good criminal mind."

"You must be wearing off on me."

"Well, it makes some sense that Malcolm might be involved. Phil certainly didn't sound like the kind of guy who could mastermind a fraudulent million-dollar claim by himself. Do you know where we can find Malcolm?"

"He was supposed to leave tonight to escort a body

to Mexico. If he hasn't already left, he's probably at his house or the funeral home."

"How long will it take you to get to the airport?"

"I can be there in twenty minutes."

"I'll meet you out front, at the departing flight drop-off." He paused and then spoke slowly, "Now Maggie, I know you're excited, but please don't break any land speed records getting here. I'd hate to have you end up in the hospital again. Your friends will come back from skiing, and you'll be the one with the aches and pains."

My mind drifted back to my recently kidnapped, bronze piggy bank that had been a gift from Cleon Cummings, the client with the IRS problems. "Tim, you remember Cleon's creative containers to smuggle money out of the country?"

"Yeah . . ."

"Maybe Malcolm has liquidated the stocks and is planning on smuggling his money out of the country in the casket. Hell, maybe he's planning on smuggling Richard out of the country in the casket."

"Calm down, Jessica Fletcher. Let's not jump to any conclusions just yet. Pick me up, and we'll go from there."

I gave him Malcolm's work and home phone numbers along with the number for the funeral home before hanging up.

Rush-hour traffic was a disaster. Since New Year's Eve was tomorrow, my guess was lots of people were stretching the holiday into a long weekend and leaving early on Thursday. A half hour later, I made it to the airport and found Tim pacing back and forth. I slid over to let him drive his own car.

"So what's the plan?" I said.

"I called my partner, Dwight. He's working with police to get an arrest warrant issued for Malcolm. I checked with Malcolm's office, and he's not there. A few officers are headed over there anyway to check the place out. I told Dwight we would meet him at Malcolm's home in Chesterfield. If Malcolm has the equipment to manufacture fake IDs, my guess is we'll find it at his house."

Traffic was bottlenecked even worse on the drive to Chesterfield as everyone tried to squeeze over the bridge to Saint Charles. We didn't talk much during the drive, I think we were both speculating about what was going to happen.

As Tim exited off Highway 40, his cell phone rang. He talked briefly and hung up.

"I don't suppose that was Malcolm calling to turn himself in?"

"No, that was Dwight. He's on the way with some uniformed officers. I told him we'd wait down the street for them."

Malcolm's neighborhood was composed of a selection of modest two-story houses. They looked to be between fifteen and twenty years old. The prerequisite Christmas decorations were everywhere. It was definitely a family neighborhood and not the place I would expect to find a single guy like Malcolm. He seemed more the type to have a loft in the city.

We parked a few houses down from Malcolm's and waited for the troops to arrive. They showed up forty-five minutes later. Tim got out of the car and conferenced with Dwight and the four officers. As I watched the men, I noticed the sun had begun to disappear, and Christmas lights had started illuminating the outlines of many of the homes.

Tim left the huddle and came back to his car.

"You stay here. We're going to check Malcolm's. We don't think he is in there, but whatever happens, your butt is not to leave this car. Understood?"

I nodded.

Tim got into Dwight's car, and they followed the other two squad cars back to Malcolm's. I watched as two officers hoofed to the back of the house and the other two officers, along with Tim and Dwight, went to the front of the house.

They knocked at the front door and waited. It didn't look like anyone answered. They banged on the door again, but still no answer.

Two of the cops lifted a battering ram they had been carrying and busted in the front door. The four men disappeared inside, and I sat and watched the lifeless house. Twenty minutes later, I jumped at the sound of my phone ringing. I checked the caller ID and it was private, so I assumed it was Tim.

"Hello?"

"Maggie, he's not here. We've checked the house and didn't find anything incriminating." His voice was calm, but I could detect his disappointment. "I'll be out in ten to fill you in. Just stay in the car until then."

He hung up.

Fifteen minutes later, I saw the men emerge from Malcolm's house. Tim got back in his car, and we followed one of the squad cars out of the neighborhood.

"What happened to Dwight?" I said.

"He's staying behind with the other two cops in case Malcolm comes home. We did a cursory search of Malcolm's and didn't find him or anything incriminating. I was hoping we might see some camera equipment, fake ID supplies, copies of claims, or something of use, but the place was clean."

I nodded. Tim's disappointment was apparent.

"I'm not giving up yet, though," he said. "Let's see what we find at the funeral home."

We reached the Vandenberg Funeral Home, and it looked deserted. The front parking lot was empty. The squad car continued to the back lot, and Tim followed.

"That's Malcolm's car!" I said, pointing at the black Lexus.

The rest of the lot was empty. The squad car parked beside Malcolm's car, and Tim parked next to them. I watched as the three men approached the doors to the funeral home. Evidently, the door was locked, because again a battering ram gave them access. The three men then disappeared into the funeral home.

I didn't particularly want to have a gun and go busting down doors with them, but sitting in the car and waiting was killing me. I watched traffic on Manchester Road pass back and forth. None of the car's occupants seemed to care about our little drama taking place inside the funeral home.

And then sirens permeated the air. About fifteen minutes after the men had entered the funeral home, an army of squad cars filled the parking lot. Two ambulances also arrived.

Most of the officers charged inside, but one came over and yanked my car door open.

"Who are you?" he said, pulling me outside.

"My name is Maggie Connors. I came here with Tim Gallen and two officers who went inside to arrest Malcolm Vandenberg."

"We have a report of several shots being fired inside and at least one fatality, so it's not safe for you to be sitting here."

Chapter 23

I sat in a squad car parked on the outskirts of the funeral home parking lot. My shattered nerves made me feel like I was in the basement of a building about to collapse.

Was Tim dead? Malcolm?

The waiting was unbearable.

Then I saw Stanley Vandenberg's stately old hearse drive up at an unstately speed. It skidded to a halt, and Stanley raced to the entrance that had been busted in. An officer stopped him for a moment and then allowed him access.

Ten minutes later, a few of the officers came out. They were laughing and slapping each other on the back. A pair of medics walked out with smirks on their faces, packed their gear into the ambulance, and left.

I couldn't wait any longer to find out what happened. I left the squad car and walked toward them. I was halfway across the lot when Tim came out the front door. Unlike the jovial officers that had preceded him, Tim was pissed.

"In the car," he said. His voice made it clear it wasn't open to debate.

Again I sat in his car and waited. Tim went over and conferred with a couple of the officers before coming back and getting in the car.

I sat silently as he stepped on the gas and screeched out of the parking spot. He clipped the curb as he left the parking lot, and my head bounced against the roof of the car.

"All right, what the hell happened?" I said.

"Malcolm is in Mexico. I'm taking you home, and then I need to go fill out a ream of paperwork."

"But Malcolm told me he was leaving tonight."

"According to his uncle, Malcolm realized when he was packing last night that his flight left at nine A.M., not P.M."

"So he couldn't have been at Stephanie's today?"

"Bingo."

"Is it still possible that he smuggled Richard out with him?"

"No, he didn't smuggle Richard or any money out with him."

"But the police said that someone was dead."

"There are a lot of dead people; it's a funeral home."

"Tim, something happened in there. I was told that there were gunshots and a fatality."

He turned onto Highway 270 and pushed on the gas pedal.

"You know," I said, "it's my life that's screwed if I don't figure out what is going on, so quit making me pull out what happened one syllable at a time."

He veered off to the shoulder and stopped the car.

"You're right, I'm sorry. It's not your fault." He took a couple of deep breaths. "The three of us went into the dark funeral home, looking for Malcolm. We searched the main floor and didn't find anything.

Someone found the elevator, and we took it down to where they prep the bodies. It was dark, hard to see, and an officer and I went into a room and heard a voice yelling, 'You're a dead man. You're a dead man.'

"The officer I was with identified himself and told the man to put down his weapon and let his location be known. Instead, there was a flurry of movement, and I fired off a shot. When the lights were turned on, I realized I had killed a goddamn parrot."

"Oh nooo, not Socrates?"

"Yes, the goddamn parrot is dead, along with my career. I was specifically told not to get involved in this mess, and it's going to be a little hard to hide my involvement when I have to go fill out multiple reports detailing the circumstances of discharging my firearm."

"What happened when Stanley got there?"

"Oh, yes. I wouldn't want to leave that out." His tone was overflowing with sarcasm. "I'm in the middle of picking up parrot pieces from all over the place and Stanley shows up. He tells us he put Malcolm on a plane this morning at nine o'clock, which I confirmed with the airline. And if he smuggled money out with the deceased, he didn't smuggle much. According to Stanley, the deceased had signed up for the bake and shake treatment. The body had been cremated and was being transported in an urn so the ashes could be spread on some Mexican hilltop. I checked, and Customs confirmed it. Richard may want to get out of the country, but I think that approach is a little extreme."

Tim pulled back onto the highway, and we drove for a while without talking.

"Well, at least we can get proof that Phil filed a false claim with Illinois," I said. "That should help my case."

"There's a problem with that," Tim said.

"What problem?"

"The director called me back and gave me some more details on the case."

"And . . ."

"And it's true that Phil Scranton filed the claim, acting as the attorney for Eleanor's estate. But the stock certificates weren't sent to him. By law they were sent to Eleanor's heir stated on the claim."

"Who was . . ."

"I'm sorry Maggie. I explained what was going on to the director before I found out there was an heir. The director wasn't too happy to hear that the state of Illinois had made a $2.5 million screw-up and is launching an investigation of their own."

"So why are you apologizing to me? The state of Illinois—Oh, my God."

"That's right. The certificates were sent to Maggie Connors. I'm afraid the state of Illinois is looking for you for theft of $2.5 million dollars."

"You're kidding me. But I didn't receive any stock certificates."

Tim didn't answer.

I leaned my head against the back of the car seat. With the tanking of Palimo, the reimbursements to my clients, and the three-million-dollar donation to the hospice, a jury would believe I had millions of reasons to kill an old woman and steal her money.

"Besides, I don't know the first thing about falsifying an identity," I said.

"Oh, really, Maggie? Or do you prefer to be called Shelly Culbertson?"

I froze.

"Maggie, did you go to Kinko's the other night and create a fake press pass for yourself using the name Shelly Culbertson?"

"Holy shit, that doesn't count. I did that to interview Eleanor's neighbors. How did you know?"

"The Kinko's clerk got suspicious after you left and called the police. Apparently, you gave him a credit card that wasn't valid and ended up paying in cash. The good news was that the clerk didn't keep a record of the credit card number or your real name. But he did have a copy of the fake press pass you made, which he faxed to the police. Dwight told me he saw the fax on someone's desk when he was getting the arrest warrant for Malcolm. He didn't say anything, but as soon as the news hits about the false Illinois claim, the cop who has this fax is going to see your picture and put two and two together. How many blessed times do I have to tell you not to break the law? Forget morality, it just doesn't work. Cops aren't stupid. You get caught."

"But wait. We know someone's behind this. And we've got Stephanie as an eyewitness. Stephanie saw someone—"

"In the dark, who she can't identify."

"But she said he had an English accent."

"Do you know how easy it is to fake an English accent? All you have to do is watch *Masterpiece Theatre* for a few hours," he said, in a plummy, upper crust voice.

"Look, someone called her today, pretending to be my lawyer. And we know someone is behind this. Couldn't we—"

"No, we couldn't. It's time to let the police handle this. You're through playing Nancy Drew, understand?"

"But all I want—"

"No, I'm taking you home. The police may be at your place in the morning to arrest you, and if so, we'll deal with that then. I can't hide you, and there's no point trying to run away from this."

I looked at Tim while he drove and watched as he clenched his jaw. He was going to be as helpful as a cadaver. Maybe it wasn't too late to join Malcolm in Mexico.

Chapter 24

The numbers on my digital clock slowly dissolved into one another. It was after midnight, and I couldn't sleep. I had spent the last several hours reviewing the week's events, and the more I thought about it, the more convinced I was that Phil killed Eleanor, probably with Malcolm's help, and maybe Richard's as well. It just fit together too neatly.

I flung the covers back and got out of bed. There was no use lying there anymore. If I couldn't sleep, then maybe I could do something productive. I was probably going to sell the condo, rather than paying the maintenance fees on it while I was in prison, so I decided to clean up all the stuff I had been neglecting. I went to the kitchen, grabbed a trash bag from under the sink, and took it out to my front porch.

The only problem with my theory was that, according to Stanley, Malcolm had gone to Mexico. Alone, unless they found a way to jam Richard into an urn.

The stars were twinkling in the midnight-black sky,

and it didn't seem fair that the rest of the world was snuggled peacefully in bed and I was picking up a week's worth of newspapers from my porch. I loaded the newspapers into the bag and then dragged the bag through the house and into the garage.

But someone had called Stephanie. Who? Could it be Richard working alone? But why would Richard kill Eleanor?

I glanced at my bag of newspapers, then dropped it to the floor and began digging inside for Tuesday's, to see if Eleanor's obituary was listed. It wasn't in Tuesday's paper, but I found it in Wednesday's. The black-and-white photo of her triggered my memory of her warm smile. I wasn't sure why I needed to read the obituary. Maybe just to remind myself that the injustices happening to me were infinitesimal compared to Eleanor's.

I collected the papers again and tossed them into the trash can. As I left the garage, I flipped off the lights—and realized I had turned the interior laundry room light off as well. The double light switches inside my garage. That's how Phil was electrocuted.

Someone else coming in from the garage turned on the lights and zapped him. Phil was too good a handyman to do it to himself.

But of course, this was another piece of the puzzle that could be equally incriminating for me.

I locked the garage door behind me and went to the kitchen. I opened the refrigerator, hoping someone had miraculously stocked it, but it was still empty. I slammed the refrigerator, which caused the cordless phone to fall off the wall receiver. I should have called Stephanie Wolf to apologize for keeping her in a hotel room and to let her know it was safe to go home. At almost one in the morning, it was a little late for that now.

Eleanor's obit picture reminded me of the awful Phil Scranton photo on the fake driver's license. I had no idea how easy it was to get a fake ID. It probably took Phil less time than doing his makeover. Actually, making a rotting corpse look good was probably an easier task than plucking Phil's eyebrows. At least Phil didn't have to contend with a lip drift problem.

And then it connected.

Corpse cosmetology. Fake IDs.

Phil didn't do his makeover, Malcolm did it for him. And Malcolm didn't go to Mexico, Richard did, posing as Malcolm. Using a fake ID would get Richard out of the country and give Malcolm the perfect alibi to stay in town and harass Stephanie. No, kill Stephanie.

One A.M. or not, I rang Stephanie's hotel. No answer in her room.

I slammed down the phone. What now? Call the cops, like Tim wanted? Like they would go out and break down another door on the strength of my new theory without any evidence. Call Tim?

I stood at the sink and debated what to do. The Vandenberg Funeral Home door was busted in and probably wouldn't be fixed until sometime tomorrow. And if Malcolm did have Stephanie, he would want to dispose of the body. Which meant the crematorium. Maybe I could sneak in and get enough evidence to interest Tim and the cops.

Besides, I was already in enough trouble. Would a little more make a difference at this point?

I shuddered. Breaking into a funeral home had the appeal of having a slumber party at a graveyard. I washed the last of the newsprint from my hands. It was time to let the party begin.

I changed into a new breaking and entering outfit, which consisted of a black sweater, blue jeans, and a black pea coat. I was walking out the front door when I heard my phone ring. I stopped and waited for my answering machine to pick up the call.

"Hi, Maggie it's Tim. I guess you're sleeping. I just—"

I walked out of my condo without listening to the rest of his message. Getting him involved now would just complicate things.

New problem.

Tim had dropped me off since I totaled the rented Escort and my Corolla was still impounded. I didn't have any wheels. And, I wasn't too sure that if I found an all-night car rental place they would rush to deliver me car keys when I totaled the last one.

I dug in my purse. Somewhere near the bottom I found Phil's keys. Was his car nearby? I spied a spotless new truck parked down the street, under a streetlamp. I didn't remember it belonging to any of my neighbors. I crunched through the snow as fast as I could to get a closer look. The red truck was a little flashy and expensive for Phil, but weirder things had surprised me this week.

I held Phil's key in my hand, hovering near the door lock. If the key fit, then it meant fate wanted me to break into the funeral home because Stephanie's life was in danger. If the key didn't work, and perhaps set off a truck alarm instead, then it meant fate wanted me to put my overworked imagination back to bed and wait for my probable arrest in the morning for unclaimed asset theft.

I jammed the key into the lock.

An alarm didn't sound, but the key didn't work, either.

Shit.

Screw fate. I needed to get to Vandenberg's.

Then I noticed a pile of snow with wheels parked even farther down the street. Of course this new truck couldn't have been Phil's. Phil's vehicle would have been parked out here for a few days and covered in snow. This truck looked like it was just driven off the showroom floor.

I hurried to the snow lump.

No more practicing.

If this key unlocked whatever was under the snow, or didn't, I would take that as fate's final message as to what I should do.

I cleared the snow away from the door lock, stuck the key in, and turned it. The lock clicked. I grabbed the door handle, but it didn't open. Apparently I had just locked the snow lump.

Minor technicality. I was sure that fate wanted me to go to Vandenberg's.

I shoved snow off the windshield and side windows. I hurried, but the snow clearing seemed to take forever. I discovered that under all the white stuff was a rust-bucket Chevy truck. If it started, I wouldn't complain.

I opened the door and climbed inside. When I sat down, the worn springs in the driver's seat bounced me up to the ceiling. I put the key in the ignition and turned. Nothing. No whine from the battery or anything.

Shit. Shit. Shit.

Then I noticed that beside me was a stick shift.

Shit. Shit. SHIT. Shit. Shit.

I had driven a stick shift once in my life, and it was only to back a car out of a driveway. There was something I needed to do to get the engine started but I couldn't remember what.

I put the shifter in neutral and tried the starter again. Still nothing.

I pushed on the clutch and turned the key again. The engine erupted from its winter sleep.

Would the coroner list the cause of my death as unbridled stupidity for trying to teach myself how to drive a stick shift while I raced across snowy streets in the middle of the night?

Time to find out.

The knob on the stick shift was worn, but I could still see the faint diagram showing where the five speeds were. I'd watched enough sports car commercials. I could do this.

I wrestled with the violently shaking shifter and after many grinding gears and abrupt starts and stops, I was moving.

My plan was to get the truck up to the fifth gear and leave it there until I got to Vandenberg's. That plan didn't last long when I realized I couldn't turn corners at that speed. Thank God I never had to stop on a hill for a stoplight. I was also thankful that at two in the morning the streets were empty so there wasn't anyone around to critique my driving ability or get run over.

I took the Manchester exit a little too fast, and the truck tires found a patch of ice that almost sent me into a snowbank. I gained control of the truck, jerked it into fourth gear, and drove a little slower to the funeral home.

The funeral home was dark, and the light posts in the parking lot gave off an eerie orange light in the late-night haze. I drove to the back and saw Malcolm's car parked next to Stanley's Packard hearse. It made sense that Malcolm's car was here if Stanley had taken him to the airport, but that didn't explain why Stanley's buggy was still here.

I tried to pull in beside Stanley's hearse, but I let the clutch up too early and the engine died before I made it into the parking spot. I abandoned the truck and raced to the hearse for a closer look. The massive back door was unlocked. I eased it open and viewed the cavernous interior. Black curtains on the tiny windows, rubber rollers built into the polished oak beds. And from the looks of it, more space than my former office at Hamilton. No sign of Stephanie. I let the door slam closed with a heavy and eery final thump.

I stared at the doors to the funeral home and tried to convince myself that what I was about to do was the right thing. I kept seeing this scene from some horror movie when the corpses all started coming to life. I was a rational, unemployed stockbroker, and I reassured myself I could outrun a dead body because they never moved very fast in the movies.

I climbed the steps to the funeral home entrance. The door hadn't been repaired and was shut but not tightly. I pushed on it and felt a resistance, almost like a body was propped up on the other side to keep it closed. I leaned into the door and pushed harder, and the door granted me access. Once inside I immediately looked behind the door and saw two twenty-pound bags of road salt that had been used to secure the door.

No bodies so far. This was a good sign.

I turned my flashlight on and surveyed the room. The atmosphere was a lot different in the dark, without the soft lighting and the pretty music playing in the background. My footsteps on the marble floor sounded loud enough to wake the recently deceased. I found Stanley's office, but there was no sign of Malcolm or Stanley anywhere.

The muffled sound of a metal pan hitting a floor startled me. I spun around, expecting to see a bad guy behind me, as had been my history of late, but the room was empty and quiet. I was sure the noise had come from the creepy body preparation area downstairs.

Damn.

I left Stanley's office and crept out to the hall. I didn't want to take the elevator and have the noise alert whoever was downstairs. Instead, I tiptoed to the door leading downstairs. I stood there with my hand on the doorknob, afraid to open it. Was Malcolm waiting on the other side with a machete in his hand? Was I about to enter the lair of some necrophiliac killer I hadn't met yet? Just what the hell was I doing here, anyway?

There was another loud bang from somewhere in the basement, which convinced me no one was waiting on the other side of the door to kill me. I turned the handle, and the door creaked open. Below I could see light coming from the room I'd seen Malcolm and Stanley arguing in days earlier. I strained forward and was sure I heard the voices of Malcolm and Stanley. Had Stanley found out what Malcolm was up to? Was he in trouble, too? Could Malcolm kill his own uncle?

I wanted to prove my innocence, but getting killed in the process would be counterproductive. I didn't think making a gun out of my finger and putting it in my pocket would convince Malcolm to give himself up. I needed help.

I took the cell phone out of my pants pocket and called Tim. The phone rang several times, and Tim's answering machine picked up.

"Tim, if you're there, pick up. I need your help." I waited, but there wasn't an answer. "It's after two in the morning, I'm at the Vandenberg Funeral Home. If I'm dead or missing Friday morning, it's Malcolm's fault."

I hung up, turned the ringer on my phone off, and stared at my phone. Should I call 911 for help? If I was wrong, and Malcolm wasn't down there, I would be calling the police on myself and was guaranteed a trip to jail. I decided to compromise and dial 911 but not push the Send button. I put the phone back in my pants pocket but kept my finger on the green button that would activate my call. If something happened when I got to the bottom of the steps, I would only have to push the button.

I began my descent, using the handrails to ease down as quietly as I could. At the bottom of the steps, I paused to check my phone. I'd waited too long to hit the Send button and the phone had cleared itself of the number. I punched in 911, put the phone back in my pocket, and walked to the doorway.

The voices had stopped, but I could hear some shuffling noises coming from within. Someone was definitely in there. If it was Stanley and he was alone, what exactly was I going to say to him? I was scrambling to come up with a story to tell Stanley when the door swung open, catching me completely by surprise.

It was Stanley.

"I thought I heard someone coming down the steps," he said.

I was fumbling for what I should say when I saw Malcolm sitting in a chair behind Stanley. Malcolm's mouth was covered with duct tape, and his hands were secured somehow behind his back.

What?

Then, Stanley jammed a wet rag over my mouth and nose. My brain stopped making sense of anything, and my finger stopped pushing on my phone's Send button.

Chapter 25

When I woke up, my chin was resting on my chest and drool was dripping down the side of my face. I looked up and realized I was sitting next to Malcolm and my hands had been duct-taped behind my back.

Stanley was frantically searching a medical cabinet at the far end of the room. I met Malcolm's eyes, hoping to get some idea of what I should be trying to do, but with his mouth taped closed, he could only look horrified.

But not as horrified as Stephanie, who was duct-taped to a chair just beyond him.

Oh, shit!

Stanley turned around and saw that I had regained consciousness.

"Oh, dear," he said. "I can't believe there isn't a single bottle of chloroform anywhere." He went to another cabinet and emptied its contents, but he still didn't find what he was looking for. "Well, ladies and gentleman, here's our situation. I used up the chloroform I had been saving for Malcolm and Miss Wolf on our little Maggie, and now I've got none left. So, while I would have preferred to have you all in a suspended state before injecting ten cc's of air into your veins, that isn't going to be possible. Instead, you're all going to have to pretend you're comatose so I can get through this. Struggling is only going to make things worse for everyone."

Stanley came toward me with a syringe. Malcolm stood up, with his hands still secured behind him, and tried to use his chair to knock Stanley over. Stanley easily sidestepped his nephew and then knocked Malcolm and his chair onto his side. He dropped his syringe and grabbed the duct tape to secure Malcolm's legs to the chair so he couldn't stand and move around. He then righted Malcolm's chair, displaying more upper body strength than I would have imagined. Next he secured my feet and then found his syringe again.

"Maggie," he said. "Let's start with you. Close your eyes and pretend you're in a restful place, filled with angels and marshmallow clouds."

"Stanley!" I said. "Are you out of your mind? What are you doing? Why are you doing this?"

My hysterical questions splintered his composure. His tranquil face became agitated and confused.

"What are you doing, Stanley?"

"Maggie, I'm truly sorry for doing this, although it will probably prove to be less painful than spending your life in prison for murdering someone Phil killed."

"Phil killed Eleanor, not you?"

"Phil's financial problems, an industrial-sized wrench, and a little old lady about to get millions are not a good combination."

"But how could Phil have known to put her in my trunk?"

"You mentioned your trunk was busted open when you stopped Sunday night. When I heard you and Malcolm making plans to go to a Mexican place near your hotel, I called Phil and told him to pick up Eleanor's body here and transfer it to your trunk. I would have cremated her body, but the crematorium wasn't working. I had to put her somewhere because the folks from the Missouri Funeral Board were coming the next day to do an inspection. Anything else on your mind? I always loved it when Perry Mason got the guy to confess at the end of the show and wrap up all the loose details."

I guessed—hoped—Stanley wanted me to ask questions as an excuse to delay what he planned to do. Well, hell, I could ask questions all night.

"But how did you get mixed up in all of this?"

"It's no secret the Vandenberg Funeral Home has been having financial problems. And Malcolm here was always on my back to sell this place. But I can't. It's been in our family for generations, and I love what I do. So one day, about a year ago, I got a letter by accident from the Unclaimed Assets Division of the Missouri Treasurer's Office. It was addressed to a man we had buried years ago, so I opened it to see what it was about. It said that he had an unclaimed asset on file with the state. I figured he wasn't going to claim it, so I did.

"The unclaimed asset turned out to be a forty-five-dollar utility deposit, but it was pretty easy to do, so I decided to try my luck again. At first, I did all my research on the Internet to see what was the smart way to go about it."

"You researched this on the Internet?"

"Just because I'm seventy years old doesn't mean I don't know how to turn on a computer. I figured if the news media are always complaining about being able to find bomb-building information on the Internet, then I should be able to find information on fake identities and false claims. It turned out it was pretty easy to do.

"So I went back through our guest registry of all the people we had buried and started searching the on-line databases to see if they had any unclaimed assets. Turns out a few of them did, and since they were dead already, I didn't think I was doing anything so wrong. Our government certainly didn't deserve the money, and this way I could afford to keep throwing fabulous funerals and letting the unclaimed assets subsidize the cost. The government wasn't going to give the assets to anyone, so I decided to exercise a little deception and reallocate the funds. Using some of Malcolm's forms from his estate work, I put together quite a few claims. Nothing extravagant, just $10,000 here, $15,000 there. Everything was going great until I got that idiot Phil involved. I regret ever meeting him."

"You met Phil at one of your Autumn Oaks seminars?"

Stanley nodded.

"He needed money, but what did you need from him?" And then I remembered Ida's comment about how helpful Phil was with the Alzheimer's patients. "Phil hooked you up with Alzheimer's patients who wouldn't question having their photos taken for your fake IDs."

"It was a good match, initially, but things got a little out of control. Phil was smarter than I thought. He discovered Eleanor had money coming from Illinois, and he tried to file a claim himself, following the approach I'd been using. The fool overlooked my main requirement, which is that the real claimant needed to be dead."

"I must have tipped you off that Phil was up to something when I told you about Eleanor's duplicate licenses."

Stanley nodded. "I confronted him. He confessed that he had ordered an ID from this company on the Internet and the damn fools mailed it to Eleanor. It really fouled things up. I invited Eleanor in to make her last arrangements, but she didn't bring the ID, and I was worried if someone found it, they would somehow be able to trace the thing to Phil. And if the police found Phil, he'd blame me. Eleanor told me she had given it to you, but I searched your office and couldn't find it."

"That's why I had forty-two clients on the bus going over, but only forty-one clients spend the night. You must have rented a car and come back early from the Palimo trip. That also explains why my stuff had been moved around in my office when I got back from Palimo. But how did you get my office key?"

"I found an extra one at the bottom of your purse when you left it in my office," he said.

I had thought my manager had taken that when he removed the one from my key ring.

"When I didn't find Eleanor's ID at your office," Stanley said, "I decided to try the next night at your house."

"So you broke in and assumed it would be treated as a burglary—which it was, when Phil attacked me—but then Stephanie saw you."

"Yes, I am truly sorry about that, too. Stephanie—like Eleanor and Phil—became another loose end. I worried that even though it was dark at your condo when we met, she might be able to identify me. I used an English accent to divert suspicion, but if someone asked her how old I was, she would have probably guessed in the seventies, not in Malcolm's thirties."

"But I had checked her into a hotel for safekeeping. How did you find her?"

"The Goldberg brothers have been trying to buy my funeral home for years so they could bulldoze it and use the land for one of their projects. From talking with the brothers at the Palimo party, I knew Stephanie had finagled a large donation out of them, but it was dependent on your donation. When Stephanie disappeared, I casually checked in with the boys, and they told me Stephanie had faxed a copy of your check from the Residence Inn business office. She was actually in my hearse, as was Malcolm, when I arrived earlier. Imagine my surprise when I found the police breaking in here. That was a close one."

"But why me? Why Malcolm?"

"Things were getting too complicated. Since Phil—that idiot—had managed to create the paperwork for Illinois claiming you were Eleanor's heir, I had to keep checking your mailbox every afternoon for a registered mail delivery notice. Luckily, you're such a workaholic that you never go home for lunch, and I didn't have any problem snooping through your mailbox until the notice showed up. Then I had to create a fake identity for a prostitute who played the part of Maggie Connors for the post office. After I got the stock certificates, I figured the best way to avoid you denying ever receiving them was to get rid of you. But you've got more lives than a damn cat. You survived Phil's attack, and after I saw your face, I started regretting my plan. I thought jail might fix the problem, but they let you out, which I didn't expect. Then you even survived your car accident after I fixed your brakes while you and Malcolm got massages."

"That was you?"

"You drive an old Packard long enough and you get to know a few things about repairing or disrepairing a car."

"But what about Malcolm?"

"As for Malcolm, he was going over the books, and I knew sooner or later he would realize I was getting outside chunks of money to pay for stuff."

"But if you and Phil were working together, why did you electrocute him in my laundry room and flood my basement?"

"Oh, I am sorry about that mess. Phil and I got into an argument over Eleanor's claim, and after that, he became paranoid that I was going to cut him out of the operation. He offered to arrange for your electrocution to get back in my good graces, and I took him up on it as a means to get rid of him instead."

"But Stanley, why? Why steal all this money?"

"Please understand that I wasn't doing this for myself, I just wanted to help ease the pain of some of the people coming here to bury a loved one. And now with Eleanor's bequest, this home can continue to deliver the lavish, fabulous ceremonies it is famous for."

I shifted in my chair, amazed at what I was hearing. I was rapidly running out of questions. "But . . . why did you tell everyone that Malcolm was going to Mexico? And we confirmed that he got on the plane and isn't due back until Sunday."

"I did that so when he didn't return, the police could do whatever searching they were going to do down there. I didn't want the funeral home involved."

To stall for more time, I started asking questions I knew the answers to. "But how could Malcolm be there and here? Especially with the tightened security at airports these days?"

"Really, Maggie, I was becoming pretty good at making fake licenses. I made one for a homeless friend using his photo and Malcolm's name, then bought a ticket and sent him to Mexico."

"Stanley, flipping a light switch to kill Phil is one thing. But Malcolm is your nephew. How could—"

"Oh he's a snobbish, British boil. I'm doing humanity and the gene pool a favor. But, I'm not killing Malcolm, Stephanie, or you. I'm just going to put you to sleep and then you won't wake up. It will be painless, I promise. I'd love to tell you about some of the other claims I've pulled off, but it's getting late. We'd better get started."

I screamed at the top of my lungs. This seemed to irritate Stanley, and he picked up his roll of duct tape and clamped a piece over my mouth. He then went back to a table and retrieved a syringe.

"I'm really sorry I ran out of chloroform. But every-

thing will be fine. Just close your eyes and try to relax."

There's nothing worse than trying to scream with
your mouth taped shut. The force of the scream I was
trying to expel through my mouth backed up and
snorted out my nose.

Stanley doused a cotton ball with some alcohol and
then rubbed the spot on my arm where he was going
to inject. Wasn't that like putting lipstick on before
blowing your face off with a gun?

I watched in horror as he pulled the plunger of the
syringe back and sucked air into the small compartment.

"Put the needle down," Tim said, walking into the
room with his gun pointed at Stanley.

Two officers quickly subdued Stanley and his needle.

"You just don't get it. Death is so overwhelming. I
was only trying to provide comfort for those in need,"
he said as the police handcuffed him and led him away.

I started to cry in relief. I wasn't going to jail. I
wasn't going to be a bake and shake victim. I wasn't—

I wasn't breathing. My emotional outburst stuffed
up my nose completely. With my mouth still taped
shut, it left my ears as the only open orifice in which
to intake air and they didn't work well in that capacity.

Tim ripped the tape off my mouth, taking my lips
with it.

I screamed in pain. Tim cut my wrists loose and then
went to the sink and soaked a towel in water. He
handed me the towel to put on what was left of the
skin around my mouth.

One of the officers approached Malcolm to remove
the tape on his mouth and he shook his head wildly.
Instead, the officer removed the tape from Malcolm's
hands and feet. Malcolm then walked over to a medical
cabinet and removed a white bottle filled with a clear
liquid. Using some cotton balls soaked in this liquid,

he started to ease the tape's gummy glue away from his skin. He had the tape off of his mouth in about a minute without taking any of his skin or hair with it.

Malcolm then repeated the process for Stephanie. When he finished, he walked over to me. His eyes were filled with despair. "Maggie, I'm so sorry for what my uncle did and was trying to do. I had no idea."

I nodded, not sure what to say, and gripped my towel tighter.

"I'd better go see what's going to happen to him," he said and left.

A hysterical Stephanie was led out behind Malcolm.

I turned the towel inside out, hoping to find a cool spot to continue comforting my face.

"I called 911 from my cell phone," I said, my voice muffled. "What the hell took so long for everyone to get here?"

"The folks at 911 knew you were in trouble but didn't know where you were."

"Then how did you find me?"

"I got your message," Tim said, working on the tape around my feet. "I'd called your place several times, and you didn't answer, which was unusual for how light a sleeper you are. I got worried and decided to drive over and make sure you weren't out breaking into places. When you didn't answer the door, even after I banged on your bedroom window, I guessed you were out furthering your crime spree—probably breaking into the already broken into funeral home. I checked my answering machine from my cell phone in the off chance you called."

"Thank God for answering machines."

"After I got your message, I called 911 to see if they could get a squad car over here any sooner than I could get here. It turns out that they were listening to your 911 call, but you never mentioned in your conversations with Stanley that you were at the Vandenberg Funeral Home."

I had to remember to be a clearer-thinking potential murder victim in the future.

"I got here just a few moments before the police did."

"So you waited outside the door until the last possible moment for my rescue?" I said, my mouth hanging open momentarily in disbelief. "If you didn't notice, Stanley's elevator stopped going to the top floor a long time ago. Anything could have happened. He could have tripped and stabbed me with his syringe."

"But he didn't, and you got a nice confession out of him."

"And another thing, next time you remove duct tape from my mouth, use what Malcolm used. That—"

"Let's hope there isn't a next time. And if there is, I'll leave the tape on."

Chapter 26

Friday, December 31

I planned on sleeping in on New Year's Day Eve, but a reporter called my house around eight in the morning and woke me up. I hung up before he got the full name of his paper out of his mouth.

Next I called Hamilton's automated system to check my account balance. After a high of $13,182,475.35, my current balance was $48,343.22. I wasn't broke, but damn close. Just like the financial depression I get after an expensive speeding ticket, I figured the best way to cheer myself up was to spend some more money. I called my spa and booked a full morning session with Stephen. I knew he had probably been booked for a long time, but I'm sure my appointment was accommodated because Stephen was more interested in the knowing the latest Saint Louis scuttle and I had lots to share.

By early afternoon, my hair was red again, my face

had been exfoliated, and my body had enjoyed another head-to-toe massage. I was dressed in a black Armani suit, and even if my portfolio didn't look good anymore, I did.

I pulled into the Hamilton parking garage and parked in a visitor space near the entrance. At least my new unemployment status afforded more convenient parking. I decided it would be better to clean out my office this afternoon so I wouldn't have to revisit old ghosts at the beginning of the new year.

I opened the front door and found my boss on his way out for a long weekend. "Maggie, I didn't expect to see you here."

"I wanted to get my stuff cleared out today so I wouldn't have to come in next week," I said, looking at the ground.

"Don't do that today, it's New Year's Eve. In fact, don't do it at all. According to the news reports, it looks like you cleared your name and they're also running a story about your three-million-dollar contribution to the Children's Hospice. I can't believe in light of what happened to your portfolio that you anted up such a large sum. You are a better person than I would be in that situation."

I decided to let him think that and not explain how another six-million-dollar contribution depended upon my three.

He led me to a seat in reception area and sat down beside me.

"I'm sorry I added to your stress by firing you," he said. "If you're still interested in Hamilton, we'd like to have you back."

Any other boss, and I would have told him to stick his job up his ass, but Mike had always had a genuine concern for me. If the roles were reversed, I probably would have acted the same way.

"That's nice of you to offer, but right now I'm not sure what I want to do."

"Leave your stuff in your office and think about it for a while. I think we could help you get back on your feet."

I shrugged. "I'll think about it. I want to go check in with Stacy and see how she's doing."

"I understand completely. Promise me you'll have a good holiday weekend and you won't worry about the financial stuff."

It was still a little too raw to talk about it so I just nodded absently.

After Mike left, I walked to my office and found Stacy sitting with her feet up on her desk, drinking a Pepsi, with several phone lines ringing uncontrollably.

"Looks like you have things under control," I said.

She jumped to her feet and embraced me. "You're all over the news! I can't believe it, what happened at the funeral home, the money for the hospice, and all this after the Palimo nosedive."

I smiled.

"So, are we working here anymore, or do I report for work at our new office on Monday?"

"I saw Mike when I came in, and he offered me my job back, but I need a few days to sort things out. I'm not sure I can afford the new office right now. Can we talk about it later?"

"I go where you go. Just keep us both out of jail and out of hell."

"Is there anything in that pile of messages that can't wait until next week?"

"Just one." She went into my office, came back with a pink message slip, and handed it to me. "Here's the address for Donna Trundle, the broker-of-the-day client you asked me to track down."

"Thanks." I looked at the address. "I'll give you a call at home over the weekend, and we can talk more. It's been almost two weeks since I've been to the new office, and I want to go check in there to make sure no one mailed me a bomb or anything."

"Even if they mailed you a bomb, couldn't it wait a few more days?"

"I just want to check in. I'll catch up with you later." I hugged her before leaving.

I drove to my new office, which was most likely not going to be my office. It was a few blocks away in a seven-story building of office suites. I took the elevator upstairs and was greeted by the receptionist who welcomed all the clients for the group of ten offices that shared this wing. I walked down the hallway to my office and unlocked my door.

Unlike the paper explosion in my Hamilton office, everything here was clean and tidy. The newness made my heart ache at what could have been.

I returned to the receptionist and asked if she had any phone messages for me. She handed me about a dozen. I flipped through them on the way back to my office. Toward the back of the pile was a message from Charles Witmer, the hospital client I had tackled out of his chair at the restaurant. It said he was sorry that given the current circumstances, the hospital wouldn't be able to entertain my proposal for their retirement account. He also said he would be praying for me. At least it was something.

I set the stack of messages down on my desk and leaned back in my chair. It would have been fun to start a business doing things the way I wanted to, but without a large account like the hospital to get me started and with my financial cushion wiped out, it wasn't really an option. I tried to appreciate that I was alive and not going to jail, but it was still somewhat painful to look around and see all the effort I had made to start my own firm. Not just in getting the office set up, but in nurturing clients and their accounts for so many years in the hopes that one day they would transfer with me.

I stood up and walked to the door. I took one last look around the place before shutting off the lights. I closed the door and was locking it when I heard the noise of the fax machine receiving something.

I opened the door and walked to the fax machine and waited for whatever message was being sent to magically reproduce itself on paper. The wheels turned and the machine hummed. I looked down and saw a letter written to me on Saint Louis General Hospital letterhead.

Dear Ms. Connors:

The delegation committee in charge of selecting the financial firm to administer our deferred compensation plan wishes to offer you their sincere apologies for having our collective heads up our asses. Please continue to service our account, either at Hamilton or in your new venture.

Happy New Year,
Sincerely,
The Board of Directors

I scanned the individual signatures on the bottom of the letter and smiled when I saw Dave King's, the man I had reimbursed from the Palimo disaster so he and his wife could travel to France for alternative medical treatments. I didn't know he was part of this committee.

I laid the fax on my desk and left the office again. Maybe I would be back after all.

Instead of doing an end zone celebration dance to the elevator, I moped along with the enthusiasm of lint. My recent successes of not getting killed, not going to jail, and still having some career options left weren't as much fun without someone to celebrate them with. Tonight was the biggest date night of the year, and the man I wanted to celebrate with would be toasting with another woman while I baby-sat his sister's kids.

If money can't buy happiness, exactly what were my options now that I was broke?

I slapped myself on the forehead.

I knew exactly what would lift my spirits and it had nothing to do with the opposite sex.

I retrieved my cell phone from my pocket, checked my log of missed phone calls, and found Stephanie Wolf's number.

"Hi, Stephanie, this is Maggie Connors."

"Maggie, I'm so happy to hear from you! Thank you for the money. Thank you for saving my life. Thank you, thank you, thank you."

"Your welcome. Stephanie, the reason I called is that I need a favor."

At six o'clock on New Year's Eve, I knocked on the Cunningham's front door. A woman wearing a strapless black dress answered.

"Are you Maggie?" she said. "Come on inside. I'm Tim's sister Amanda."

"I guess I found the right house."

I stomped my feet on the welcome mat to rid my shoes of excess snow. We stopped at a hallway closet, and she hung up my coat before leading me into the kitchen. The home was decorated in French country with another layer of Christmas decorations added on top.

"I can't believe you've been on the news all day and now you're standing in my kitchen," she said. "The kids told their friends that a celebrity is baby-sitting them tonight." She turned toward the family room. "Hey guys, Miss Maggie is here. Turn the TV off and come in here and introduce yourselves."

Three kids bumped and busted their way into the kitchen, and I was introduced to Nick, seven; Alexandra, five; and Kate, two.

"And this is my husband, Thomas," she said as a man in a tux entered the kitchen.

"Nice to meet you Maggie, and thanks again for watching this bucket of trouble while we're out. Trying

to find a baby-sitter on New Year's Eve is murder—"
He stopped and looked dumbstruck. "I guess that
wasn't—"

"Don't worry about it. And don't worry about these
guys; we'll be fine."

Amanda explained that the kids had already had dinner and outlined their bedtime rituals.

"We've got to get going, if we're going, honey,"
Thomas said to Amanda.

"All right, kids, be good. Miss Maggie is the boss
tonight, and I want you to keep your listening ears
attached."

Everyone promised to keep their body parts where
they belonged, and Amanda and Thomas disappeared
out the door with a promise to be back around one.

Over the next two hours, the kids put on a parade
of Christmas toys. Then it was snack time, followed
by a hosing off of the snack in the tub. A little after
eight-thirty, they were tucked in bed. Twenty minutes
later, the final bathroom breaks and drinks of water had
been delivered, and the three settled down for the
night.

I was scrubbing fluorescent yogurt off the kitchen
floor when the doorbell rang.

Instinctively, I stiffened. The psychos and wackos
had all been accounted for except for one. But it
couldn't be. I walked to the front door and looked out
the peephole.

It was Tim.

I threw open the door. "Thank God," I said, whispering so I wouldn't wake the kids. "I thought it might
be Richard."

"No chance," he whispered back. "Some friends of
his sailed his yacht into Newport News yesterday. It
set sail again this morning, with him on it. The Coast
Guard nabbed him a mile offshore."

I relaxed. Last psycho present and accounted for.
"So what are you doing here?"

"Are they asleep?" he said.

"No, we're whispering to sound sneaky."

Tim looked confused.

"Yes, they're asleep," I said.

He came inside carrying bags of Chinese food and several bottles of champagne. I followed him to the kitchen and watched as he offloaded his supplies onto the table.

I put my hands on my hips and frowned. "I thought you had a date."

"I do. With you."

"But you said—"

"I said I was spending New Year's Eve with an old girlfriend I wanted to get to know again. That's what I'm doing." He kissed me full on the lips. "You did real good with the hospice. That donation saved your life."

I frowned, not getting the connection.

"Maggie, if you hadn't called Stephanie, Stanley would have killed her. You never would have known about him breaking into your place before Phil did. You might have spent your retirement in jail for stealing $2.5 million from Illinois and killing Phil Scranton."

"Yeah, but I'm broke."

"Broke can be good for you."

I raised one hand to the Girl Scout pledge position. "Resolution. If ever I get a fortune again, I'm going to use it rather than just accumulate it."

"Good for you."

He pulled a container of sweet and sour chicken from the brown bag and handed it to me.

I set it on the counter. "Now it's your turn."

"What?"

"A New Year's resolution—not to be such a stickler for rules."

"Now, Maggie—"

"Tim, if I'd called the cops with my theory about

Malcolm and Richard, do you really think they would have raided the funeral home again?"

"Well, no. And they would have been right. Your theory was wrong in every major respect."

"I knew it was a Vandenberg, I just had the wrong one." He raised a questioning eyebrow, and I decided not to argue that point further. "But if I hadn't broken the rules, Stephanie and Malcolm would be dead, and who knows what Stanley would be doing now."

"Well . . ."

"And what's more important? Following the rules or saving a life—correction—lives?"

"I . . . will allow you that there are times—rare times—when the consequences of following the law justify breaking it."

I grinned. "I'll take that for now. And now you can tell me why the hell I had to put the kids to bed by myself?"

"Because baby-sitting is no way to spend New Year's Eve. Now my sister is happy, the kids are in bed, and we can have a romantic night together."

"Sounds like you planned the perfect evening," I said. "You manipulative bureaucrat."

He smiled smugly.

"Let me do the honors." I picked up a bottle of champagne and loosened the wire fastener. I nudged the cork up and then pointed the bottle at Tim. The cork exploded from the bottle, and Tim ducked in time to avoid a lobotomy. The cork ricocheted off the refrigerator and then broke an innocent vase of flowers that had been sitting on the counter.

Laughing and hissing at each other, we jumped to contain the mess from the broken vase and the erupting champagne bottle.

"We heard a noise," said a small voice.

Tim and I looked up from the mess to see three little kids standing in the doorway, squinting their eyes at the kitchen lights.

"Ahhh, let the romance begin," I said.

Chapter 27

Post Log

Earlier That Evening

Although the sun hadn't set yet, it was dark in the one-room apartment. The electricity had never been turned on. Little light crept in from the apartment's only window that had a view of a brick building ten feet away. The light was blocked even further by several of the windowpanes that had been busted out and replaced with cardboard.

A woman sat on the floor in the corner and rocked a small child. Somewhere in the darkness she heard a rat scurry across the floor. It must have been a young rat because the older rats had already foraged through the empty apartment and learned that there wasn't any food to be had.

Both mother and child whimpered slightly with each

rock. The child whimpering because of the hunger in her stomach and the pain of a disease that was eating away at her small body. The woman's pain wasn't just from her empty stomach but from the stress of seeing her little girl suffer and being unable to relieve that pain.

What extra clothes the two had were piled on top of them to keep the winter weather at bay since the temperature in the tiny room was close to freezing. People were arguing in the hallway, and a stereo blared from next door. Over the noise, she heard the sirens of an approaching ambulance and wished it would stop to help her child. But the sirens faded away.

It was just as well. She knew any social service that could give Elizabeth the medical care she needed would also take the child from her. Health care red tape required a permanent home address, and she was only hours away from homelessness. Elizabeth was going to die either way, and she would not let that be in the arms of a stranger.

Someone banged on the door.

The woman didn't move and didn't answer. Whoever it was probably wanted money for something, and money she didn't have. The only thing she did have was the warmth of her body to offer her young daughter, and she would not interrupt that to answer the door. The super had promised to wait until tomorrow to evict her, and she planned on savoring every last minute of the apartment before moving out to the snowy streets.

The person at the door banged, yelled for a few more minutes and then finally went away.

The woman and child continued rocking and whimpering until ten minutes later when another bang on the door rattled the apartment.

"We're coming in," a man said.

The woman clung tighter to her child. There was nothing to defend herself with, and gang violence was an everyday occurrence in this neighborhood.

She heard the sound of a key unlocking the door to her apartment. A few seconds later the door banged open.

She could see the silhouettes of four people standing in the doorway, no doubt letting their eyes adjust to the darkness.

"I don't have anything of value." Her voice was high-pitched from fright and exhaustion. "Please go away and leave me alone."

"Donna, it's okay. It's Stephanie Wolf. No one's going to hurt you. We're here to help."

A flashlight cut through the blackness. Donna could see that with the woman were two paramedics pushing a gurney and carrying medical bags. The building super who had let them in stayed in the doorway.

"You're not going to take my child from me!"

"Donna, we're not taking Elizabeth from you."

Several more flashlights illuminated the room. The woman named Stephanie crossed the room and bent down to where mother and child were huddled.

"I have a message from Maggie Connors. She said to tell you belated Merry Christmas."

"Maggie who?"

"Maggie Connors, the financial consultant you met with at Hamilton Securities about two weeks ago. She's been looking for you ever since. She's made arrangements for you and Elizabeth to come with me, to the Saint Louis Children's Hospice. We're—"

Donna gasped. "I know who you are. I applied to your program, but they said there was a six-month waiting list."

"We've had a change in funding. You and Elizabeth are welcome to stay at the hospice for as long as necessary. Elizabeth won't suffer anymore and will get the best medical attention available. Your housing, food, and medical costs will all be paid for. And later, well, we'll talk about later when we get there."

This time there was no stopping the tears, and the

woman cried, as hard as when she had first learned of her daughter's cancer. This time though, the tears were from relief.

"Momma?" the little girl said, a frightened look on her frail, hollow face.

The mother bent down and kissed the girl on the forehead. "It's going to be all right sweet child. It's going to be all right."

About the Author

Malinda Terreri lives in St. Louis with her husband and three children. Ms. Terreri is a professional sales trainer known for her fun, interactive training exercises. Her articles on sales training have appeared in publications around the world. You may visit her at her website: www.MalindaTerreri.com